Praise for *Somebody on This Bus Is Going to Be Famous*

A Junior Library Guild pick

"A great and fast read about finding yourself and making friends that will be enjoyed by even reluctant readers."

—*School Library Journal*

"Like E. L. Konigsburg's *The View from Saturday* or Wendy Mass's *The Candymakers*, Cheaney's tale weaves together a quirky cast of characters and seemingly random details, all the while dishing out clues to the mystery…a middle-grade reader with both substance and complexity that is also truly fun."

—*VOYA*

"Cheaney effectively combines multiple layers of mystery with an uplifting message about resilience."

—*Kirkus Reviews*

"A heartwarming, engaging story filled with discovery, hope, humor, mystery, and even an unexpected twist you won't see coming unless you take your seat on the bus and go along for the fun ride."

—Karen Harrington, author of *Sure Signs of Crazy* and *Courage for Beginners*

"J. B. Cheaney should be famous for this book! Wrapped up in the mystery that drives this story is a compelling tale of heroism and redemption that shows readers that you should never judge a kid by reputation alone."

—A. LaFaye, winner of the Scott O'Dell
Award for Historical Fiction for *Worth*

"Knowing there will be a bus wreck doesn't prepare readers for the final twist. So, who becomes famous? Few will be able to guess."

—*Booklist*

"With her spit-spot perfect ear for dialogue and eye for telling detail, Cheaney creates a wonderful cast. My only fault with this book was that it had to end."

—David L. Harrison, award-winning author of
The Boy with a Drum and *The Book of Giant Stories*

"[A] diverse cast of characters…[Cheaney] renders them with realism, respect, and even judicious tenderness."

—*The Bulletin of the Center for Children's Books*

I Don't Know How the Story Ends

J. B. Cheaney

sourcebooks
jabberwocky

Published by Sourcebooks Jabberwocky, an imprint of Sourcebooks, Inc.
P.O. Box 4410, Naperville, Illinois 60567-4410
(630) 961-3900
Fax: (630) 961-2168
www.sourcebooks.com

Library of Congress Cataloging-in-Publication data is on file with the publisher.

Source of Production: Worzalla, Stevens Point, Wisconsin, USA
Date of Production: August 2015
Run Number: 5004597

Printed and bound in the United States of America.
WOZ 10 9 8 7 6 5 4 3 2 1

To Melissa,
for those early days
and the footsteps I so often followed in.

Chapter 1
How We Came to California

The first I heard of Mother's big idea was May 20, 1918, at 4:35 p.m. in the entrance hall of our house on Fifth Street. That was where my little sister ended up after I pushed her down the stairs.

It wasn't all my fault. She pushed me before I pushed her—figuratively, I mean.

She'd picked a bad time to tangle with me, for I was in a drippy, dismal mood, like our Seattle weather that day. While walking from my room to the stairs with an open book—*Jane Eyre*, my new most-favorite—I heard a moaning noise behind me, starting low and growing louder: "*AhhhhWOOOO!*"

I turned around. "Whatever you're doing, stop it."

A cobwebby ghost was creeping up behind me: Sylvie, draped in gauzy curtains she'd somehow pulled down from our parents' bedroom window. "*AWOOOO!* I'm the ghost of the battlefield. No—I'm Daddy's lonesome spirit come back to haunt you, and... Quit it, Isobel!"

I had smacked her on the shoulder with my book. She smacked me back, so then I pushed her against the banister and she stumbled on the wads of curtain under her feet. The next moment, she was bouncing down the stairs, howling at every bump.

The noise brought Mother from the study and Rosetta from the kitchen. Both could only stare at first, flummoxed by the noisy cocoon I was frantically trying to unwrap. Sylvie had made it all the way to the bottom without breaking anything, I was pretty sure. Father used to say he was going to take her on the road as a scientific curiosity because her bones were made of rubber. But the fact remained that she had been pushed, and someone had done the pushing.

"Isobel," my mother said accusingly.

"I'm sorry! But she was acting silly, as usual, and saying she was Father's ghost, and we know that Father's alive and well, but I can't stand it when she…" Et cetera. And all this time Sylvie was yelling that it wasn't her fault—she was just playing, and I hit her before pushing her, and so on.

Rosetta stepped in to lend a hand, and finally Sylvie was standing on her own two feet, both of us waiting for Mother to send us outside for a switch from the forsythia bush. But she just looked at us, lips pressed together, the silence lengthening like the long shadow that had fallen over us ever since Father left for France.

"That does it," Mother said at last. "I've had enough of dreary days and melancholy daughters. We're going to California for the summer."

Once the idea was in the open, I learned it had been building for a while. Mother was California born and bred, and her sister, my aunt Buzzy, had been begging her to come for a long stay ever since Father volunteered to serve his country in the Great War. Father had left in November, and now it was almost June—a very wet and gloomy almost-June, all the wetter and gloomier without his quiet smiles and bad jokes. But that didn't mean I was ready to turn my back on home.

"We always spend July on San Juan Island!" I protested when Mother bought our train tickets. "And what about digging clams with Grandpa or taking Sylvie to Pike Street Market? You know Rosetta needs me to do the shopping for her when school's out. And I don't know anybody in Los Angeles!"

"You soon will. Your aunt married a very wealthy man with a child about your age. Thirteen, I think."

"He's a *boy!*"

"Boys can be human. You have fog and rain in your soul, Isobel. As for me, I've been longing for the sunny hills and orange groves of home. A trip south will wring us both out."

"I don't *want* to be wrung out," I whined. "And California is not my *home*." To no avail: in Father's absence Mother had swung about and pointed south, like a contrary compass needle.

I didn't understand it. The calling of a Seattle doctor's wife had always suited her like gravy took to a roast. (Even though Mother photographed much better than a roast, with her dark

3

eyes and stately beauty flawed only by a slight vertical scar on her upper lip.) Hardly a month went by without some item in the newspaper about a tea or charity show hosted by Mrs. Robert F. Ransom, Jr. And now she was ready to throw over all those radiant good works for a dollop of California sunshine!

She did have a point about the melancholy daughter though. All winter and spring, I'd moped about the house and snapped at Sylvie when she got unbearable, which only made her more unbearable. *Jane Eyre* was teaching me to accept new challenges—and besides, there's not much a twelve-year-old can do about her immediate destiny. So I tried to think like Jane Eyre, setting off for Thornfield Hall and a fated meeting with Mr. Rochester. Perhaps I was destined for my own fated meeting, and besides, we'd be back by the end of August.

But that didn't mean I should not feel a little teary when we gathered at King Street Station on a drizzly afternoon, the tenth of June. Granny kissed us one more time, and Grandpa stood aside, looking like he didn't care all *that* much, even though I knew he did. He took a swipe at his eyes as Granny told us to get lots of sunshine.

My stiff upper lip trembled, for I couldn't help remembering the last time we'd lingered on a station platform. That was the day Father left.

He is just the best, kindest man in the world—tall and handsome too, especially in his uniform with the captain's bars on the shoulder—and the harder he worked to cheer us up with his jokes and ha-ha's, the worse we felt. Finally my mother said, "For heaven's sake, Bobby—" and grabbed his shoulders and boosted herself on tiptoe to kiss him, right on the mouth! Firmly too.

Father was as shocked as the rest of us, but at least it stopped the ha-ha's. Some honest and dignified sniffling followed the kiss, and Father wiped his glasses, after which he picked up Sylvie and bear-hugged me. Just before letting me go, he whispered, "You're the responsible one, Isobel—look after your sister and be good for Mother. I know you'll make me proud."

That was last November. Now it was June and we were the ones climbing into the coach, California-bound, saddened by farewells past and present. At least I was. Mother, who took her seat and faced resolutely forward, seemed no sadder than the proverbial clam. As for Sylvie, any excuse to get on a train thrills her to no end. While I waved through the window at my grandparents receding from view, Sylvie was climbing the brakeman's ladder on the back platform. The porter pulled her down before she could kill herself.

I will admit to cheering up somewhere south of Portland, as we dined on oyster stew and filet of sole while gazing out our dining-car window at an orangey sunset. After dinner, Sylvie wandered up the aisle making the acquaintance of all our fellow travelers, including a gentleman in a soldier's uniform three seats ahead on the opposite aisle. Being the responsible one, I kept an eye on her in case she overstayed her welcome, which usually didn't take long.

There was something odd about the soldier's face: while he seemed to be speaking, his mouth never moved. With a start,

I realized that it wasn't a mouth. It was a mask. When Sylvie's hand went out to touch it, I jumped out of my seat and started up the aisle, saying, "Sylvie! Don't be rude—"

"It's all right, miss." The soldier's muffled voice came through a narrow slit in the mask. His eyes tried to smile as he touched his painted-tin jaw, which was attached by almost invisible threads to his ears. "She means no harm. Unlike that exploding shell that got me in France."

I smiled sickly as I murmured an apology and pulled Sylvie back to our seat. "Well done," Mother said when I explained. "Sylvie, I think you can stay put until time for bed."

"I wonder where he was when he got hit," I mused. "Maybe Father was the first one to treat him!" This thought, dreadful as it was to contemplate, made me think of striking up a conversation with the wounded soldier myself.

"Who knows?" was Mother's only comment as she turned a page of the *Ladies' Home Journal*, adding, "Leave the poor man alone."

I didn't just miss my father—I was slowly starving for him. Or I was living each day in the half dark, without the light of his easy smile. (Mother's smiles were not so forthright; I guess you would call them ironic.) Every week we faithfully sent letters to him, and at first he'd written back long, detailed replies about roughing it in a barn and trying to buy fresh vegetables from the Frenchies and the funny things his orderly said and how he'd improvised a scalpel from a British colonel's penknife and helped the nurses put up a scraggly fir tree at Christmas, decorated with cutouts from sardine cans. He was at pains to reassure us that his ears were within range of the fighting but the rest of him wasn't: *Bullets won't get me but the bedbugs might, ha–ha.*

Since January his dispatches were much shorter and farther between. "Maybe there'll be a letter waiting for us in California," I said.

"Don't count on it." Mother still gazed at the magazine but her eyes weren't moving. "We've talked about this, Isobel. He's extremely busy and too exhausted after a long day of patching up soldiers to write anything funny." She turned a page with a snap. "And if he can't write anything *funny*, he can't write at all."

She sounded almost angry at him for trying to keep a cheerful countenance, but then, she was angry at him for going in the first place. It would have made more sense, it seemed to me, to be angry at Kaiser Wilhelm II of Germany, who started the whole thing. Still, her irritation showed almost every time I mentioned Father going to the war, so I usually didn't.

But I longed for someone to talk to about it. All through the winter, my school chums and I had sold war bonds and marched in parades and knitted socks for soldiers, but the war felt so far away, and so did Father. What was it really like, tending to the wounded in a field hospital lit by the rockets' red glare?

Grandfather Ransom would know, since he had served as an army surgeon in the Philippines back in '98. But he never wanted to talk about that part of it—only steaming into Manila Bay with Admiral Dewey, banners flying and artillery roaring. When I asked about his work, he usually just chewed his mustache and looked preoccupied.

Before long, Sylvie started kicking the seat, and Mother put her magazine aside. "When the seat-kicking begins, it's time to get ready for bed. Suppose I read not one but two chapters of *Robin Hood* tonight?"

For one so proper, Mother is a very good read-alouder, giving a bearlike growl to Little John and a thin sinister tone to the Sheriff of Nottingham. Sylvie begged for a third chapter, but by then the porters were coming through to turn down our beds—literally I mean, pulling down upper berths from the walls and nudging lower seats together to be made up with starchy sheets. I took an upper berth, with Sylvie opposite me. Mother tucked us in and kissed us good night before settling below.

Sometime in the wee hours, a rare thunderstorm rolled up and Sylvie tried to leap across the aisle from her berth to mine. I can't say why she thought this was a good idea, and she couldn't either. That may have been because—after the hubbub caused by her catching her foot in the drapery pull and hanging upside down hollering like a banshee until the entire coach was awake and scrambling to her aid—it slipped her mind.

"Hoo-law," the porter said, chuckling as he unwound the cords she'd wound herself in. "Derrin'-doin' like Mister Douglas Fairbanks."

He meant the Mr. Fairbanks who was renowned for derring-do in the moving pictures, but Sylvie did not get it.

"I'm not a mister!" she cried, still undignifiedly upside-down. "I'm a *girl*!"

"Oh, for heaven's sake." Mother was holding Sylvie up by the waist and trying to keep her nether half decently covered while gravity ruled otherwise. "As if every roused soul in this car didn't know that by now!"

In the confusion, I blundered into a shape behind me and turned to meet a horror: a ghostly face with no jaw and a shapeless lump of a mouth: "*Ahhhh!*"

"Sorry, miss!" the soldier slurred. He'd forgotten his mask. "So sorry—trying to help—"

He backed into his berth, pulling the curtains closed, and I felt as small as a shrub for hurting him like that. But really, what other response was possible for such a face? Those soldiers my father was patching up—how many of them looked like him?

That was enough excitement for one night, even for Sylvie. She crawled in with me so I could talk her to sleep with a story, though I was hardly in a storytelling mood. Thunder boomed and lightning throbbed through the window blind as I tried to launch a plot: "Once upon a time, there was a little girl, six years old—"

"Just like me!" she interrupted, as usual.

"…who lived happily by the Northern Sea with her mother and father—"

"And sister too?"

"Sylvie, can't you just go to sleep for a change?"

She insisted, so I made up something about the girls

traveling south to the mysterious land of California, and fortunately she was asleep before I could get very far. I almost never got a chance to end my Sylvie stories, which might be why I wasn't good at endings. As Sylvie snored softly, my surroundings took on a sinister character, looming like a ghost.

Trains have a special kind of aloneness about them, especially at night in the sad glow of dim lights with restless sleepers all around. Our little bed, closed off by heavy curtains, began to feel like a box. It reminded me of Jane Eyre being locked up in the Red Room and made me glad of Sylvie's company, twitchy though she was.

The locomotive whistle moaned in the night and the iron wheels clacked relentlessly over the rail joints, their sharpness muffled by the rain: *ch-click, ch-click. Ch-click, ch-click.* I drifted off in the middle of a prayer for Father's safety, but sleep for me was iron-riddled and trembling with the shaky glow of the ceiling lamps.

In my dream, the earth turned, rotating to a field of splintered trees and plowed-up ridges. As cannons rumbled and bombs flashed, the ridges became bodies, tossed like grain sacks. And lying apart, a body in a uniform, the captain's bars still smartly gleaming. I knew who it was even while knowing it couldn't be: *Bullets won't get me, bullets won't get me, bullets won't—*

His cap was knocked aside and his face turned away, but as I came nearer, the gleam of wire drew my attention to an object on the ground by his head: a pair of glasses, both lenses shattered in the light that flashed behind them.

Sorry, miss. Sorry—

I jerked upright in the berth, clutching my throat. Just a dream—Father never got that close to the fighting—but my fear felt as real as if he were leading every charge. Sylvie moaned and turned to one side. The wheels rolled on, inexorably: *ch-click, ch-click...*

⌒⌒

The soldier got off at his stop sometime in the early-morning hours. Later, I awoke with sunlight bursting through the blind and Sylvie taking up most of the berth. My body felt like it had been wadded up and pushed in the corner. Later still, rumpled and blinking, we three stepped down from the coach at Los Angeles Central Station.

No one rushed up shouting our names. We walked down the platform, away from the chuffing locomotive with its shroud of steam and coal smoke that smells the same wherever you are. At the end of the platform, the midmorning sun leaped upon us.

It wasn't just strong—it was *muscular*, like a burly masseuse at a Turkish bath, kneading our arms and faces and backs with such energy that Mother arched her back and almost purred, "Ah, California..."

When I tried arching my back and breathing deeply, the sweet, dusty air just made me sneeze. Meanwhile, the sun was poking fingers (in a manner of speaking) into my very bones.

"Mattie!" came a cry from the other end of the platform,

and we turned in that direction. Aunt Buzzy was flying at us, followed by an Oriental fellow in a blue uniform, who managed to not look like he was rushing, though of course he was.

Aunt Buzzy's real name is Beatrice, but the story is her brother started calling her "Buzzy" when she was born because he was only three at the time and couldn't manage three syllables. Now that same brother, my uncle Moss, is a banker in Santa Barbara and can manage any number of syllables, but Buzzy's nickname stuck. Everyone calls her that except Mother. Buzzy doesn't buzz, but she is busy as a bee, so the name is not too amiss. Also, she's honey-colored from her ankles to her golden hair, with a clover field of freckles (whence Sylvie gets them) scattered across her nose.

She sped toward us with such determination that I felt a breeze. "Little Sylvie, how you've grown!" Our aunt squeezed my sister's arms until she peeped like a baby chick. "Belladonna!" This was her pet name for me, after Mother put her foot down on *Izzy*. "I declare, you look more like your mother every time I see you!" I got my face squeezed instead of my arms, which mangled my smile but didn't hurt.

"Dear Mattie." This is short for Matilda, which Mother doesn't like but puts up with. The sisters—who don't look like sisters because one is fair and flyaway, while the other is dark and reserved—embraced while Aunt Buzzy whispered a few words in Mother's ear. Probably regarding Father, for both looked solemn for a moment.

"But *now*," said my aunt, as if one solemn moment was quite enough, "we're going to have *such* high times. I can't wait to show you the house and introduce you to my new family, and, *oh!* to begin with, this is Masaji, our chauffeur."

Still catching his breath, the denizen of the exotic East bowed to us, and Sylvie and I bowed back. Mother tipped her head, but I could see she was much impressed. We knew Buzzy had *married well*, but didn't know it was well enough to employ a chauffeur—and where there was a chauffeur, there was bound to be a large, shiny automobile.

There was—and what an auto! My father owned a Model T, black and plain as his medical bag, to get around to patients in Seattle. But Aunt Buzzy's vehicle was a long, pearl-gray Packard Town Car with morocco leather seats and a fold-down top, now open to the dazzling sunshine. Mr. Masaji tucked Sylvie and me into the rumble seat, snug as birdies in a nest. Then he handed the ladies into the backseat, clucked around to the front, and sped away as Sylvie shrieked in delight.

"Well!" Mother remarked, adjusting her veil against the wind, "I must say, Bea, you've done well for yourself."

Mr. Titus Bell had hired my aunt some years back to tutor his only child and finally ended up asking for her hand in marriage. It was just like Mr. Rochester and Jane Eyre, although we were pretty sure Titus Bell kept no mad wives in his attic to complicate matters. Thus with an "I do," my aunt became Buzzy Bell, a name I thought I would never want to be saddled with—although, on second thought, if it came with a vehicle like this, it might be worth considering.

Bare brownish hills rolled along both sides of the highway.

13

"Look!" Sylvie squealed, pointing. "Palm trees, just like in the Bible!"

Her christening Bible has a picture labeled "O Little Town of Bethlehem," in which gigantic palm trees tower over houses that look like building blocks. Aunt Buzzy turned sideways in the backseat, reached around, and squeezed Sylvie's knee with an affectionate smile. "It will be so lovely to have little ones in the house again. It's too quiet with Titus gone half the time and Ranger acting so serious and grown up. I miss the madcap he used to be."

(She meant Mr. Titus Bell's son, her former pupil. I had never met him, but soon would, and "serious and grown-up" were not the first words that would come to mind.)

"What's that smell, Bea?" my mother asked. "Not the orange blossoms. Something spicier I don't recall."

"Pepper trees. Ten years ago they were all the rage. When Titus built his house out here the scent was overpowering, but they're starting to go now. The new people don't care for them."

"New people?" Mother asked.

Aunt Buzzy nodded. "From back east. Titus has become quite thick with some of them for business reasons. Very interesting...people."

Mother, sitting directly in front of me, raised her eyebrows— that is, I only saw one eyebrow, but I know her looks, and this one indicated that "interesting" meant something you didn't talk about in front of the children. "So I hear."

"Look!" Sylvie shrieked again. "Cowboys!"

In the direction she pointed, four horsemen were galloping along the crest of a barren hill. "Where are the cows?" I asked.

"They're chasing *him*." Our auto was pulling even with a lone rider, galloping desperately. As the other four gained on him, they drew pistols and began firing!

"Oh!" I bolted upright in the rumble seat. But Aunt Buzzy just glanced in that direction before assuring me, "It's nothing, dear—I'll explain later." Then, turning back to Mother: "Now, where was I? Oh yes, the queerest look came over his face, and *then* he said…"

Our touring car passed the lead rider, who was now hanging over the saddle as though wounded. I noticed an open auto on the ridge, keeping an even distance while another man stood behind the driver's seat. His face was obscured by some kind of box on a tripod. Sylvie and I stared at each other—my eyes, I am certain, as big and round as hers. *What kind of place is this?* I wondered.

Abruptly Mr. Masaji turned onto a narrow unpaved road, bumping over railroad tracks. Our shining chariot crested a small, round hill and looked down on a valley of orchards and meadows, crisscrossed by straight roads. Inside each square or rectangle was a house, surrounded by outbuildings and gardens, all very picturesque.

Aunt Buzzy turned to us again, beaming. "Welcome to our little paradise, loves. Welcome to Hollywood!"

Chapter 2
The Boy with the Hat

*A*fter the grandeur of the auto, I expected no less of the house. But when Mr. Masaji bumped the car down a long, sandy drive and stopped, my first thought was, *Is this the house or the garden shed?* Columns and towers were what I expected—what I saw was a low, rambling structure that seemed to be mostly roof. The peak began somewhere out of sight and sloped forward so far it might have forgotten there was a house underneath. Bright-red chili peppers festooned the rafters and grapevines twisted up the wooden posts of a wide porch. From its deep shade, double glass doors stared out flatly.

"Here we are!" Aunt Buzzy chirped. "Our hacienda!"

Disembarking from the auto, Mother, Sylvie, and I followed her across the porch and through a rustic entrance hall. When we stepped into the front room, our jaws dropped as one.

Mr. Titus Bell, my new uncle whom I'd never met, was an importer of exotic goods. I didn't know exactly what that meant until now: his house was like an Oriental/Near Eastern/Mediterranean/Polynesian/Eskimo bazaar. Taken all in a gasp, as we did, it assaulted both sense and imagination.

The room was big enough to play red rover in. It ran the width of the house, with a high, sloped ceiling and a huge stone fireplace. Indian silks shimmered in the windows, and Persian carpets rioted on the polished floor. Bronze lanterns beaten with Fiji hammers glared fiercely from the rafters, and Chinese statuary crouched in every nook. And then there was the furniture, to which every creature on earth might have given a horn, hide, bone, or feather. At first sight, it stunned me like a whack to the head. I took a step back, only to be poked in the ribs by the tip of a large, wooden palm leaf—a mail tray, mounted on a real elephant's leg.

"I know," Aunt Buzzy said, laughing. "It's like a museum. Or like a museum *warehouse*."

"Very…impressive" was the word my mother chose.

"The trouble with Titus is he can't say no to any little pretty that catches his eye. And I can't either. I just adore everything he brings home. We were hoping you could help us decorate, Mattie. You're the only one of us with any taste." Aunt Buzzy raised her voice to call, "Solomon! Esperanza! We're home!"

Dropping her voice again, she added, "Now where could Ranger be? I told him to stay nearby to welcome you. Though it's hard to keep him close these days, he's always wandering… Esperanza! I'm afraid they step a lot more lively when Titus is the one calling. But he's back east until the end of June. *Solomon!* Oh, thank you, Masaji."

The chauffeur had dragged in our trunk and was just now setting our two suitcases beside it. He touched his cap to Aunt Buzzy, who was darting from one doorway to the next, peering, calling, taking off her hat, and pulling off her gloves one finger at a time. The doorway on the left side of the fireplace stood open, and from it drifted a jaunty tune played on the gramophone. I wondered if there was a dance going on in the servants' quarters.

"I may have to go to the kitchen myself and... Oh, Solomon. There you are."

A dark-featured man with straight, black hair like an Indian's had appeared in the open doorway, no expression on his face whatsoever. "Señora," was all he said.

"These are our guests: my sister, Mrs. Ransom, and her daughters, Miss Isobel and Miss Sylvia. Please ask Esperanza to bring some lemonade and tea cakes and...do we have any melon?"

Instead of answering the question, he just said "Señora" again and departed with scarcely a glance at us. My mother would have settled his hash in a hurry—and wanted to, I could tell. But Aunt Buzzy just kept flitting, unfazed by surly housemen. "Where *is* that boy? I told him to... There he is. RANGER!" she hollered out one of the open windows on the west side. "We're home. Please come in and say hello!"

Then she turned to us with a radiant smile, as though her main problem had just solved itself. "He's a good boy. Just a little preoccupied these days. Goodness, what am I thinking? Let me take those jackets and hats, and we'll act like you're here to stay."

While shrugging off my coat, I noticed a youth framed by the doorway on the right of the gigantic fireplace. This door had to be reached by three flagstone steps, enough to give him a commanding height from which to survey us.

He stood quite still, his wire-rimmed glasses flickering as he sized us up. His right arm was in a sling. When Aunt Buzzy said, "Come and join us, dear," he sauntered down the three steps.

"Sauntered" is a show-offy word, but it suited him. He wore corduroy pants stuffed into Western boots, a herdsman's jacket with deep pockets, and a hat just big enough to give his game away: he was dressing up. And, with the sling and all, I must say he was the picture of rugged Westernness until Aunt Buzzy asked him, "What do I always say about wearing hats indoors?" He tugged it off with an irritated sigh, just as the heel of his boot snagged on the bottom step and he barely saved himself from landing on his face.

While Aunt Buzzy was making introductions, he recovered his dignity, bowing in a downright courtly manner to Mother and smiling indulgently at Sylvie. Coming around to me, he took my hand and bent his head, then looked me square in the eye. Without the hat he wasn't so tall, and with that crinkly, gingery hair going every which way, he wasn't so old either. But his eyes behind the glasses were so dark and keen that they startled me, and they were set in a face of exotic hue. I had thought him to be merely tan, but the color was deep-dyed, a smoky bronze that whispered of foreign shores.

Then he bugged his eyes at me.

Which seemed very fresh, but I had it coming, staring at him like that.

"Oh, thank you, Esperanza," said my aunt as a partridge-plump woman with long, black braids brought in a tray of tea cakes and icy-green melon balls. Solomon followed with a frosty pitcher of lemonade. Suddenly I was ravenous, but we had to go another round of introductions for Esperanza's sake, after which she made a little bob and smilingly excused herself.

We tucked into the refreshments and conversation languished, save for small talk about the weather. After two tea cakes and a half-dozen melon balls, I asked Ranger, "Have you been out riding?" That getup made him look as horsy as Buffalo Bill.

He opened his mouth to reply, but Aunt Buzzy intercepted: "His father's declared the saddle off-limits until September, since Ranger took that tumble and broke his collarbone."

"Very sensible," Mother commented as Ranger shifted awkwardly in his chair and draped one leg over the arm—which seemed to be made from the horn of a yak.

"That explains the sling," Aunt Buzzy went on. "If you're wondering about the outfit, he's adopted the style of his latest hero, Mr. D—"

"*Please*, Buzzy," Ranger interrupted.

Mother's eyebrows, which were certainly being worked today, jumped again. I wondered if, when my aunt was tutoring him, Ranger had at least addressed her as *Miss* Buzzy.

But the lady herself didn't seem to mind. "Oh, all right. I'll admit you're much less trouble since school let out for the summer." She smiled at him with affection and he managed a weak grimace in return.

Talk then turned to Mr. Titus Bell and what he was doing back east—something to do with investors and a new company. It went over my head but I was further distracted by the boy's behavior. For one thing, the foot on the floor couldn't hold still, but hammered out a restless tattoo with the heel of his boot. For another, he kept looking at me. Glances at first, then more intently, and finally through a circle made by the thumb and forefinger of his left hand. Like he fancied himself as Leonardo framing the *Mona Lisa*, for heaven's sake.

"Ranger, *please*," said Aunt Buzzy, noticing at last. "You'll absolutely spook poor Isobel. Put your lens away."

Lens? I wondered. Meanwhile Sylvie had finished her lemonade and gone looking for mischief. She found it by pulling a rose from a vase on the table, which upset the whole arrangement in a thump of pottery and a splash of petals. Mother sent an imploring look to her sister.

"Children," Aunt Buzzy said, "wouldn't you like to explore our quaint little town? Ranger is a wonderful guide—he knows all the interesting places." Ranger sprang up from his seat like a jack-in-the-box.

"Remember you're responsible for your sister, Isobel," was Mother's parting words to me.

Once we three were in the great outdoors, that California light was what Granny would call a tonic—like you could take it from a spoon for a jolt of well-being. The air was warm but not sultry, and the breeze caressed with a scent of orange blossoms. Sylvie whooped and raced ahead of us down the long drive.

"What did Aunt Buzzy mean about you being less trouble since school let out?" I asked Ranger. It sounded abrupt, but I needed to know if he was a fit guide for two young girls in a strange town.

He shrugged. "Just that I'm not trying to get myself expelled anymore."

"*Expelled?*" I squeaked. "How?"

"Oh, burning down the gym, things like that. School is stupid."

"But…" Did he mean for me to take him seriously? "What about when you have to go back in the fall?"

He looked at me with a peculiar glint in his eye. "Who says I'm going back in the fall?"

"Well…your father, for one. You're only thirteen—you have to go."

"My father and I will have a day of reckoning," he said rather grandly.

"Oh." I was trying to decide what to make of that, when Sylvie called out:

"More haciendas!"

We had come to the end of the long drive, where Ranger turned east onto Eighth Street. The houses here were either one-story bungalows or Spanish-style ranch houses with red tile roofs. In Seattle, the tall, stately houses reared over you with glassy, watchful stares, but these dwellings seemed to lay back and regard us lazily. Ranger raced to catch up with Sylvie, calling over his shoulder, "Come on!"

"Where are we going?"

"You'll see."

He crammed the hat back on his head. The swooping brim cast a shadow that made him look older and wiser—not like a wild-haired, piercing-eyed boy. Catching up with him, I panted, "Is it a decent place for girls?"

His laugh jumped out like a frog from a pocket and startled me just as much. "Heck *no*—come on!"

He took off running again with a whoop and a holler, dropping a good seven years from his attitude. His broken collarbone did not appear to slow him down at all, and Sylvie was only too glad to keep up. I held myself to a ladylike trot and wondered if we were trespassing on the sunny fields he led us across. Soon we were back on the street, past spurting lawn sprinklers and a long, white building with a circular drive ("Hollywood Hotel!" Ranger called over his shoulder).

He turned at the corner and turned again at the next, and soon was loping along beside a long plank fence. When he picked up a stick and trailed it along the boards with a musical clatter, Sylvie did the same. They paused at the next corner for me to catch up. "Took your time, didnya?" Ranger said and immediately sprinted away too fast to see the tongue I stuck out at him.

We had come to the edge of town, where citrus groves stretched as far as the eye could see on the other side of the street. On our side, the fence ended at the corner of a salvage yard. Or that's what it appeared to be, with stacks of lumber, piles of door and window frames, and sawhorses scattered like a grazing herd. Farther in, carpenters were putting up a house—at least one side of a house: a flat front with painted bricks and columns, propped up from the back with wooden trusses. Is that how they build houses in California, I wondered: one side at a time?

"We're here," said our guide. "Follow me and keep quiet."

"Where're we going, Ranger?" Sylvie cried, her voice sticky with adoration.

He just put a finger to his lips, with a half smile to show he accepted her worship. Then he turned and led us into the wreckage.

I couldn't see the need for silence; the place was as noisy as Pike Street Market on Saturday morning. The lot itself looked like a cyclone had passed through. Two crews were building things, but another crew was just as busily tearing things down. We picked our way past floors without walls and walls without floors, whole sections of buildings standing or leaning or flat on the ground. Hammers thudded, saws rasped, voices called, and over it all I thought I heard the tinkly tones of a piano.

"What *is* this place?" I finally burst out.

Ranger had stopped at a high wooden fence and tapped his lips again in that secretive way that was beginning to aggravate me. On the other side of the fence, a blast of jaunty piano music began, silenced abruptly when a sharp voice shouted, "*Cut!*" A murmur of voices, then a pause. The piano changed its tune to ominous rippling chords.

Ranger motioned us closer and pointed to a crack between the planks where I could peep through. He chose his own peephole, and Sylvie squeezed herself in front of him. While squinting through the crack, I noticed him watching me again, lips moving as though he were describing me to companions unseen.

"*What* are you—" I whispered as he whirled back around and peered through the crack. Sighing, I turned my attention to whatever was behind the fence. The sight unfolded in pieces as I shifted my position.

There was a platform built up about a foot from the ground. It was shaded by a roof made of bleached muslin. Soft light fell on two men in buckskin and Stetson hats who were shouting at each other. The music grew in intensity. From their clothes and makeup and the way they stood, it looked like a play. That would make the platform a stage, but where was the audience? The fence cut off my view, but the area it surrounded seemed much too small to hold an audience of any size. And voices chattered continually in the background— theater patrons wouldn't be so rude. I began to notice a sound that had been going on for some time, a whir and a click, and I was wondering what it was when one of the cowboys punched the other—*smack!*

He received a hard shove in return, which sent him staggering against the bar. Then he launched himself on his rival's neck, and next thing, the two of them were rolling on the floor. There was a woman standing by—not a very nice one, by the way she was dressed—and she recoiled in horror when one of the men rolled on top of the other and raised a very large knife—

"*Stop!*" I screamed. I'm not the kind who screams for show, but what came out of me was showy and loud enough to stop the fight. The cowboys glanced around, startled. A voice came from the other side of the fence, alarming and close: "What the—"

Ranger shot a poisonous look my way before grabbing my arm and pulling me away so fast I nearly fell over. I was speechless until we were back on the street: "Unhand me, you—villain!"

"Didn't you know what that was? Didn't you hear the camera?" he hissed. "It wasn't a real fight—they were just making a picture."

"Of course I knew that!" And indeed, I was beginning to recall hearing somewhere how Southern California was fast becoming the nation's motion-picture capital. But that was a bit of information like Akron, Ohio, being the rubber-tire capital—it had nothing to do with me. That is, until I'd made a fool of myself.

"I knew it was some kind of performance. It looked like a play. But then it happened so fast—and we saw a gunfight earlier today—and—"

"Huh," he remarked, shaking his head sadly at my denseness. "Come on."

Sylvie was sticking to him like a wet lollipop, so I had no choice. We picked our way out of the lot and were soon back on the street, where she plied him with questions. "Why were they fighting, Ranger? What was making that clickety noise? Did that man get stuck with the knife?"

"It was a picture," he said again. "The clicking noise was the camera. The action goes on a film that runs through a projector, and you see it on a screen. Haven't you ever been to a picture show—or a nickelodeon even? Keystone Cops? Mary Pickford or Charlie Chaplin—you've never seen *Charlie*? He's the most famous man in the world!"

"Not to us," I said with a sniff. "Mother thinks he's silly. And vulgar, the way he chases women."

"Nuts!" Ranger scoffed rudely. "She should talk to her sister. Buzzy's seen lots of Chaplin pictures, and she laughs as loud as anybody."

"Why does he chase women? He could chase me all day and never catch me!" As if to prove her point, Sylvie raced ahead of us.

"Mary Pickford is perfectly all right," I told Ranger, defending Mother's taste. "We've seen *Rebecca of Sunnybrook Farm*."

"But didn't you know that Mary Pickford works here in this town? Lives here too—I can show you her house."

"So what?" His scorn was becoming tiresome. "Famous people live in Seattle too, like…" But I couldn't think of any at the moment.

"*Ranger!*" Sylvie yelled, as she pelted back toward us. "It's wondrous, it's magnificent! What is it?"

I looked where she was pointing and gasped in spite of myself.

Towering above the ordinary little houses surrounding them were the massive walls of an ancient temple. Its arches reared against the sky, with golden fretwork spun between them, painted frescoes, elephants prancing on the tops of columns—far too much to take in one glance. I merely stood like a pillar of salt, dumbly echoing Sylvie: "What is it?"

Ranger's face glowed with satisfaction as though he'd built the whole splendid structure with his own hands. "*That*, my dear, is Babylon."

Chapter 3
Tales of Babylon

*B*abylon has fallen," I said, being too overwhelmed for the moment to think of anything smarter.

"Looks like it rose again," Ranger told me smugly. He led us to a plank fence directly under the towering walls. "This is Belshazzar's Court. The gates of the city used to stand here, but they got pulled down to make room for this."

"Who's Belshazzar?" Sylvie asked in a hushed voice. "Is he home? Will he let us go in?" She was overcome—perhaps by the elephants, which were awe-inspiring indeed, even though a close look showed the gold paint peeling off.

"But what *is* it?" I asked yet again.

Ranger leaned against the fence, gazing up dreamily. "You've heard of *Intolerance*, right?"

"Of course," I said, wondering how ignorant he supposed me to be.

"What's intolerance?" Sylvie asked eagerly.

"You know," I told her. "There are lots of things Mother

won't tolerate, like running in the house and sneezing at the table and—"

Ranger thumped his back against the fence, gazing upward with a sigh as though beseeching the gods for patience. "You girls are pitiful. I mean the picture *Intolerance*. The greatest epic ever produced. D. W. Griffith made it—that's his studio, right across the street."

I glanced in the direction he pointed, at a sprawling barn of a building I wouldn't have noticed otherwise, even with *Fine Arts* grandly proclaimed on the sign across the entrance. "Oh, the picture. We didn't see it. My parents heard it was unsuitable for children."

In fact, Rosetta had told me about seeing *Intolerance* with Ralph the iceman, but the meaning of the greatest epic ever produced was apparently lost on her. "I couldn't make heads or tails of it," she complained. "All that shuttling back and forth between old times and new times—my head was spinning. And it was pret' near four hours! The Good Lord never meant for folks to set that long. My tailbone like to petrified."

When I asked if it was unsuitable for children, she'd snorted. "I'll say this: those dancing girls in Babylon didn't wear enough clothes to dry a saucer with. Ralph sure sat up and took notice at that part."

"*Intolerance* is a masterpiece," Ranger told us fervently.

"What's it about?" Sylvie asked, willing to take his word on just about anything by now.

"It's about man's inhumanity to man."

"Which man?" she persisted.

He sank on his heels and motioned us to sit beside him. The Griffith studio seemed quiet today; no clamor and bustle behind the barn door, unlike that other junkyard—I mean, motion picture factory—we'd visited. "It's really four stories, and each one happens in a different time and place."

With that, he launched out on choppy narrative seas, telling all four stories, which soon tangled hopelessly in my head. Sylvie's too, even though she listened with raptness. Ranger's hands were large for the rest of him, with long, slithery fingers that jabbed and poked and embroidered his words. On the Babylon parts, Ranger became so excited that he twitched, bouncing on his heels: "Then there's a *huge* battle! And you should have seen King Belshazzar driving his chariot along the top of the walls! With arrows falling around him like rain! You can almost feel your head getting bigger, trying to take it all in!"

I had felt like that once, on the ferry bound for Vancouver Island, gazing back at the tumultuous mountains of the Olympic Peninsula. But that was nature, not flickers. "You must have seen it more than once to remember all that," I observed.

"Seven times," he said, and my mouth dropped open.

"How could your parents take you to see the same picture *seven times*?"

"Who said anybody took me? In fact, I wasn't even supposed to see it once. In fact," he added with a wary glance, "you don't have to repeat that."

"Hah," I said.

"It was only fair I get to see it. After all, I was in it."

Sylvie jumped up in excitement. "You were *in* it? What did you do, Ranger? Did you get to drive the charet?"

"Chariot," he corrected. "My father knows Mr. Griffith, see. Invested money in his pictures. So we came down here a couple of times when the Babylon scenes started shooting. D. W. was talking to Pa one day, and he noticed me. 'Titus,' he says, 'that boy of yours has a Babylonian look. Do you think he'd agree to appear in a scene?'"

"But what did you do exactly?" I was trying to picture him as a Babylonian, which his foreign-looking darkness may have suited.

"I got to hold the chariot horses for the Mountain Girl when she drives to the Persian camp to learn their secret plans. Remember, I told you that part?" I nodded uncertainly. "After that, a ten-foot pole couldn't have kept me away." (Wild horses, I thought he meant, but let it go.) "I was down here every chance I got, just to watch. And once"—he started bouncing on his heels again—"when they were shooting the last battle, I sneaked into some armor and grabbed a helmet and joined right in! One of the Persians stabbed me, and I died a bloody death. That's one reason I had to see the picture so many times—to find myself getting killed."

"And did you?"

"I think so, but it's hard to tell with the helmet and all."

Sylvie blurted out, "Could we do it, Ranger? Is D. W. making another picture that we could be in?" *Speak for yourself,* I thought.

"He's always making pictures," Ranger said. "Great ones. But there'll never be another like *Intolerance*." Sylvie's face fell at the unlikelihood that she would ever get to die a bloody death on the walls of Babylon. "You should have seen all the people it took," he went on dreamily. "Hundreds—*thousands*, even. And every one had to have a costume and weapons, and a place to stand and something to do—and the director has to keep it all in his *head*. D. W.'s the king of directors. He never gets flustered, even when the walls are shaking and the horses are nervous and half the soldiers can't find their helmets and spears. Why, one day—"

A sudden breeze sprang upon us like a Persian spy, making the palm leaves rattle overhead. "Can't you tell us on the way home? It's getting late; Mother will be worried."

Heaving a sigh and casting a last longing look at Belshazzar's palace, he rose to his feet and stuck out a hand to Sylvie. I followed them through an alley and out to Sunset Boulevard, where he turned north.

"Aren't we going home?" I asked.

"Not yet," he replied. "We're taking a little detour. I have to see a friend."

"*Now?* Can't you take us home first and then go see your friend?"

A sharp *ding!* sounded behind us, and Ranger turned his head as a streetcar approached. Then he broke into a gallop, slipping his elbow out of the sling and waving both arms wildly overhead. The streetcar slowed, and he jumped aboard the rear end, pulling Sylvie behind him.

"Come on, Isobel!" she yelled.

I ran a few steps and hopped on, thankful for the ride. "Your collarbone doesn't seem very broken to me," I remarked to Ranger.

"It's all healed up now, but nobody needs to know that just yet. I can get out of some chores that way."

"Well, of all the—"

"Fares!" bawled the streetcar driver.

We worked our way slowly to the front of the car, Ranger fumbling in his pockets. "I think... No, just a minute... um... Looks like I only have enough for one. You have any change on you, Isobel?"

"If you'd told me we were going to be using public transportation, I would have brought my pocketbook—"

"How about you, Sylvia?"

"I'm Sylvie," she corrected him. But she had no pocket change. She didn't even have pockets.

"Come on, kids," the driver prompted us.

"Could she ride for half fare?" Ranger asked with a jerk of his thumb at my sister. "She's small."

"Any time now," the driver said as houses and palm trees sped by.

"Or how about a promissory note? I'll send you the money as soon as I get home. What's your name?"

"No dice, Jake." The driver slowed down for a ragpicker's wagon directly ahead while tapping his horn impatiently. "Aren't you that Bell kid? Can't your old man ride you around in his fancy town car?"

"My father and I have some philosophical differences. That's why—"

"You got a philosophical difference with the LA County Transit Company, pal. Off, all three of ya."

He stopped at the corner. Ranger took his time stepping down, turning to offer a hand to each of us so it didn't seem like we'd just been thrown off, though of course we had. "Thanks for the lift."

Shaking his head, the driver buzzed on.

"What philosophical differences?" I asked Ranger.

He shrugged. "Big words stretch the ride out. Got up to four blocks this time. Only a few more to go."

"And how do we get back?"

"I'll worry about that later. The Keystone Studio is straight ahead; that's where we're going. I want to show you something."

At this rate we'll never get home! I thought despairingly, but Ranger was already five paces ahead of me, hands in his pockets and elbows out, the disregarded sling hanging around his neck like a cowboy's bandana. Or an outlaw's. It was almost four o'clock and the sun slanted down from its westerly trek, still warm but not so intense. We passed cottages and storefronts, truck gardens and eucalyptus groves, and street vendors selling from carts, including one with a sign that read *I don't know where Mom is, but I've got POP ON ICE.*

"Ha!" Ranger remarked to the proprietor, a boy no older than himself. "Good one."

He turned a corner, with Sylvie close behind. Sighing, I could do nothing but follow, since he was the only one of us who knew his way around.

Next minute, he was charging right at me. Then he blazed on by, pulling Sylvie by the hand. He hesitated for a half second at the Pop on Ice stand, then pushed my little sister behind it and crouched down beside her. They were hardly out of sight when two boys pounded around the corner, one yelling, "We've got you now, Bell!"

Only they didn't. They slowed down, looking around confusedly, until the Pop on Ice boy pointed to the alley beside a florist shop and yelled, "*They went thataway!*"

With a wave of gratitude, the boys took off again. When their steps no longer sounded, Ranger crept out from behind the stand and painfully stretched his legs. "Thanks, Coy."

"Anytime, Ranger." The boy nodded as though this was not the first time he'd provided cover.

"We were hiding!" Sylvie skipped to me, ecstatic.

"From what?" I asked, as Ranger joined us with a quick look over his shoulder.

"Nothing," he said. "Just chums from school."

"And what did these *chums* want to beat you up for?"

"Not sure. Maybe the peach-pit incident. Or it could be the cayenne-pepper incident. Better hoof it."

He stepped up his pace, and I had to do the same, while he led us on such a meandering route that I had to wonder if it was an evasive action. "How likely are we to run into any more 'chums' from school?" I asked.

"Not very, if I keep a sharp lookout. Half of 'em are gone for the summer anyway."

"Did you happen to have any friendly friends at school?"

He failed to answer as we turned yet another corner. I was completely lost by now. Only the lowering sun indicated which way was west. A dusty haze turned the sky yellow, and the pepper-tree smell thickened up like spicy cream-of-tomato soup, and everything seemed so strange I was suddenly, sharply homesick.

Motorcars passed in swirls of dust. A few were long and grand like Aunt Buzzy's, but many more were tin lizzies like my father's. Amid the hum of wheels and rattle of fenders I made out a clip-clop of hooves coming up behind us. Ranger turned around and raised his hat with an elaborate sweep of his arm. "Evening, Mr. DeMille."

The gentleman on the chestnut horse touched his own broad-brimmed hat in reply. "Same to you, Mr. Bell. Ladies."

Ranger paused to let me catch up. "That's one of the biggest directors in town."

"Can't he afford a car?"

"Sure he can. When he first got here, his studio was a barn at the end of a mud track. He needed a horse just to get to it."

And that's what Hollywood calls *big*? I thought. But I was too tired for a dispute.

"How much longer?" whined Sylvie.

"See up ahead?" He pointed at a collection of long, white buildings, some of them stucco and some no more than sticks and muslin. *Mack Sennett Comedies* read the biggest sign. "That's where we're going."

While we waited to cross the street, Ranger swerved his head and gave me another of his piercing stares.

"Why do you keep *looking* at me like that?"

He faced front again. "Here we go." At a break in the traffic, we scampered across the street and passed the main gate as a sleepy doorman waved Ranger through. "My friend works here in the afternoons. They'll be cranking up their evening shoot schedule pretty soon so we can't stay long, but let me show you the—"

Sylvie gave yet another cry of wonder. "Look, Isobel!"

I looked but could not tell what I was looking at. Like a gigantic top hat, it stood about twenty feet high, as big around as a house, with a wooden platform circling it like a brim. The cylinder was painted with low rolling hills, trees, and blue sky. A couple of workmen near the back of the platform were fixing a tree in place. They took no notice of us as we walked up to the edge.

"It's called the panorama—they just finished it a couple months ago," Ranger explained. "The platform here stays in the same place, but the background moves. Just the opposite of a carousel."

I couldn't see the point. "What's it for?"

"Shooting road scenes and chases. If you put an auto right here"—landing on the platform with a hop—"and a camera there"—pointing to the ground beside us—"you can shoot the car in place while the background rolls along behind it. So it looks like the car's moving. Sennett used to shoot all his car chases on the real street, but he kept getting in trouble with the natives."

"It's *delicious*," Sylvie said breathlessly, quite overwhelmed.

I was skeptical. "It's too big to move."

"Oh yeah? I've made it move by myself—that is, me and a bunch of the neighborhood kids. One night we snuck under the platform and lined up along one of the struts inside and started pushing. It takes a little muscle, but once you get it started… I'd show you now if I could, but I've got something important to do."

He jumped off the platform. "Wait here." With no more instruction than that, he ran around the curve of the panorama and disappeared.

"Well!" I exclaimed. "How do you like that?"

Sylvie seemed to like it fine. "He's the wonderfulest boy I've ever met."

We found a pair of orange crates to sit on and were debating that point a few minutes later when the wonderful boy reappeared in the company of an older fellow. The stranger appeared to be about fifteen or so, with a bony face and straight brown hair that might have been cut with a pair of garden shears. He carried a broom over one shoulder.

The two of them stopped about ten feet away from us. Dragging on a cigarette, the older boy looked me up and down with gray eyes as pale as dimes. It was the height of rudeness, which I was just about to mention when Ranger asked him, "Well?"

"Yep," the other boy said. "Good eyes, good hair. Can she act?"

"Haven't asked her yet."

That did it for me. I jumped up and folded my arms and stamped my foot like an overtired child who's been told she can't have the last cookie. "What is this about? Tell me *right now*, or I'm leaving this instant and taking Sylvie with me, no matter where we end up."

"She can act mad," the stranger observed.

Ranger turned to me with eyes so animated that they could have jumped out of his head. "This is about art," he told me, "and life, and truth and beauty too, if we can pull it off." He paused for effect. And then:

"How would you girls like to be in a picture?"

Chapter 4
Truth, Beauty, and Flickers

*B*eing in a picture was the last thing I could think about wanting in my life, but to Sylvie, it was the best idea since corn plasters. "Can I be in it too?" she begged Ranger. "Pleeese?"

"Absolutely," he said. "We'll need you for the pathos."

"More like the pathetic," his friend observed—ironically, I suppose.

"What do you need me for?" I asked Ranger. "And"—turning to the friend—"what did you mean about my eyes and hair?"

"Oh," he said, condescending to take the cigarette out of his mouth, "they're dark. Dark shows up better on the film we have to use. Blue eyes just looks spooky."

Like his, if he ever bothered to open them all the way. And if *dark* was all I had to offer, they'd be better off with a weasel. "Excuse me," I said politely, "but we haven't been introduced properly."

He shrugged. "Ain't been introduced any way that I recall." His voice had a slight rasp, with flat vowels that sounded more East Coast than West.

"This is Sam," Ranger explained.

"Samuel Patrick Service." The tall boy stuck out his hand in my direction. "At yours."

"Isobel Ransom," I replied with a very quick shake. "And this is my little sister, Sylvie."

"Nice to meetcha 'n all that," he mumbled. Then, to Ranger: "Maybe you'd better cue some people."

"We're making a picture," Ranger told us. "Sam's the cameraman, I'm the director, and you girls… Oh, come on, say you'll be in it." His face broke out an unexpected smile, bright as the white crest on a wave. "Please?"

"What's it about?" Sylvie piped up. "Do we get to be Bablionians?"

"No Babylonians." He sighed regretfully. "But other than that, we're not sure. Depends on who's in it."

"But we just met," I protested. "What makes you think I'd be any good in pictures?"

"Because you've got a camera face," he said.

That took me aback, I can tell you. "What do you mean?" I asked, blushing in spite of myself. "Pretty?"

"More than that. But yes, that." He smiled again, even wider this time.

"What am I?" Sylvie demanded.

"You're lively," Ranger assured her.

"We still don't know if they can act," Sam reminded him.

44

"Leave that to me. A good director can get a rock to act."

"Sure. 'Long as it's acting like a rock."

"Trust me—I've got a hunch. So what do you say, Isobel?"

My head was spinning. I *could* act—everyone said my portrayal of Beth in our school production of *Little Women* was the soul of the play. And it was fun too. But this was uncharted territory, and I could also hear my father saying, *You're the responsible one, Isobel.*

"Let me think about it," I said.

Sam made a little snort, as though thinking was only for sissies—and girls, of course.

"*I'll* do it," Sylvie volunteered.

"Not without me," I told her. "And you know Mother doesn't approve of the pictures."

Both boys rolled their eyes, and Ranger even groaned, bending almost double in frustration. "She doesn't *understand.* Some people think film is just Keystone Cops crashing cars or somebody's pants falling down. But it's a lot more. It's the new art: telling stories with light and motion. This"—he waved his arms grandly, taking in the Keystone lot with its fabulous panorama—"is going to be bigger than the Sistine Chapel. D. W. Griffith, Cecil B. DeMille—they're the new painters, as great as Michelangelo." He was now soaring on wings of exaggeration, in my opinion. "And someday, R. A. Bell."

He meant himself, I supposed. "What's the *A* stand for?"

He waved away the question. "Doesn't matter. I was named for my grandfather."

"But 'grandfather' starts with a *G*," Sylvie pointed out.

"Never mind! What I'm saying is, we've got a chance to get in at the beginning of something really big. It's the opportunity of a lifetime—"

"So what do you say, girlie?" Sam interrupted as he ground the stub of his cigarette underfoot. No romantic, he.

Sylvie was tugging my jacket. "Yes," she whispered. "Yes, we can."

"Stop pushing me! We just got here, for heaven's sake!"

"How about tomorrow then?" Ranger suggested. "You give us an answer by noon tomorrow."

"Well, I suppose…"

"Peachy. Just a minute." He grabbed Samuel Patrick Service's elbow and pulled him aside, where the two conferred in knife-sharp whispers. One insisted, the other resisted, while Sylvie whined to me that we *had* to do it because it was the chance of a lifetime, bigger than a chapel, and so on.

Finally, the boys came to terms, and Ranger strolled back with a casual air that didn't fool me for a minute. "Right," he said. "We'll take this up again tomorrow. Oh, and, Sam?" He bit his lip, abashed. "Do you happen to have a couple nickels for the streetcar?"

Ranger escorted us home, only to desert us at the head of the drive. His explanation was so hasty I barely caught it: "Tell-Buzzy-I've-got-an-important-errand. I'll-be-back-in-time-for-supper. She'll understand."

46

Sylvie objected, but as Ranger raced off down the street, I found myself grateful for the breathing room. He had a certain dash—not "dashing" like Mr. Rochester in *Jane Eyre*, but "mad-dashing," like Mr. Toad in *The Wind in the Willows*. Life appeared to slow down with his sudden departure, which was a good thing because even though Sylvie had made up her mind about him, my mind was rather quandarified.

Aunt Buzzy had company. Two ladies from the San Fernando Neighbors Association (whatever that was) had stopped by to ask for her signature on a petition of complaint against Thomas Ince (whoever he might be). As we paused in the entrance hall to assess the situation—some might call it "eavesdropping"—I learned that Mr. Ince was a director of Westerns.

Pictures again! Didn't anything else happen in this town?

One of the ladies was waxing very indignant about an outlaw band that had trampled her carrot patch twice in the last month while staging a shootout. "Don't these movies understand *No Trespassing*? I declare, Mrs. Bell, something must be done. And that is why…"

"I'm hungry," Sylvie complained, pulling me into the front room.

Aunt Buzzy jumped up as we entered and, after brief introductions and curtseys, offered to show us to the kitchen. That left Mother in the company of Mistresses Busy and Body, but she didn't seem to mind.

Aunt Buzzy led us through the left-side door, which opened to a long hallway with windows on one side and storage closets on the other. At the end of the hall, she pushed open a black swinging door into a huge kitchen gleaming with chrome. The gramophone was playing "Sister Susie's Sewing Shirts for Soldiers" while Esperanza sat at the counter shelling peas and swaying to the music.

"Please don't get up," Aunt Buzzy told her, then took her time getting Sylvie happily perched on a high stool with two ladyfingers and a bowl of strawberries. "Do you want anything, Belladonna?"

When I said no, she motioned me back into the hallway. "Now I must figure out how to graciously not sign that tiresome petition," she confided as we walked slowly toward the front room. "Every few weeks they bring another one by. Everybody's up in arms, but if you ask me, the movies are the best thing that ever happened to this poky little town."

"What are 'movies'?"

"People who work in the moving pictures. They've certainly livened things up around here. Did Ranger come back with you?"

I shook my head. "He said to tell you he'd be here for supper."

"Did he take you to Babylon?" I nodded. "He'd live there, if he could. And I'm sure he told you all about *Intolerance*? For someone who wasn't allowed to see it, he can certainly hold forth on the subject."

"Um." She asked me no questions so I told her no lies. "Aunt Buzzy? Did he really burn down the school gym?"

She stopped. "Oh no, dear. He only tried to. Pretty much gutted the broom closet, but that was all. Between that and

48

painting black prison bars on the classroom windows and setting off firecrackers during the awards assembly, he's had a difficult year."

It sounded to me like the school had had a difficult year. "Why?"

"I expect it was hard to adjust after all those years being taught at home, but his father decided it was time for Ranger to get out of his own little world. And I agreed, but it appears that process will take some time. He's very bright, but he doesn't think like other boys, and he's not good in sports, and he can't sit still..." She tapped a windowpane hesitatingly. "He may tell you this, or he may not. But it will help you understand: his mother was Indian. Not red Indian, the other kind from India. That's why he's so dark, and...well, it's not easy, looking different."

I blinked in surprise. The boy was so different in numerous ways that I'd forgotten he *looked* different. "But there's something else I'd like to tell you in confidence," Aunt Buzzy continued. "Ranger is on probation at the moment. After the firecracker incident, his father was ready to ship him off to military school for some discipline. I mean *at once*." She shook her head, frowning at the memory. "Such a battle of wills going on around here! I'm surprised the walls aren't pitted. I've known only one person more stubborn than Ranger, and that's his father."

Then the worry lines between her eyebrows disappeared, and her natural sunny countenance returned. "Fortunately, he's settled down quite a bit since April. Has a new hobby. I'm sure you noticed!" She seized both my hands in hers. "I was *so* excited to hear you were coming, Belladonna. You could be a real friend to Ranger. I'm not sure he's ever had one."

I wondered if she knew about Sam or the extent of Ranger's new hobby, or if I should say anything about either. But she settled that last question for me: "Back to the fray! I'm so glad you girls had a pleasant afternoon—the first of many, let's hope."

Then she squared her shoulders and marched into the front room, the back pleat on her skirt swishing like a pheasant's tail. I didn't recall mentioning a pleasant afternoon.

In fact, within five hours of meeting Ranger, I'd embarrassed myself on a studio lot and had been thrown off a streetcar, chased by vigilantes (or at least my sister had), and propositioned to be in a motion picture. "Pleasant" was not the word. Nor was I especially fond of motion pictures.

My memory of the first I'd seen flickered like the screen in the stuffy little nickelodeon with creaky chairs, where Rosetta had taken me while we were supposed to be shopping for shoes. The story was something about policemen chasing robbers and continually falling down until the robbers got caught almost by accident. I was so confused by the end that I could hardly tell who was chasing whom, but Rosetta laughed uproariously all the way through. Even though she got in trouble later when we came home without shoes.

The next picture I saw was with Father—*Rebecca of Sunnybrook Farm*, featuring wholesome Mary Pickford. I liked her just fine, but the film was so jerky the people on the screen looked like they were being poked with sticks.

"The projection speed is all wrong," Father kept muttering. "I'm *that* close to lodging a complaint with the management." But of course he didn't. Father would have to be on fire before lodging a complaint with the management, as Mother has said more than once.

And last fall, Millie Kemp and Alice Russell and I skipped a French lesson to catch a matinee at the Variety: a Western picture followed by a comedy called *Coney Island*, with Mr. Roscoe Arbuckle (better known as Fatty). *Coney Island* was rather amusing. In fact, we nearly had unfortunate "accidents" from laughing so hard, especially when Mr. Arbuckle dressed up in a lady's bathing costume and… Well, anyway, it wasn't worth the switching I got when Millie's mother telephoned mine.

"If a story is not worth reading, it's not worth seeing," Mother said. And given other factors, like a burned broom closet and a sleepy-eyed, cigarette-puffing partner, Ranger's new hobby sank lower in my estimation the more I thought about it.

The next morning, as Esperanza served broiled grapefruit, scrambled eggs, toast, and fresh-squeezed orange juice in the sunroom, Ranger nudged me with an elbow.

"The answer is *no*," I said. My mood was shaky after a restless night during which I dreamed about the battlefield again, complete with ravaged earth and a body on its side and light flashing behind a pair of broken lenses.

"Firm and flat?" Ranger didn't seem disappointed. He even smiled a little as he shook Heinz 57 Varieties on his eggs over easy.

"Yes, firm and flat." It's a good thing Sylvie was at the other end of the table getting her nose wiped, or she would have raised 57 Varieties of Cain right then and there.

"We gave you until noon to make up your mind."

"But if my mind is already made up—"

"Do me a favor." He leaned forward earnestly. "Go on a little excursion with me."

"But—"

He raised his voice. "Say, Sylvie? How 'bout an adventure after breakfast?"

The sneak! Mentioning "adventure" to my sister is like waving a red flag in front of a bull, even though Mother imme-diately said no: "We need to go shopping for summer clothes."

"Oh, Mattie," Aunt Buzzy said. "There's plenty of time to shop. Let them go exploring. Remember our golden summers in the mountains when we were young?"

I would not have believed it if I hadn't seen it with my own eyes, but Mother grew a little misty and gave up her shop-ping plans for the sake of our golden childhood. I could have kicked Ranger.

"If you think this is going to change my mind..."

"I'm not looking to change your mind," he replied sweetly, adding with his face half turned, "just your heart."

I was still wondering what he meant when we boarded a northbound streetcar. "Where are we going?" Sylvie asked, to which Ranger replied, "If I told you, it wouldn't be an adventure, would it?"

Aunt Buzzy had supplied transit passes for Sylvie and me so we could explore to our hearts' content, but I pretended to pay no heed while Ranger pointed out local points of interest. "This is the street in *Tillie's Punctured Romance*, where Tillie and the City Slicker nearly get run over by the trolley… There's the road to Echo Park, where Mr. Griffith shot the battle scenes in *Birth of a Nation*…"

Finally, he pulled the bell cord, and we stepped off at the next stop. We were on a street lined with sun-blasted, blocky buildings and spindly palm trees. *Vitagraph* read the sign over the main gate. Ranger led us down an almost-deserted street, turned at an alley, and paused to exchange a few words with the little man who was sweeping trash into a pile. The man pointed to a door, and out of the corner of my eye, I saw Ranger slip something into the man's pocket. It looked like a cigar.

Stenciled on the door was *Projection Room 2*. Ranger's knock was answered by Samuel Patrick Service.

"Are we set?" Ranger asked him in a not-quite-whisper.

"Almost." Sam stood aside to let us into a small, windowless room that reminded me of a nickelodeon. There was a screen on one wall and two short rows of chairs facing it, and at the opposite end was a gray, blocky machine I took to be a projector. Sam went straight to it after letting us in, and I watched him mount a round reel, like a bobbin, on the front of the machine.

"How does it look?" Ranger asked him.

"Not bad. Some of the cuts are jumpy." Sam pulled a strand of film from the front reel. Holding Sylvie by the hand, I drew nearer while he threaded the film through the projector as deftly as Mother threaded her sewing machine. The loose end went onto an empty reel, which he spun until it snapped taut. "Ready."

Meanwhile, Ranger had been winding up an old gramophone and searching through a stack of records. Finding the one he wanted, he set it on the turntable and pulled a chair close. "Ladies? Please take your seats."

Sylvie whooped with glee. "Are we seeing a picture? Is it *Babylon*?"

Ranger held up a finger, signaling for silence. "Ladies and gentlemen, thank you for the pleasure of your company at this exclusive, private showing of *The Mother and the Law*, directed by D. W. Griffith." His voice deepened on the great man's name.

Right away, I suspected I was being set up somehow. "Where did you get the film?"

"From a friend," Ranger explained (unsatisfactorily), then hurried on: "We only have the last reel, so I'll tell you what happens in the first part. There's a girl, called Dear One, and a young man called the Boy, and both their fathers work in a mill. But there's a strike, and when the strikebreakers come in, there's some shooting and the boy's father gets killed. The mill closes, so they all have to move to the city to find work. Dear One's father dies, and the Boy falls in with a bad crowd, but they meet and fall in love and he goes straight. Roll it, Sam."

Ranger pulled the overhead light cord, and Sam threw a lever, causing the projection machine to lurch into a loud whir. Light blazed from the screen as Dear One and the Boy appeared, poor but happy in their little home. Ranger placed the needle on the record, and strains of a "To a Wild Rose" helped mask the noise of the projector. After a while though, I stopped noticing the noise so much. The figures on the screen seemed almost real—not like the antic Cops of Keystone.

Trouble soon heaves over the horizon. The Boy's old partner in crime, known as the Musketeer of the Slums, tries to lure him back to shady ways. When he's refused, the Musketeer plants evidence on the Boy's person to make it appear he's been gambling illegally. The Boy is arrested and goes to jail, leaving his wife with their baby, her only joy—until some upright society ladies take the baby to an orphanage, because a woman with a jailbird husband is no fit mother.

The Boy gets out of jail. But that very day, the Musketeer comes to their apartment and tries to take advantage of Dear One! The Boy appears just in time, and there's a fight. A shot rings out, and the Musketeer falls dead!

(Ranger had a wooden block ready and slammed it on the table when the shot was fired—*bang!* Sylvie and I jumped a foot.)

The shot was not fired by the Boy but by the Friendless One, a woman who's jealous of Mrs. Boy. She (Friendless) was crouching on the fire escape during the fracas. But when the police arrive, they assume the Boy is guilty, and back he goes to court. In spite of his wife's pleas for a pardon, he's sentenced to hang!

"Oh no!" I gasped, immediately embarrassed that I'd said the words out loud. Out of the corner of my eye, I caught Ranger's smug smile.

Finally, tormented by her conscience, Friendless confesses to Dear One that she pulled the trigger. The two of them, with the help of a kind policeman, set off in pursuit of the Governor, who's bound somewhere on a train. Meanwhile, the Boy receives last rites from a priest and leaves his cell for the gallows.

"But he's not going to hang, is he?" Sylvie whispered.

"Hush!" I whispered back as the scene switched to Dear One chasing the Governor's train in a borrowed automobile.

"Faster!" Sylvie shouted.

Back to the gallows, where the Boy is slowly climbing the steps—

Back to the auto, which is catching up to the train. I vaguely noticed that Ranger had moved the needle to the overture from *William Tell*—

"Huuuuurry!" Sylvie was almost in my lap by now.

Back to the gallows (sad violins) where three hangmen pause, each with a knife, ready to cut the drop.

"No," I whispered. "No, wait—"

Back to the Governor's train, which has stopped. Everyone piles out of the auto and crowds into the Governor's car, where Friendless makes her confession.

But how will they stop the execution? Back at the gallows, the Boy has a black scarf tied around his eyes and the noose settles around his neck.

"Arrrgh," Sylvie groaned. I noticed my fingernails were in quite a sorry state.

Then a loud bell jingled next to my elbow, startling a cry from my agitated throat. On the screen, the prison warden stopped the hangmen so he could answer the telephone, and I realized that Ranger had rung a bicycle bell.

I also realized that he had arranged this whole performance to soften me up.

What's more, he succeeded.

Chapter 5
A Start in the Pictures

*S*uch is the power of art—I was swept up. What I had just seen was so large and real (while it lasted) that it blocked out sensible questions, like where did the boys get their camera and film, and what did their parents think of this, if they even knew?

"When can we start?" Sylvie asked.

"Well." Ranger knitted his brow while sliding the gramophone record into its sleeve. "Your sister hasn't said she'd do it yet."

"But she has to!" Sylvie cried, as though someone had to make me.

You're the responsible one, I kept telling myself. "How do we know you can even do this?" I asked. "Motion-picture-making takes a lot of costly equipment and experience—"

Ranger just said, "Roll it, Sam."

The projector whirred again and the screen flickered. I threw myself back into my chair with a flustered sigh. Were we ever going to get an answer by just *talking*? The screen flashed with countless little flags of gray and white, or perhaps ripples on a pond.

"This is our first attempt," Ranger said. "The light's all wrong—too much contrast. All that shows up at first are leaves in the trees—it was a windy day—but keep watching…"

Even as he spoke, I saw a spot of black take shape in the center of the screen and quickly grow larger. And something else: something that sprouted arms and legs and resolved itself into human form. A running human form. And as soon as I recognized that much, the setting resolved to a bridge and the thing he was running from became a locomotive, bursting with steam and rushing right at us!

Sylvie screamed, and I clapped a hand to my mouth. The runner's face blazed with terror, just before he reached the end of the bridge and dived off to one side. The picture jumped violently and the screen went gray.

"Ranger…was that you?" The scene had passed so quickly that I wasn't even sure.

"Yep. Durn train was coming on faster'n I thought."

"Nearly lost the camera right out of the gate," Sam said from the darkness.

"Stop crabbing—you had plenty of time to get out of the way. Now *this*," Ranger remarked, pointing at the screen, "could have been a real disaster."

The light was much better; we could comprehend the scene, a creek flowing between the steep sides of a canyon. Nothing seemed to be happening at first, but as we watched, a small figure swung across the creek on a rope or vine. After reaching the other side, he disappeared into the brush. A few seconds later he swung back again, and with a sharp intake of breath, I realized he was wearing nothing but a loincloth.

"Ranger!" Sylvie cried out delightedly.

"Here's the best part," he said. The view changed; instead of downstream we were at the edge of a cliff, with the water barely visible below. A movement on the opposite bank caught our eye, coming directly toward us. It was, of course, Ranger on the vine, still practically naked, with a look of exhilaration that quickly changed to dismay as he appeared to be swinging right into our laps. *Look out!* he silently cried, just before the screen went blank.

"Told ya to wear your glasses," Sam said.

"Does Tarzan wear glasses? But here's the best one yet." On screen, a figure on horseback galloped along the edge of a pasture. Next, in closer view, he reined in his mount and peered over the horizon like a frontier scout.

By now we knew who it was. Sylvie squealed, "Ranger! Is that your horse?"

For once the camera was taking its time, and we got a good look at him (Ranger, that is, not the horse). Without his glasses he looked a little older but not much. I recognized the khaki outfit, disguised though it was with a pair of epaulettes, as the proud apparel of the American Boy Scouts. I could not describe the surpassing strangeness of having Ranger in two places at once—on the screen, and living and breathing not five feet away.

On screen, Ranger bolted upright in the saddle as though he'd spied something worthy of note. Then he kicked his horse's sides and set off galloping heck-for-leather. The camera swung, a bit jerkily, as he rode by.

"Watch this," Ranger said. The camera had changed position; we appeared to be on the other side of a ditch, and he was galloping straight toward it and us. Like the locomotive, at almost the same speed. Next—as my breath caught—we seemed to be *in* the ditch, and the horse sailed right over our heads! Then we were upright again, just in time to see all four hooves strike the ground on the other side. It was a rousing finish, until the horse shied and Ranger fell off.

The horse then lost interest in acting and moseyed to one side of the screen, while Ranger got painfully to his feet, clutching his shoulder, and addressed the camera. I don't read lips, but it looked like he was yelling "*Stop!*"—along with other words that probably were best left unyelled.

"Sam!" he complained now. "You were supposed to cut all that."

"Might be useful sometime," Sam remarked, palming the end of the film as it went *flap-flap-flap* on the take-up reel. He must have been lying in the ditch to get that view under the horse, but I couldn't understand how he'd leaped up quickly enough to capture the landing.

"It was wonderful!" Sylvie exclaimed, jumping up and down. "Is that how you broke your collarbone? Will it be in our picture? Can I fall off a horse too?"

"Ask your sister if you can even be in it." Ranger was packing the reel with *The Mother and the Law* in its round metal case.

Sylvie turned to me with eyes wide as a puppy's. I was tempted, like the time I let Millie talk me into that afternoon matinee in lieu of French class. Ranger himself was part of the temptation. His spirit was infectious, fizzing up in his snappy eyes. He would take any risk for his art, but that spice of danger, I had to admit, only added to the appeal. As long as he didn't get us killed.

"Do you expect us to swing from trees or be chased by trains?"

"No, no, no," he assured me. "No adventure, just a quiet little family drama. We can't risk the camera anymore." No word about risking *us*.

"Where do you get the camera? And how do you develop the film, and who lets you use this projection room, and—"

"Don't worry about all that. Everything's jake. All we need is you. What do you say?"

"Well…" No doubt about it, my earlier resolutions were unraveling. What would it hurt to spend a few hours posing for a camera and then seeing oneself on a screen? "I suppose if Mother says it's all right—"

"No!" the boys cried out as one. My suspicions spiked up again like porcupine quills.

"That is," Ranger went on, "the picture is supposed to be a surprise for Buzzy and my father and…some other people too. They don't know about it. Yet."

"A *surprise!*" Sylvie was even more delighted, if that was possible. "Please let's, Isobel! Say yes!"

Good sense said no. But against a pesky little sister and a very determined boy, good sense never rose above a whisper. "Perhaps we could try it," I said gingerly. "But we reserve the right to back out at any time."

That is why, on Saturday morning, we found ourselves on the red streetcar going over Cahuenga Pass. We were fully fared after Ranger begged the money from Aunt Buzzy to take us sightseeing. "I'll give it to you this once," she said, "but you know your father wants you to manage your own funds for things like this. Where does it all go?"

Actually, we were bound for a "shooting." And who was to get shot? Me. With Sylvie, of course. Much to her disappointment, we had seen little of Ranger over the last few days. He was either "scouting locations" on streetcar or bicycle, or shut up in his room writing "scenarios" for the picture.

What he had come up with involved two sisters whose mother had passed on and whose father was neglectful of them. One day, the girls are wandering in the woods—maybe lost, maybe abandoned—when some danger (as yet undecided) threatens. Ranger would rescue us from it, and after confronted with near-tragedy, the guilt-stricken father would reform on the spot.

"Is that all?" I asked after a pause.

"Well…that's just the simple outline. We'll add details later."

I was far from impressed. "If so much of the story isn't decided yet, how can we act it or shoot it, or whatever we're doing?"

"All we're doing today is two babes in the woods being distressed."

"But…" I began once again.

"She thinks it's supposed to be like a stage play," Sam remarked from across the aisle, where he sat with arms folded and feet firmly clamped around a bulky carpetbag. "Where you start at the beginning and go straight through."

"No!" Ranger vigorously waved both hands in negation. "That's the beauty of film. See, it's all on lots of little pictures strung together, and each one—"

"I *know* what film is."

"But what I'm telling you is that the film can be cut at any point and spliced to another piece of film at any point. At the end of each day's shooting, you have long strips of film with bits and pieces of the story on them. When you have enough, you put them together in the order you want the story told."

"Oh." Honestly, it had not occurred to me that moving pictures were made in this piecemeal way. Once explained, it made perfect sense. "But still…if we don't know why we're wandering lost in the woods, how can we act distressed? What are we distressed *about*?"

He heaved an elaborate sigh. "Distressed is distressed. It doesn't matter why. The earlier scenes will explain that, or we'll put in a title card." (I was about to ask what title cards were, but then realized that they must be the captions that appeared at the beginning or middle of a scene to explain the action.) "So all we need today," Ranger went on, "is to get some shots of the two of you in the woods. You'll hear a noise and look frightened, and Sylvie can cry—you know how to do that, right, Sylvie?"

Rocking back and forth on the wooden bench, my little sister assured him she could weep with the best. "But you should get Isobel to make up a story for you," she added. "She makes 'em up for me all the time."

"Don't worry about the story," Ranger said, a little miffed. "We'll see to that later. Just be glad we didn't go with my original idea: a tale of passion and murder in Belshazzar's Court. With monkeys, borrowed from a fellow my pa knows. I had it all written out, but Sam absolutely nixed it."

Though he never turned his head, one side of Sam's mouth went up. "Monkeys are nothing but trouble."

"See?" Ranger waved a hand. "You girls are perfectly safe. Sam's the level-headed side of this partnership. He keeps me from getting too carried away."

"Huh," came from across the aisle. "If *only*."

We got off at the last stop and parceled out our equipment. Sam carried the camera, Ranger the tripod and film canister, I a satchel with makeup and costume items, and Sylvie a piece of heavy cardboard covered with tinfoil, which Ranger called a "reflector." A block down from the streetcar stop, we turned onto a sandy path. Dwellings were few and far between; the last one we passed was a shabby, white cottage with a peeling picket fence.

"Dead empty, near as I can tell," Ranger called over his shoulder. "I'm planning to use it for exterior shots."

"Where are we going?" I asked after several more yards of the path growing steadily steeper.

"Place called Daisy Dell," he answered.

The name certainly sounded flowerish, but what met our eyes, after we'd struggled up the path, was a huge slope-sided bowl of cactus and sage, with boulders big enough to hide any number of outlaws waiting their chance to pop up and fire away.

"We'll set up over here by the woods," Ranger announced, marching toward a scruffy little stand of pine and juniper.

While he tramped into the "woods" with Sylvie, Sam leveled his tripod and opened his carpetbag. "What kind of camera is it?" I asked.

"A moving-picture camera."

I folded my arms patiently. "What make? Eastman Kodak? Bell & Howell? Burke & James?"

"Kodak only makes still cameras," he said, heaving a squarish wooden case to the tripod and lining up the anchor bolts. But he seemed to regard me with a little more respect for knowing those names. "This is a Prestwich, Model 14. British made."

"Does it belong to you?"

"B'longs to my dad. Jimmy Service." He paused and added with obvious pride, "Best cameraman in the business."

"And he's letting you borrow it?"

"Um." He seemed very intent on the lens, opening it to peer through and blowing off a speck of dust. "Yeah."

"But how do you develop the film? Where do you get the chemicals and the hypo fixer?"

He was so surprised he almost opened his eyes all the way. "You know about that?"

"My father—who's serving his country right now as a field surgeon in France—is an amateur photographer. I help him in the darkroom." Though in fact, I didn't help him much. I liked watching the picture emerge on the print paper but could barely tolerate the smell. "It takes a lot of chemicals to develop a roll of still pictures. How do you manage a whole reel of motion-picture film?"

Sam snapped the lens shut. "It ain't easy."

Ranger called from across a clearing where he'd been pacing off distances and kicking away branches. "Ready, Sam?"

Unfortunately for me, the most interesting part of the day had already passed.

Imagine being dropped into a wilderness where the few people you see keep calling upon you to do things that make little sense, while carrying on conversations entirely over your head. Even Sylvie was getting enough of "No, move closer... Now back... Let's have that scream again—but not so loud! Put your arm around her, Isobel... *Comfort*. You know, 'There, there' and all that. Now cry... C'mon, Sylvie, you did it before."

By noon the sun was beating down like a vengeful god and everybody was a bit snappish. When Sam said, "Film's out," in the middle of another stroll through the wooded glade, Ranger threw up his hands like the frustrated artist he supposed himself to be. We trooped down the path in a bedraggled mood, and once on the streetcar, Sylvie slumped against my shoulder and dropped off to sleep.

"Sam and I have to develop the film and look it over," Ranger told me. "Tell Buzzy I'll be home in time for supper."

"Don't I get to see the film?" I asked. That was the only thing I was looking forward to after this long, long morning.

"We'll arrange that later."

"What's to arrange?"

He rolled his eyes. "It's like this. Saturday afternoon is the only time that part of the Vitagraph lot is empty. The janitor lets us in, in exchange for a few Cuban cigars. Sam can get in at night sometimes, but not me, unless I sneak out. So Saturday afternoon is the only time we can both count on working together, and we have to work fast. You girls would just be in the way. Savvy?"

I did, but when the boys got off the bus without a backward glance, I stuck out my tongue at them.

Sylvie was cranky when I woke her to change streetcar lines and whiny when we reached our stop. She sounded like I felt, but as we trudged up the long drive to the hacienda, Aunt Buzzy's sleek, gray auto swept alongside and paused, motor purring. The door opened and her voice pealed, "Hop aboard, you weary souls!"

Gratefully we squeezed in beside her and Mother. They both looked flushed and startled, as though happily surprised. Mother especially. She took off her straw hat to tuck loose strands of her hair back over her ears. "We've had an adventure!"

"We did too!" Sylvie replied. "We were up in—"

"What kind of adventure?" I interrupted.

"The Hollywood kind," Aunt Buzzy said, laughing. "We were just motoring home from a sedate luncheon at the Plaza with Mrs. Armitage and her stuffy friends. I asked Masaji to take the southern route so we could see the orange groves in bloom. Coming up on the intersection at Seventh and Vine, I noticed an auto that looked like Celia Travers's, and I told Masaji to step on it because I didn't want her to wave me down and bend our ears for two hours about her latest gardening triumph. But when we hit the intersection, I barely had time to notice that it wasn't Celia after all before we were spinning around in a maelstrom!"

"What's a maelstrom?" Sylvie inquired.

"Like a whirlpool, dear—just a figure of speech." Mother's voice was calm, but her eyes sparkled with something I might have called manic glee if I didn't know her better. "We had sped right into a Keystone Cops picture!"

"Yes, and Mack himself was there, and he got the whole thing on film."

Masaji parked the car in front of the hacienda and got out to open doors for us, his lips tight and face pale. As we went into the house, Aunt Buzzy supplied the details. Mr. Sennett, chief director of Mack Sennett Comedies, had actually greased the intersection to add a comic touch to a chase scene. He had posted a watchman down the road to warn unwary travelers, but the watchman wasn't minding his business, or else Masaji had not noticed him. When Aunt Buzzy ordered him to speed up, he did—with results, everyone agreed, that could have been tragic. But they weren't, and everyone seemed just fine.

It was the kind of thing that would have made Mother quite livid if it happened in Seattle. But it was also the kind of thing that didn't happen in Seattle. It was a Hollywood thing. And in Hollywood, Mother was not quite the same person.

"Of course," she remarked while putting her hat away, "Mr. Sennett apologized profusely, but there was no harm done."

"No harm done" was not what she'd said when Sylvie had tobogganed her red wagon down a hill and barely missed smashing into an ice delivery truck.

"Mack offered us a personally guided tour of the lot," Aunt Buzzy added. "And we may just take him up on it in a few days. If the film develops well—or however they put it—we may end up on the silver screen in a Keystone Cops picture!"

Mother raised her eyebrows but did not deny it. Both ladies then disappeared into the east wing to change their clothes.

Belatedly I searched the palm-leaf mail tray for a letter from France. But there was no overseas postmark among the bills and cards. Had Mother even looked?

Chapter 6
Interiors

C ut!" Ranger yelled a few days later. "What's wrong with you girls? When I say fear, I want *fear*!"

I sighed; even Sylvie sighed. Sam straightened up from his camera crouch and opened the lens, then squirted a puff of air inside with a rubber syringe—his habit after every take, to blow dust off the film.

"It looked okay to me. We don't have that much film stock to waste," he said.

"I know. But I'm not getting what I want. And I didn't like the angle much either." As Ranger paced up and down, two fingers pressed against his brow in a way that signaled *Genius at work*, I grabbed Sylvie's hand to keep her from rubbing at the makeup—really just flour dusted over a thin coat of lard. It made us look like we'd blundered out of our untimely graves, but Ranger insisted: "The film makes you too dark, especially in the shade." Shade and light were two of the things that had to be worked out, which was the reason we met earlier in the morning this time, before blazing noon made us glare in the sun and disappear in shadow.

Sam yawned hugely and leaned an elbow on the tripod. Morning was not his best time; Ranger told me he often slept until noon, which gave him less than an hour to get to his job at Keystone, where he ran errands and cleaned up sets until seven. *Did he go to school?* I'd asked. *Not since he was fourteen,* Ranger had replied enviously.

"I've got it!" Ranger cried now. "Instead of just standing here under the tree, you girls go down the path—see where that stump is? Go to the stump and then back into the trees so we can't see you. When I holler, step out on the path and start walking toward the camera, not too fast. I'll talk you down. Savvy?"

For an answer, I put a hand on Sylvie's neck and marched her up the path toward the aforementioned stump. Behind me Sam muttered, "You're going to have to make up your mind because—"

"I know!" Ranger muttered back snappishly. "But who's *paying* for the film?"

That must be why he was always cash poor, I thought. We kept marching, and when Ranger called, "Now disappear!" I pulled Sylvie off the path with me.

"How much longer?" she whined.

"Just until Mr. Art decides his muse is done for the day."

"Who's Mr. Art?"

"Don't touch the makeup! We'll just have to slap it back on. Don't forget, you're the one who wanted to be in a picture."

"I already was in a picture, and we didn't even get to see it."

"That's because we're just decoration."

"What's that over there?" Sylvie asked, pointing through the trees, at the very moment Ranger yelled, "*Now!*"

I got a firm grip on her hand, whispering, "Ask me later. Let's get this right, or we'll have to do it again and again and again."

"Look scared!" Ranger called, as we emerged from behind the trees. I didn't see him, but of course Sam was at the end of the path, turning the camera crank at a steady pace, counting under his breath for every full turn: *one* one hundred, *two* one hundred…

A high-pitched scream from the bushes made me almost jump out of my skin. Sylvie clutched me in a suffocating grip. "What was that?"

"*Good*, Sylvie!" came Ranger's voice from the brush on our right. "Look in the other direction now. Isobel, you're jumpy. You've been hearing noises—*Arrrrrgh!*" He made a gurgling noise in his throat. "It might be a mountain lion or a bear!"

"But I saw it," Sylvie said to him. "It looked like—"

"Stop looking this way! I'm not here! Squeeze close to Isobel!"

"Talk to *me* if you have to talk," I murmured.

She answered, just as murmury, "Back in the trees. It looked like—"

"Put your arm around her, Iz!" Ranger commanded, keeping pace with us. "You're trying to be brave, but these noises are getting to you. Like this one: *Arrooooo!*" I pulled Sylvie closer, barely keeping a straight face. "*Bully!* As you come closer, let the camera see your eyes get wider—no, not too fast! A little at a time. And your mouth like an O. Closer…closer… ready… Cut!"

By then, my eyes were as wide as they could go without falling out. Sam emerged from behind the camera, almost smiling. "Looked good, except the kid kept talking to you."

"Yep, I thought that might have blown it. Let's do it again."

My hands flew up in exasperation, which freed Sylvie to dash back up the path. While the boys engaged in camera talk, I sulked, staring at Sam's cap, which he always turned backward while shooting so the bill did not bump up against the viewfinder. Very practical, but I thought it looked silly. Like so much else in the moving-picture business. They were coming to some sort of agreement (I could tell by the voices, not the words), when Sylvie screamed from the woods: "*Come look! Come look!*"

When she lets loose like that, it can mean she's just excited or she's being mauled by a very large animal, so I took off at a gallop with the boys close behind. What we found, after crashing through the brush and wire, was Sylvie doing a clog dance on the floor of an abandoned shack. It was about the size of an auto garage, with one door and two windows, a wall missing and the roof partly caved.

"See?" Sylvie crowed. "I'm in a show!"

I sagged, gulping for breath. "Is that all? I thought you were being killed."

Ranger stared, then smiled, then walked all the way around

the pitiful structure, his smile broadening. Finally he burst out, "Look at it!" as though we hadn't been.

Sam sounded equally awestruck. "Wonder who owns it."

"Nobody! Or nobody who cares. See how it's falling in? All we'd have to do is pull down the roof—"

"Take the broken glass out of the windows—"

"Replace a few boards on the floor—"

"Clear the brush away—"

"For what?" I broke in. "Are we going into the real estate business too?"

Ranger turned to me, his dark eyes fairly crackling. "Don't you see? It's perfect for interior shots. We haven't been able to put any of the story inside because we had no place to shoot it."

"Can't you use a room in your house?"

"No, no, no. Not enough light. Light's the problem. You remember that Western we watched them shooting last week?" I nodded, hoping he wouldn't tell Sam how I'd interrupted the scene. "That's how interiors have to be shot, in a house with no roof and one wall missing—just like *that*." He stabbed a finger at the building, giddy with glee.

"Unless you have kliegs," Sam said. When I looked at him, he added, "Klieg lights."

"You can't 'borrow' any of those?" I asked, not really joking.

"Lenders have their limits, girlie."

Ranger meanwhile had taken another turn around the house with Sylvie clinging to him and asking what we were going to do next. "This is *bully*. We can use the wood from the roof to build furniture. A bed, a table—"

"Pictures on the wall?" Sam suggested.

"I suppose," I said slowly, "if you could tack up another kind of wall cover, like a sheet or something, you could use this for more than one…um…interior."

The boys looked at each other, possibilities multiplying like lice. "A store!" Ranger shouted.

"A saloon?" Sam offered.

"A church—"

"A barn—"

"A *railroad station*," Ranger concluded reverently. "How's this for a scene? We go down to Culver City station and set up the camera to look down the track. You shoot the train coming in. We see Isobel step off the passenger coach—"

"Me, too!" Sylvie clamored.

"Isobel *and* Sylvie step off the passenger coach. Then we see them go into the station. Next scene, that door opens"—he pointed to the door in the center back wall of the shack—"and they're inside!"

What we would do once inside the station, or why we were on the train in the first place, were sensible questions that it did not occur to me to ask. Because for the first time, I was beginning to catch a ray of Ranger's shining vision. We could go anywhere on the streetcar route and shoot anything, and by cutting and splicing the film, we could make it look like this little house was part of that same place, even though it was miles away.

Motorcars and flying machines were supposed to be annihilating time and space, but film could actually do that. Or create the illusion anyway. Like in the well-known fable, I was plodding up to the starting line, a poky tortoise to those eager hares. But if Ranger and Sam had a long start on me, I was at least heading in the same direction.

When they stopped for breath, I said, "Hadn't we better get started?"

When the three of us returned home, much later in the day than we'd said, Aunt Buzzy threw up her hands. "Where on earth have you *been*? I was almost ready to call the police."

She didn't look all that disturbed; more like she thought she should be worried but couldn't quite work up to it. Ranger said, "We've been building a playhouse over in Daisy Dell."

That line suited our looks if not our ages, for even though I'd tried to keep Sylvie and myself reasonably tidy while clearing away brush and boards, those nails seemed to reach out and grab us. We were more than a little grubby, and Sylvie had managed to get two rips in her dress, which I'd hoped to sew up before anyone noticed.

"All the way over to Daisy Dell?" remarked Aunt Buzzy in surprise. "That's a wasteland. What on earth brought you—"

"Where's Mother?" I interrupted. This was the first time since our arrival that Mother wasn't stuck to her sister like a Siamese twin.

"You'll never guess." Aunt Buzzy's eyes danced. "Remember how Mack Sennett invited us to visit his studio? We decided to take him up on it, *but* just as we were starting out the door, Mr. Bell phoned and needed me to find some papers for him. One thing led to another, so I told Mattie to go on to Sennett's by herself if she wanted to, and darned if she didn't!"

"Can we go make ourselves a sandwich?" Ranger asked.

I had been entertaining similar thoughts, but Aunt Buzzy's news, which she seemed to think delightful, made my stomach forget it was hungry. Why should my mother, a respectable lady with a husband in the service, go gallivanting off by herself to visit some fellow who made a living by getting people to fall down for no good reason in front of a camera?

And what would Father think about that? I glanced at the elephant-foot mail tray beside the door: empty. What should *I* think?

It was all very confusing, and Mother herself did not help to dis-confuse when she returned shortly after, with that flustered-but-pleased expression I'd noticed after her encounter with Mr. Sennett's greasy intersection.

"Bea, Isobel, you'll never guess!"

"What, Mattie?" Aunt Buzzy dutifully inquired.

"Who do you think is going to appear in the next Keystone comedy feature?"

"Not *you!*" Aunt Buzzy's voice rose as my heart descended.

"Where and how do you get to fall down?" I asked when the excitement had abated.

"Oh for heaven's sake, Isobel. I couldn't achieve such an exalted status in my first picture—and last, no doubt. My part is already finished. Masaji and I arrived just as the Cops were chasing an ice wagon down a studio street, and Mack recruited us to be part of the astonished crowd looking on. I very much doubt you'll see more of me than my hat."

"What fun!" Aunt Buzzy exclaimed, while I thought, *Mack?*

On Thursdays Aunt Buzzy volunteered at the Red Cross, rolling bandages for soldiers overseas. This Thursday Mother and I were going along, and on the way we planned to leave Sylvie at the home of one of Aunt Buzzy's friends, who had a little girl just my sister's age. I hoped Aunt Buzzy would still have that friend after Sylvie's visit.

Shortly before lunch, Ranger took a telephone call, after which he looked me up with that eager expression I would soon recognize as *Sam's got the camera.*

"We're going to Daisy Dell," he told me.

"Have fun," I said.

"No—you, me, and Sam are going. It's a chance too good to miss. We'll spend a couple hours setting up the place, and when the sun starts getting low, we can work in some interior shots."

"But we won't have Sylvie."

"Exactly."

"And I was going to the Red Cross today."

He was ready for that, launching a full-frontal assault on my commonplace ideas of patriotism. "You can roll bandages any day of the week! But the opportunity to serve your country as an artist only comes around once in a full moon—"

"Blue moon," I corrected him. "And what's patriotic about two girls lost in the woods?"

"Don't worry about that. This picture's going to be more red, white, and blue than the Stars and Stripes. Just don't tell Sam."

"Why not?" I asked.

"Because he doesn't want to make a war picture. Too complicated, he says. But he'll come around. You'll see. I have plans."

Suffice it to say, I came around in time. Soon after lunch, we were on our way to Daisy Dell carrying a broom and a saw and a hammer, along with curtains and a tablecloth and a few dishes to make our shack look like home, be it ever so humble.

Ranger smuggled almost everything in a guitar case, but the broom wouldn't fit. I had to carry it, and endure the inquisitive stares of transit patrons. "Next time wear a cap and apron," Ranger suggested. He was bouncing with anticipation at trying out our new "studio"—his name for the tumble-down shack.

When we had struggled up the path to Daisy Dell, Sam was already there with his own tools, plus camera and tripod. His first words were, "Got a story yet?"

"I'm working on it," Ranger breezily replied.

"You can work *on* it all you want, as long as it's in your head. But we don't have that much film to play around with, and I don't want to get stuck with fifteen beginnings and no end."

"All right, all right—by the end of the week. I promise."

We set about making the shack presentable, and with no little sister to get charmingly underfoot, we made quite a bit of progress. In just a couple of hours, the floorboards were pounded down and the window frames repaired, and a crude table had been thrown together to go with a rickety chair. The boys did most of that, while I swept and hung curtains.

By then the sun was at a decent angle for camera work. The scenes we shot were of the kind Ranger called "establishing"— meaning to set a mood or location. So there was the girl in her miserable home, searching in vain for something to cook for dinner. Then a scene where the hero came to call and I made the best of our poor hospitality. Wanting comic relief (which would have been easy with Sylvie around), Ranger hit upon some business where he finds a cockroach in his soup and I am mortified.

Sam would have to get a close-up of an actual roach in a bowl sometime, but he said their house had no shortage of them.

On the way back to the streetcar stop, we paused to shoot a scene beside the little white house. There wasn't much to it. I merely stood beside the picket fence looking sad. Then I stood beside the picket fence weeping into a handkerchief, and as usual, Ranger couldn't tell me why. "It doesn't matter—could be anything. Pop's on a bender or Little Sister's lost or you're sad to see the hero go—say, let's get one of me going."

To my mind, none of it amounted to much, but Ranger seemed pleased. Sam took a different route home, and on the streetcar Ranger told me tales of "the business." Such as Mr. Griffith's methods of direction: "I heard that when he met Lillian and Dorothy Gish—they're sisters and two of his favorite actresses now—at first he couldn't make 'em understand what kind of emotion he wanted. So, unbeknownst to them, he loaded a pistol with blanks and invited them into his office, and started chasing them around the room firing shots into the air. He got his response, all right."

"You'd better not try that with us!"

"Whatever works. And another time, I heard…" Though I was not convinced his stories were completely true, I had to admit they made the time speed merrily by all the way to the hacienda.

At the end of the drive, Ranger took my broom and suggested we separate. He would circle around to the back so the grown-ups wouldn't wonder about our domestic implements. "I'll meet you in the kitchen."

I had expected the ladies to be back from the Red Cross, but the house seemed eerily empty when I walked into the entrance hall. Wondering if they'd had to take a little girl to the hospital to get stitched up (with Sylvie, one never knew), my eye fell upon the mail tray. Dead center on the palm leaf was an envelope stamped with a U.S. Army postmark. I pounced. *Yes!* It was from Captain Robert Ransom, our first letter in over a month!

Back in Seattle, Mother would have perused it first, then

gathered me and Sylvie to read it out loud. But here... After a slight hesitation, I slit open the envelope, shook out the contents, and scanned the date: June 2, when we were still in Seattle.

His handwriting shocked me: sprawled like a drunken sailor, with many unfinished words and cross-outs. Some lines were blacked over completely. It was as if Father himself, always so neat and well-groomed, had wandered through the door in a bathrobe with his hair in his eyes. I made out the meaning slowly:

Dear ones,

By this time I expect you are enjoying the sunshine. I don't get much, seems the sky is always full of smoke. Sleep is a distant memory, but I am in good health thank God. Much to do here. [a sentence blacked out] Ambulance brings in stacks of wounded. I have never [more crossed out] Sorry to be making such a mess. I would start this letter over but no time. The food here leaves much to be desired. I've shed all that extra wait Rosetta's cooking put on me. Once I've served my time you will not recognize the ~~scarecrow~~ trim figure who bounds off the train to swoop you all up in his arms. One good thing about the work here I have so little time to miss you.

Love to Buzzy and best to all her house—
Your devoted, etc.

Chapter 7
By the Beautiful Sea

The ladies arrived within minutes, and I was partly right in guessing where they'd been—not to the hospital, but to the cleaners to try to salvage Sylvie's dress after she'd spilled half a bottle of ink on it. The other half, I gathered, went on the hair of her new little friend Agnes—whose hair was already black, thank goodness, Aunt Buzzy observed cheerfully. Though Agnes's mother did not take such a philosophical view.

Cheer abruptly fled after Mother snatched up the letter and read it, first to herself and then out loud. A moment of silence followed. "Poor Bobby," sighed Aunt Buzzy. "Such a shame he had to go."

"He did *not* have to go," Mother snapped. "He was poked and prodded into it by—" She stopped abruptly, remembering little pitchers with big ears nearby: namely me, gazing at her with my mouth open.

Prodded by whom? Could she mean Grandfather Ransom,

who spoke of his own war service in the Philippines as his noblest hour? Memories of certain strained moments around my grandparents' dinner table came back to me, making me wonder if the whole business of Father's enlistment was more complicated than I had thought. And if he didn't *have* to go, why did he, and leave us with all this worry and unsettlement?

I didn't sleep well that night. The old nightmare of the battlefield returned with the blasted landscape of splintered trees and mucky ridges. Father kept telling us he was in no immediate danger.

What if he wasn't telling us the entire truth?

The next morning we met at Griffith Park (no relation to the great D. W.), where Sylvie found three little boys who almost matched her for rowdiness. While they played variations of hide-and-seek, Ranger read his scenario to Sam and me. It was only three pages long, or less if one didn't count the cross-outs. But it took him a while to explain because of interruptions. For instance, after he began with, "There are these two girls, see, and we'll call them Matchless and Little Sister," Sam responded with an impatient *humph*.

"Those aren't names," he pointed out, while trying to roll a cigarette in a gusty breeze.

"No, they're qualities. Mr. Griffith does that because—"

"I know he does that, and I think it's stupid. If they're supposed to be real people, give 'em names."

"They're more than real people. They're ideas too."

"All right—if Matchless is an *idea*, better make that clear at the beginning. Somebody wants to beg a match off her and she doesn't have any. Get it?"

That's why it took so long for Ranger to get through his scenario, but finally the story was laid out for our inspection:

"Matchless and Little Sister live in a rundown shack with their worthless father who's cruel to them when he's down on his luck, which is—"

"I don't like that," I interrupted. "Most fathers are upstanding gentlemen" (like mine, I didn't say) "who work hard for their families."

"It's just part of the story, Isobel," Ranger explained patiently. "Every story needs some problem to solve, right? In this story, Dad's the problem."

"But—"

"To continue: while the two girls are on an outing at the beach—we'll go down to Santa Monica—Little Sister falls off the pier and is saved from drowning by a dauntless youth."

"Is that his name?" Sam smirkily asked. "*Dauntless Youth*?"

"—who becomes friendly with the girls. He calls on them at their home when their father is away, and Matchless falls in love with him."

"But I'm only twelve!" I protested.

"In the picture, you're closer to sixteen, and I—the youth, I mean—is eighteen. He has to be that old because he's just enlisted."

"Wait a minute," Sam interrupted again. "I already toldja we can't make a war picture. We don't have the money or the—"

"No, listen." Ranger's dark eyes crackled as he sat eagerly forward. "Thursday after next, there's going to be a huge bond rally during the Lasky Home Guard drill. If you set up right next to the street with a good angle, it'll look like the boys are marching off to war."

"I'm not gonna risk—" Sam began.

Ranger raced on: "I know a prop man at Lasky who just enlisted for real. He said he'd lend me his Home Guard uniform. So we get a shot of Isobel and Sylvie waving like mad, and I can run over to them in my uniform, and it'll look like I just stepped out of the ranks to say good-bye."

Sam was shaking his head. "Too risky. All those people."

"What's the Lasky Home Guard?" I wondered aloud, meanwhile wondering silently what Sam was afraid to risk around "all those people."

"It's the Famous Players Studio volunteers," Ranger told me. "They drill every Thursday night with wooden rifles and uniforms from the wardrobe department. Mr. DeMille is the captain because he has military experience."

Sam *humphed* again. "He went to military *school*. As a kid."

"So what? The point is, with a bond rally going on at the same time, there'll be a big crowd and lots of cheering and flag-waving. It's too good to miss, so don't be a stick-in-the-mud, Sam."

Sam clearly looked stuck. He opened his mouth to speak a couple of times, then stopped himself after a glance at me.

"But back to the story," continued Ranger. "The Youth has already enlisted when he meets the girls, so he has to go, but there'll be a touching farewell scene where Matchless gives him a seashell from the beach where they met. Then a scene of him in France, scouting for the Allies. That's how we'll use the horse footage—how's that for an idea?" He punched Sam on the shoulder. "And what would you think if we got some newsreel film of the actual war and cut it in. Wouldn't that be bully?" Sam's expression softened a little, as though the idea was worth considering.

"Meanwhile, back home, the father loses his job and that puts him in a worse temper than before. There's a scene where he knocks Little Sister around and accidentally kills her—"

"*What?*" I exclaimed, as Sam groaned.

"It'll be terrific," Ranger insisted. "Here's the Youth fighting for his country in Europe, and it's the dear little tot back home who gets killed. Real pathos."

"No," I said quite firmly.

"But wait'll you hear. Next scene, she'll appear as an angel to the Youth on the battlefield, like at the end of *Intolerance*—"

Sam stopped him. "Wait a minute; let me guess. You want to hang her from a tree with piano wire?" At Ranger's nod, he put his own foot down. "No piano wire. If you don't know what you're doing, you could cut somebody's head off."

That was enough for me. Trying as she could be, I preferred Sylvie *with* her head rather than without. And the notion of a tyrannical father made me queasy. Ranger put up a spirited defense, but faced with our united opposition, he had to back

91

down. "All right, so the father doesn't *kill* her. He can still knock her around."

I was going to object again, but Sam spoke first. "And who plays dear old dad?" he asked. Ranger looked at him with beseeching eyes, but to no avail. "I already told you I'm not going to be in this thing. I'm a cameraman, not an actor. And who would man the camera? Matchless?"

"Why not?" I asked. "Just for a minute."

"Nobody touches it but me."

I decided to make a point of touching the camera the next time we went shooting.

Ranger mused, "Maybe I could put on a beard and lifts. But there's one scene where Dad and the Youth appear together."

"Put one of the girls in a beard and lifts."

I sputtered, not entirely sure that Sam was joking. "Do you mean to tell me, Ranger Bell, that you don't have any other friends you can twist the arms of?" Unlike most boys, Ranger never had to meet the fellows for a baseball game, and his schoolmates were more inclined to run him down on sight, as I knew from experience.

He waved aside the question. "We'll work it out later. The Youth gets an honorable discharge after some heroic deed and hurries home because he's been going all moony over that seashell so we know he's in love. He gets off the train, but she isn't there to meet him. I was going to have the station agent tell him that there's been trouble at home... You wouldn't mind being a station agent, would you?" Sam just looked stony.

"Anyway, the youth rushes down to the shack and

discovers… Well, I'm not sure what he discovers *now*. It was going to be the old man on a rampage, and the Youth could lay him out flat. At any rate, the girls are in peril and he rescues them, and he and Matchless declare their love and live happily ever after. How's that?"

"Can't the girls just be orphans?" Sam asked. "You could still cook up all kinds of peril to rescue 'em from."

"But there has to be a villain," Ranger insisted. "Somebody for the audience to hate."

"What audience?" I gasped in alarm. I had forgotten that my "acting" might actually be seen by anyone.

Ranger looked flustered. "You never know."

Sam's eyelids lowered farther. "We know who your audience is."

"*I* don't," I said—usually not so eager to admit ignorance, but I was getting lonely out there in the dark all the time.

"The great D. W.," muttered Sam. "That's who."

Ranger flared. "*You* wouldn't mind if he saw your work."

"No, but you haven't told me how you're going to get his attention."

"I thought your father and Mr. Griffith were friends," I said.

No answer, and after a brief silence, Ranger awkwardly changed the subject. "We'll figure out the villain problem later. In the meantime, when can we go to Santa Monica?"

Not any time soon, as it turned out. The first two mornings we set, Sam was "busy." That probably meant that the camera was busy.

The delay gave me an opportunity to write two letters to

93

Father and meet the local librarian and wile away the lazy afternoons with *Ivanhoe* and *The Scottish Chiefs*, while Sylvie became very tight with Bone the sheepdog. Ranger went out "on business," which I gathered had much to do with the war bond rally he hoped to shoot the following week. Or he worked on his scenario, wadding up page after page of notepaper—attempts, he told me, to either get by without a villain or suggest one without showing him. By the looks of things, it wasn't going well.

But he seemed downright cheerful the morning we finally made it to Santa Monica. The beach was a lively place, with a long arcade at the water's edge and a calliope jauntily wheezing out tunes. We found Sam on a bench near the boardwalk, the tripod behind him and the carpetbag, as always, firmly clasped between his feet.

"I've only got an hour," he told us without preamble. "Already took some shots of the ocean in case we need 'em. There's a fishing pier up north a little ways. Tide's going out— we'd better move quick, while there's enough water for a little girl to drown in."

We were all breathless by the time we hiked down to the fishing pier, burdened with equipment and extra clothes. A grandfatherly gentleman with a pole took one look at us and decided to quit the premises.

Sam set the tripod and mounted the camera while the rest of us made each other up. For Sylvie and me, this was a matter of lip color and eye paints, which Ranger had purchased from the local five and dime. Here on the beach, we could forego the flour and lard, but Ranger plastered himself with a free hand, after which he outlined the scene: "We have to get a few shots of the girls walking along the beach while Sylvie's clothes are still dry. So you two go up that way and wait for my signal. Act happy. Matchless got a few pennies from somewhere, and you've decided to take Little Sis to the arcade. Maybe we can get some arcade shots—"

"No arcade shots." Sam's voice held a warning tone, again making me wonder why he was so shy about crowds.

"Okay, never mind. Sylvie—you see the fishing pier and run out on it. Isobel yells for you to come back and you don't, because you're feeling naughty. So she starts for you, and you do a little dance right on the edge of the pier." Ranger raised his hands and pirouetted to show what he meant. I hoped nobody was watching. "Then you slip and fall in. Remember all that?"

Sylvie not only remembered all that, but threw in some business of her own. When we started our walk with the camera cranking, she plopped down in the sand, to my consternation, and started peeling off her shoes and stockings.

"Good!" Ranger yelled through his cupped hands. "Iz, unbend a little. Remember you're on a holiday—take your shoes off too!"

So I did, unbending enough that Ranger shouted, "Bully! Don't forget to pick up the shoes. Sylvie, look this way: *Oh joy! Let's run away from Big Sister!*" He acted this out with pattering baby steps. "Isobel, yell at her to come back."

Sylvie ran exuberantly toward the pier, and Sam managed

to follow her onto it, turning both the film and the panning crank. When Ranger shouted, "*Cut!*" he closed the shutter and cranked one full turn to create space between takes.

For the next shot, Sam positioned the tripod right on the pier for a direct view of Sylvie dancing like a little maniac on the edge. At Ranger's signal, she slipped off—and landed on her bottom in a mere six inches of water. The tide was going out faster than we expected.

"Criminy," Ranger fumed. "Sam, move the camera down the pier. Sylvie! Go out a little farther and start flailing around."

"She can't swim!" I protested.

"Doesn't have to. She only has to move out far enough her knees don't show. Besides, I have a scout badge in lifesaving."

Sylvie was already bobbing out to deeper water, so I yelled, "Be careful!" and kept my eyes on her while she thrashed and shrieked. I looked away only long enough to do my own shrieking while the camera was on me. Then Sam turned his lens toward the beach, where Ranger heard our cries and determined in his resolute heart to come to our aid.

Meanwhile the pitch of Sylvie's yelling had shifted, and when I looked back to the water, she was farther out than before. "The tide's caught her!" I screamed. "She's going out to sea!"

At least Ranger wasted no more time striking poses. Already divested of his shoes and jacket, he charged the surf like a locomotive and flung himself into the waves. I ran into the water up to my knees and stood there wringing my hands. Even with the sound of the camera grinding in my ears, I was hardly acting.

Sam just kept on cranking, and soon he got something unexpected: another body in the water, emerging from the left of the lens and paddling toward Sylvie with as much resolution as any lifeguard. It was a golden retriever, long silky ears streaming behind him. The dog reached her first, grabbed her collar with his teeth, and began paddling back toward land. Ranger was thus cheated of the actual rescue, but he lent a hand when the dog's strength waned and looked just as heroic when he staggered onto the beach with a coughing and sputtering Sylvie in his arms.

I ran to her while Ranger whooped like a savage. "Did you see that? We'll leave the dog in. *Cut*, Sam—you're wasting film. We'll shoot Sylvie throwing her arms around him while Matchless and the Youth make eyes at each other, and then—"

At that moment we were joined by the owners of the dog—two boys, one about Ranger's age and the other a few years younger. The younger one was shouting, "Good boy, Champ! We didn't even know where you was until Danny heard all the hollerin' down here. We're gonna tell the mayor and get you a medal..."

While he prattled on, the rest of us became aware that Ranger and the older boy recognized each other—first with surprise, then growing hostility. "I shoulda known," the boy finally growled. "Half-breed Bell, grinding out his big picture. Now I know why you like the flickers. They give you a chance to look white."

"He saved my life!" Sylvie piped up loyally from the nest of towels I had wrapped her in.

97

"Get lost, Prewitt," Ranger said, scrubbing the flour from his face with a wet shirttail.

"I've got as much right to be here as you. Anyways, since you're already half stripped-down for a fight, remember I owe you one for pasting that shiner on Tom Pigeon last spring."

"He had it coming," Ranger muttered.

"For what? For callin' a spade a spade?"

"It was three against one! I just got in a lucky punch!"

"You feel lucky now?" Danny raised his fists and made a practice jab while his little brother shouted encouragement from the side of the noble Champ. Ranger darted forward and made an ill-considered swing that left him open to a hard punch to the ribs. The sound of air bursting from his lungs was so sharp I felt it.

Sylvie would have charged in, but Sam moved faster. He dropped from the pier and grabbed Danny by the collar band, twisting until the boy gasped for air. "Pretty day, ain't it? Why don't you go throw some sticks for your dog—who's got better manners than you."

He punctuated *you* with a shove, and Danny stumbled on the sand. The boy picked up his cap and crammed it on his head, shifting his glare from Sam to Ranger. "You still owe us one, Mud-face!" Then he hauled up his little brother and marched back toward the arcade, Champ frisking after them with never a backward glance.

Even Sylvie knew enough to keep her mouth shut. In the silence, busy fingers of ocean foam drummed away from the wooden piles of the dock, leaving them naked in the oozy sand.

"Don't let those twits get to ya," Sam said softly.

"I'm not." Ranger suddenly kicked up a geyser of sand. "What gets to me is a whole day's work wasted because of that damn dog!"

"Oh." Sam stepped back on the pier and began dismounting the camera. "We might be able to use some of it—you never know. In the meantime, watch your language around the ladies."

"I'm no lady!" Sylvie sputtered indignantly. As for me, I was glad he noticed.

Ranger was rather taciturn on the bus. I might have said "sulky," except for being unsure if it was the insult from Danny or the loss of a good day's footage that galled him more. When Sylvie finally leaned her damp head against my shoulder and drifted off to sleep, he burst out: "All right, I know you're wondering. My mother was Indian. As in 'You're a better man than I, Gunga Din.' That's why the 'half-breed.'"

I was about to tell him I already knew that, but he had taken out his wallet and was thumbing through it. "Here's a picture."

Not just *a* picture. What he thrust at me was none other than Mr. and Mrs. Titus Bell—the first Mrs. Bell that is, a dark petite woman with a shy smile and velvety eyes. Mr. Bell towered over her. With his long face and wide mouth, he reminded me of Tom Mix the cowboy actor.

99

"I can't decide who you look like more," I remarked after a moment.

"That's easy—Pa, from the scalp up. Her from the skin out."

It was more complicated than that. Ranger was an odd combination. He had his father's mouth and crinkly hair, but his mother's small build and melting eyes.

"She was very beautiful," I said, handing back the photograph.

"Uh-huh." He tucked it in his wallet. "One of Pa's exotic imports, like the African drums and Jap prints."

"What a thing to say about your own mother!" I was truly shocked.

Ranger rubbed his cheek hard, as though trying to lighten the color. "Sorry. It's just that I don't remember her at all. Everybody else seems to—and they'll never let me forget. But I was doing all right until Pa made me go to St. Michael's Preparatory Academy."

"Does he know you get picked on?"

"Sure. I've told him, and Buzzy's told him."

"What does he say?"

"He always throws some Kipling at me: 'You'll be a man, my son,' all that." Ranger stood up, steadying himself with one hand on the overhead grip and the other hand clutching his jacket lapel. "And then something like, 'Your mother was a lady of elegance and breeding, and it's to my sorrow you don't remember her. But you must learn that those petty slings and arrows can't make a dent in the inner man.'"

He stuck his chin out, much to the amusement of the little

boy who sat across from us with his mother. Ranger's imitation was quirky enough to recognize a real person in it, though I'd never met the person. "They've made plenty of dents in the *outer* man," he added, "but Pa doesn't talk about that."

"Under the circumstances, it's probably good advice," I told him.

"Maybe." Ranger glanced out the window. "Here's our stop. And say, Isobel…" Our eyes met, like shy forest creatures blundering together before jumping apart. "You don't have to feel sorry for me. Savvy?"

I assured him I didn't feel sorry in the least. But that might not have been quite true, or else I would never have agreed to his next harebrained scheme.

Chapter 8
Buy Bonds!

Ranger's next scheme involved the war bond rally, which had become his beautiful blue-eyed baby after he was inspired to work it into his picture. He spent three whole days setting it up: figuring out the locations and when to get there and where he would change into his uniform. Also what lies, fibs, or prevarications he would have to tell to pull it off.

His latest great idea was to slip into the actual ranks of the Lasky Home Guard. With luck he could even march with them for a block or two before anyone noticed. That's one reason why the camera positions were so particular. Sam, who got permission to take off work for the rally, was to shoot the Home Guard, with Ranger among them and a forest of waving flags in the background. The grand scene would be followed by a touching farewell once the three of us had rendezvoused in a nearby alley. Ranger informed me of these details on Wednesday morning while I was curled up on the window seat with my favorite book.

"What if Sam's father refuses to let him use the camera that day?" I asked, keeping a finger in *Jane Eyre* to hold my place.

"He won't. Wait 'til you hear what I—" He broke off.

"What you what?" I asked, suspicion rising like fog over the moors. But he changed the subject to the terrific spot they'd found in an empty building, where Sam might be able to get an overhead shot, if they could just arrange to get inside…

With all these "arrangements," he was late for supper on Wednesday, sliding into his seat just after we all bowed our heads for grace. "You are pushing your luck, young man," Aunt Buzzy remarked as Esperanza served the tomato soup. "This is the second night in a row you've been late for supper. Next time you'll do without."

"Sorry." Ranger blew on his soup. "I was down at the armory watching them build the platform for the rally; forgot the time."

"Indeed. But on that subject: your scoutmaster telephoned this afternoon. The visiting troop from Santa Barbara has a shortage of boys in their color guard, and Mr. Monroe wants you to fill in during the parade tomorrow."

Ranger promptly gagged. "But, Buzzy—" he managed to croak, "I have *plans*."

"Oh? Like what?"

"I, um, might have to stand by to march with my own troop."

"That's unlikely, since Mr. Monroe informs me your troop is at this moment camping at Arrowhead Lake."

"Oh."

"He seemed surprised I didn't know that, and I was

surprised too, needless to say. But since you are obviously not camping, you're available to serve in the color guard."

"Why can't they get somebody else?"

"Don't argue with me, Ranger. I'm not in the mood. Mr. Monroe and I went on to have a very interesting chat during which I learned for the first time that you're behind in your dues and you've attended no meetings since April." Ranger was giving extraordinary attention to chasing a speck of pepper around his bowl. "Well? How do you explain that?"

"Come *on*, Buzzy," he pleaded. "I outgrew scouts about when I outgrew knickers."

"If you think you're beyond scouting, you must take the subject up with your father—and I hardly need to remind you that you're in enough hot water with him already. For now, Mr. Monroe is offering you a chance to redeem yourself, and you *will* take it."

Her unusual firmness led to a miserable evening, with Sylvie whining that Ranger wouldn't play with her, and Ranger sulking, and me suggesting he could perhaps look just as heroic in the Boy Scout color guard, which he did not take very well. But at bedtime, after we had said our prayers for Father's safety, and Mother had read a chapter of *Kidnapped* and kissed us good night, he made a clandestine visit to our bedroom.

"I've got an idea," he told us.

"For heaven's sake, Isobel," my mother remarked late the following afternoon as we joined the thronging crowd on its way to the rally. "Are you gaining weight?"

Sylvie piped up, "No, she's—*ouch!*" That was in response to a sharp kick delivered to the shinbone. By me.

What made me appear so voluminous was Ranger's outgrown scout knickers under my dress. He suggested I put them on to save time when changing clothes. And where would we do that? "I've got it all figured out," he'd told me. "Don't worry."

Why was I starting to feel that when Ranger said, "Don't worry," worrying was the very thing I ought to do? Those were also his last words of the night before, and as a result I hadn't slept much. *How on earth*, I asked myself for the thousandth time, *had he talked me into this?* What mysterious power did he wield over my better judgment?

The sparkly day made Mother hook her arm in Aunt Buzzy's and exclaim, "To think it's still raining in Seattle!"

"Ranger, hadn't you better find the troop?" Aunt Buzzy asked.

"In a minute." Ranger took my elbow as the crowd condensed along Hollywood Boulevard. I could see the tall, bunting-draped speakers' platform up ahead, where a band of studio musicians blared out the "Washington Post" march. He pointed. "See that flagpole? Wait two minutes after I leave, then work your way over to meet me there. And stop chewing on your lip—this'll be *fun*."

His dark eyes glittered like a firecracker fuse. After

saluting the ladies, he passed me with a half wink. He had made it sound like fun the night before, while flattering my acting ability and telling me I was his angel muse. He actually said that, and in the soft glow of moonlight with Sylvie eagerly seconding everything he said, I half believed it.

Now, in the blinding light of day, my supposed angel wings dragged like lead. Once he was out of sight I heaved a sigh and started counting seconds. I had counted up to ninety-eight when we came to a reviewing stand not far from the stage.

"Why don't we find a seat here?" suggested Aunt Buzzy. "I see space near the top."

I took a deep breath. "Mother, I need to be excused."

She turned to me in surprise. "Whatever for?"

I made the kind of eye signals we used for a necessary function, and she looked even more surprised. Usually it was Sylvie who "needed to be excused."

"Well...is there a ladies' room nearby?" she asked Aunt Buzzy.

I already knew there was, because Ranger had scouted this part of the plan too. "At the streetcar station a block east." Aunt Buzzy pointed. "Not far."

"All right," Mother told me. "Look for my wave when you come back—"

I tried to sound eager. "But if I can find a spot closer to the stage, could I watch the rally from there? I'll meet you after the parade."

"Oh, I don't..."

"The seats are filling up, Mattie. We must seize the day," said my aunt. "She'll be fine."

"All right. I suppose. But don't talk to strangers—and meet us at the auto *immediately* after."

Sylvie glanced back at me with a look like a cat-swallowing canary as they started up the bleachers. Though she envied my part in this scheme, Ranger had convinced her that her part was every bit as important and dangerous.

I fought my way through the crush to meet him at the flagpole. "What a mob!" he crowed. "Sam's here. He got some shots of the Home Guard drill, and he's in position for the parade now. You'd better hold on to my arm so we don't get separated."

I barely had time to do that before he dove into the crowd. He didn't hear my anxious, "Where are we going?" as the speakers' platform loomed large in view.

The crowd around it was so dense that we had to dribble our way like sand through pebbles. I gripped his arm, suddenly aware that the band had stopped playing and a tall man had stepped forward with a megaphone. The platform was so high that I could only see the top half of him, and the megaphone muffled his voice. Soon he stepped aside for a slight, dark-haired fellow. A solid roar almost flattened me.

"Who's that?" I yelled at Ranger, but could not hear the reply he threw over his shoulder. "Who?"

"*Chaplin!*"

The most famous man in the world looked nothing like the Little Tramp I'd seen on posters—though I saw little of him before the edge of the platform cut off my view entirely. A policeman stood at the rear corner, rocking on his heels. A gust of laughter from the crowd made him crane his neck to see what the Little Tramp was up to, and Ranger suddenly pulled me between the sheets of canvas that skirted the platform. Dust motes swirled frantically in a shaft of sunlight slanting in from a crack in the canvas. Mr. Chaplin, directly overhead, had begun to speak, but I couldn't make out the words.

"Here we are," Ranger announced, unbuttoning his shirt. "Now let's get cracking."

I turned my shocked gaze to him. "*Here?* We're changing clothes here in front of everybody?"

"Pipe down! Nobody's going to see you, silly. Come on, we don't have time to—" As I lunged past him, he grabbed my arm. "You *promised*!"

Then I heard a sound that chilled my bones: a man's voice coming from the back of the platform. "What's this? Unhand the lady, villain!"

I turned to see a man in a pearl-gray suit hanging from one of the steel struts that supported the stage. Even though the ground was only an inch or two below him, he remained suspended, swaying gently.

"Wait—don't I know you? Are you Titus Bell's boy?"

Ranger let go of me, looking somewhat abashed. "Yes, sir."

The man strode forward for a better look—that is, he reached for the nearest iron bar, then the next, like a monkey swinging through the jungle. He came on amazingly fast, his suit meanwhile stretching in ways it was never meant to. "So you are. As a friend of your father's, I must ask if you're up to mischief, young man."

"It's nothing, Mr. Fairbanks. I mean, nothing important. Just a prank. No harm to anybody. She—my friend here—said she'd go along, but now she's getting cold feet."

I glared at him, and he glared back.

Mr. Douglas Fairbanks—for it could be none but he, hero of many a screen adventure—dropped to his feet and straightened his jacket and tie. He was trim and slight as a rapier blade.

"You intrigue me. What sort of prank?"

"She's pretending to be me, while I... It's perfectly harmless, sir. Scout's honor."

"Ha!" Mr. Fairbanks tilted his head toward me. "A failure of nerve, eh?"

"No, sir," I stammered. "That is—well, maybe."

He smiled with a flash of stunningly white teeth. "Here's a word of advice. If you're having second thoughts...ignore them. Just think of the stories you can tell when you're old and gray."

The roar of the crowd almost swallowed his last words. Mr. Fairbanks held up a hand and said, "'Tis my cue. Farewell, fair maid." Then, to Ranger: "So long, laddie. And don't do anything I wouldn't do."

As the cheers continued, he ran toward the back of the platform, leaped at a horizontal strut, and with a mighty swing he flipped himself right up over the edge. And landed on his feet on the platform. I could tell by the way the cheering intensified. As for me, I was pretty well bedazzled.

"Let's get moving," Ranger said, handing me his shirt.

"Is he like that in his pictures too?"

"You bet—I'll take you to see one, my treat. Step over in that corner there, and I'll turn my back. And hurry up! The parade starts right after Mary Pickford speaks, and she's next."

"Mary Pickford?" I squeaked. "She's up there?" America's sweetheart, right above my head!

"Don't stop! Sure she's up there. Chaplin, Fairbanks, and Pickford—they're just back from a coast-to-coast tour of Liberty Bond rallies. That's why there's such a crowd today." He bent to stuff a pair of lifts in his shoes.

"I would have come just to see her. But I won't see a *thing*."

"'Course you will. You'll pass right under the reviewing stand. You could spit-polish her shoes. Now pull up your socks."

He meant literally. After I pulled them up, he knelt in front of me to re-buckle the knickers, which I didn't have tight enough. Meanwhile I pinned up my hair and stuffed my dress and shoes in his knapsack and pulled the straps over my shoulders. He plopped his hat on my head and pulled a gunnysack from the corner where he'd stashed it earlier. From it, he donned a tunic and a helmet that made him look very soldierly, even though both were biggish. Finally he slung a wooden parade rifle over one shoulder.

"Oh—I almost forgot." From his pocket he took an extra pair of glasses and put them on me. "Somebody might have told them I wear specs. These are reading glasses, but you should be able to see all right."

"Somebody might have told them you don't have a milky

111

complexion either," I snapped. It may have been small of me, but I was feeling small.

He tightened his lips. "Not much we can do about that. Good luck, Isobel. And thanks." He leaned forward and kissed me quickly on the lips. I nearly choked.

My very first kiss from a boy! Under circumstances I could never imagine, and I had to be dressed in a scout uniform!

"It'll be worth it. You'll see." He flashed one of his brilliant smiles and saluted.

Police were clearing the street in front of the platform when I made my way, all fluttery inside, to the parade staging ground. Another of Ranger's thoughtful provisions was a towel doused with Mentholatum to wrap around my throat, so I wouldn't have to talk much. But I had to peer assiduously over the rims of the blurry-making glasses before I finally caught sight of the Santa Barbara troop banner in that milling throng of musicians and Home Guard and mounted police.

"Are you Ranger Bell?" the flustered scoutmaster demanded when I presented myself. Nervously I nodded; it didn't seem so much a lie if it wasn't spoken. "About time you got here. Are you sick?"

I nodded again and coughed for good measure.

"Well, don't breathe on any of the boys. Jamie! This is Ranger Bell. Where's his flag? Fall in, scouts!"

A Golden Bear flag was thrust into my hands, and I was shuffled to the right of a row of three. "Pee-ew," muttered someone behind me. "Who brought the Mentholatum?"

The boy in the center, whose honor it was to carry the Stars and Stripes, eyed me curiously. "What was your name again?"

I coughed to make my voice raspier and told him.

His eyes narrowed. "Really?" he asked, making me wonder if he knew Ranger Bell by face or reputation, even though the latter had promised me he didn't know a soul in Santa Barbara, and vice versa. The scoutmaster's whistle shrilled out, and orders started flying too fast for me to keep up with the drill we'd practiced that morning. I tried to watch my neighbor out of the corner of my eye, meanwhile feeling him watch me likewise.

Suddenly he turned to me and stuck out his hand. "I forgot to introduce myself, Bell. I'm Ted Spoonerman."

A trap, I thought. And sure enough, when our hands met, he wrapped the thumb and pinkie around mine. I managed to do the same, mumbling, "Pleased to meetcha," like a boy would.

I passed the secret-handshake test, but Ted still eyed me suspiciously as I fumbled through the drill, trying to recall the many flag-etiquette rules Ranger had told me. The scoutmaster seemed to have his doubts too—if only about whether the Hollywood troop had sent one of their better examples of scouting. Desperately wishing the parade to begin, I almost dropped my Golden Bear banner when he blasted my eardrums with his whistle, calling, "Form up!"

The troop jostled itself like a centipede while a smartlooking unit of new recruits marched by. I peered into their ranks, letting the flag slip until the scoutmaster shouted, "'*Tention, Bell!*" Ted was glaring at me. *Please let's go*, I prayed.

"You know what I think?" Ted said. "I think you're not—"

"Ready, men! Left face! Forward, march! Left, right, left..."

We forward-marched into the parade ground, then right-faced and stepped out smartly. I was getting the hang of it—or thought so, until Ted hissed at me, "*Left, right!* Not right, left." Hurriedly I reversed my steps to match his as he went on, "You march like a girl. I think you *are* a girl. Waddaya say to that?"

I would have said it was a good observation but croaked instead, "Eyes forward!"

He didn't have any choice, unless he wanted to draw down shame upon the Santa Barbara visiting troop. Eyes forward, I mustered up a pretty good imitation of military style, but I knew once the route was completed I'd have to cut out in a hurry, before the odious Ted had a chance to snatch off my hat and cry, "Behold the imposter!"

We right-faced again onto Hollywood Boulevard and the cheering started. In the red-white-and-blue flutter I squared my shoulders as the parade master called out "Left...left... left, right, left..." and the drums of the Triangle studio band beat out a heart-stirring rhythm. *Maybe Mr. Fairbanks was right*, I thought. This would be a tale to tell my posterity, if I lived long enough to have them. Now that the parade was underway and I felt safe from scrutiny—for the moment—it was almost fun. No, it *was* fun, just as Ranger said. Though I would never tell him that.

I found myself thinking of Father, hoping he would get to march in a parade when he came back. Preferably one with confetti, like the crowd started showering on us when we right-faced for the final time. In the reviewing stand ahead of us were Mr. Chaplin, Mr. Fairbanks, and Mary Pickford in a fetching gray suit and a hat with a long, white veil. Red Cross nurses flanked them, waving white streamers that looked like bandages. "*Buy bonds!*" they called as we passed. "Buy bonds!" echoed Miss Pickford in a silvery treble that carried like a bell.

I tore my gaze away from her in time to notice the camera just ahead, aimed at me. There had been cameras all along the route, but I recognized the square wooden box with its cherry hue—and who else but Sam would have raised his left arm to wave at me?

Then a shocking thing happened: he was seized from behind! It happened so suddenly that he seemed to explode backward. I couldn't see who had done it and could not look back because another peril lay ahead, namely the reviewing stand where my kin sat.

Sylvie was supposed to distract the ladies as we approached, so they wouldn't notice that the face under the scouting hat didn't belong to Ranger. As soon as I was close enough to make her out, waving both hands from the third bench from the top, she threw herself forward into the lower benches, thus distracting the whole upper quarter.

I barely restrained a girlish gasp. Honestly, she was afraid of nothing. Instead she terrified everyone around her, including me.

I managed to keep in step all the way back to the parade ground. We hadn't even received the "Fall out!" order before

Ted announced, "All right, *now*—" and grabbed for my hat. But I was ready for him. I whacked the flagpole down on his arm. Ted yelped in pain, and a whole troop of Boy Scouts cried out in dismay when the Golden Bear dragged on the ground. I tossed it to the boy behind me, as Ted called out, "I *knew* it!"

Aunt Buzzy would hear from the scoutmaster tonight, I thought grimly as I dodged various marchers to get to safety. Meanwhile there were other problems to worry about, such as what had Sylvie broken and what had befallen Sam?

Chapter 9
Hearts of the World

*A*mazingly, we got away with it. At least Aunt Buzzy received no scoutmaster calls the next day. Either the man was deceived by my crude disguise, or Ted Spoonerman was one of those irritating tattletales who had cried wolf too often. I suspected the latter.

The other good news was that Sylvie suffered no injury in her dive from the bench because she landed on a gentleman with a rather large, cushiony lap. The switching she got from Mother that day must have hurt, but Sylvie stopped yelling soon enough and was eager to hear how many feet of film Sam had cranked into his camera.

That led to the bad news. The mysterious force I had seen separating Sam from his camera belonged to none other than Mr. Service, a very irate father. I should have known. Sam had no permission to use the Prestwich Model 14, and now that he'd been caught, the precious box was under lock and key. Ranger discovered this later that night, after making a visit to Edendale under cover of darkness and speaking with the culprit through his window.

Next morning we held a conference on the front porch.

"Just the rottenest luck." Ranger savagely kicked at the gravel as he paced back and forth on the drive. "Sam's old man wasn't even supposed to be there."

"Why?" I asked. "Where was he supposed to be?"

Ranger paused. "Well…"

"Did you cook up some kind of scheme to get him out of the way?"

"It was perfectly harmless! I just sent him a letter on Los Angeles County stationery about money owed to the water company, and he could contest the bill in court on June twenty-ninth. I figured by the time he went all the way down there and found out he didn't owe anything, he'd be so relieved it wouldn't matter."

"Ranger! He could have lost a whole day's work. And he has a family to support!"

He whirled around impatiently, holding up his index finger. "First of all, we can't take any chances. Half the time he's not working, because he has this drinking problem everybody knows about. Second of all, the only family he's got is Sam."

"There's no Mrs. Service?"

"Not that I know of. When they moved out here from New Jersey a few years ago, the rumor was she stayed behind. Or wait—there was a family tragedy, I think."

"A family tragedy?" Sam didn't seem the tragic sort. "What kind?"

"How would I know?"

"He's your friend, isn't he? What do you talk about?"

"He's my business partner. We talk business."

"Where did you two meet anyway?"

He threw up his hands. "You girls. All you care about is personal stuff!"

"I don't care a bit," Sylvie stoutly affirmed. "How do we make the picture?"

Ranger kicked up a shower of pebbles. "There's got to be a way. I might know where I can get hold of a camera at Triangle. Don't think it's being used. If we could sneak in one night and—"

He was beginning to alarm me. "We're not helping you steal equipment, you hear? And no more feats of derring-do for me. Why don't you just tell your folks what you're up to? I'll bet Aunt Buzzy suspects something already."

"Naw... If I told her, she'd think she had to do something about it. Maybe stop me, or maybe help me. And I don't want anybody's help. I want them to see I can do this on my own."

"'Them'? Including Mr. Griffith too?"

"Mr. Griffith too. And then they'll see that I should drop school and go to work at Fine Arts so I can learn the business."

This didn't seem the kind of thing parents could be made to see, but I didn't mention it, since the picture looked unlikely to get made anyway. My own feelings surprised me. To a point I felt relieved—who knew what I might be talked into next? But beyond that point, a haze of sadness glowed, as if some of Ranger's fairy dust had rubbed off on me. Now I could get all nostalgic about hours spent under a hot sun plastered with flour in front of a camera. Nevermore, alas!

Because what could we do without a camera?

"There *has* to be a way," Ranger vowed again, as though I'd asked the question out loud. "In the meantime, we need inspiration."

He knew where to get it too. A new Griffith picture had just opened, and that evening at dinner, after some raised-eyebrow communication with Mother, Aunt Buzzy gave her permission for us to see it. "I hear from Maybelee Thompson that there are no nude dancing girls in it, like that Babylonian bacchanal of D. W.'s. So, because you did your duty in the parade, you may take the girls on Sunday afternoon—that is, if their mother agrees."

Mother nodded. "But Isobel only. Sylvie will stay home and consider her naughtiness in frightening us all to death."

Guilt descended on me then, because of course I was the one who had done Ranger's duty. Sylvie looked like she might be winding up to make that very point, but Ranger leaned over and whispered in her ear, and whatever bribe he offered was enough to unwind her.

I hinted rather broadly that he owed me for putting my reputation on the line, and he admitted that the afternoon should be his treat. Until I pressed my luck by asking for an ice cream soda at the world's longest soda fountain in Pin Ton candy store on Broadway. With a woebegone look, he dug in his pockets to count the change.

"I thought you got an allowance," I said.

"You could call it that. If Pa wasn't such a tightwad."

"That's no way to talk about your father!"

"It's true. For my own good, of course. But darn it, Isobel, it's not like I want to blow money on candy or the penny arcade. Every spare nickel goes for film. At two cents a foot, it adds up."

"Sam doesn't contribute?"

"Sam contributes the camera—or he did. And he usually has less money than I do. Anyway, looks like I have a dollar seventy-five and the picture's a dollar a ticket—"

"A whole *dollar*?" I'd paid ten cents to see Fatty Arbuckle at the Variety.

"That's 'cause it's new and they show it with a full orchestra at Grauman's Egyptian. If I can borrow two bits from Solomon, then maybe Buzzy could—"

"Never mind." I sighed. "I'll give you the quarter and pay for the sodas too."

He gallantly offered to drink root beer instead, saving me twenty cents. And we decided to go to Clune's Broadway in Los Angeles instead of the Egyptian, because matinees were sixty-five cents there.

As it turned out, the afternoon was worth the expense on my part, because Ranger for once behaved like a normal boy instead of a crank. Although he still insisted on wearing his slouch hat everywhere, in spite of the stares it attracted. I'd come to suspect that the purpose was partly camouflage for his notable darkness, though Buzzy had mentioned to me that Mr. Griffith wore a variety of wide-brimmed hats. He cut the crowns out of some of them to allow sunlight to stimulate his balding scalp, according to her. At least Ranger didn't go that far.

On our way home from church, Aunt Buzzy asked Masaji to let us off in downtown Los Angeles so Ranger could show me the sights, like Central Park and the Sing Fat Oriental Emporium and the Los Angeles Times Building, which had been dynamited by anarchists in 1910. Ranger was too young to remember the incident, even though it changed his life: "That's when Pa decided to move out to Hollywood. Thought it would be more peaceful."

At the world's longest soda fountain we both sipped root beer while Ranger commented on the characters we saw: Indians and Chinese and Mexicans, and a couple of fellows in spurred boots spooning up ice cream from tulip glasses.

"Are they real cowboys?" I asked. I'd come to expect motion-picture characters on every street corner.

"Sure they're real. They ride in when work is slow on the range. What do you bet those two spent Saturday morning down at the Universal pens, and the casting clerk told 'em to show up for work tomorrow? They're here to celebrate."

That, amazingly, was as close as he came to shoptalk until he glanced at the clock over the fountain and said, "Let's hoof it—show starts in thirty minutes and there's going to be a line."

The words on the marquee outside Clune's Broadway read:

D. W. Griffith presents HEARTS OF THE WORLD

with smaller letters below:

Charlie Chaplin in THE BOND

Hearts of the World was a war picture; I knew no more about it. The line at the box office was mostly ladies out for the afternoon. "One of these days they'll be lining up to see pictures by *me*," Ranger whispered as we crept forward in the line. He laid out the money for our two tickets with the assurance of one who threw quarters about like confetti, then took my arm and escorted me to the doors, which a uniformed doorman opened for us.

Once inside, I hardly had time to admire the lavish lobby before he grabbed my hand and made a dash for the balcony to get seats in the front row: cushiony, velvety seats into which I sank up to my chin almost.

"It's like a palace!" I whispered.

I had not yet seen enough motion pictures to count on my two hands, and all of them were seen on hard chairs in small, dark rooms with a pounding pianist. Today I was looking down on gilded panels with cut-velvet wallpaper and candelabras that gave off a quivery glow. The curtain over the screen was painted with a Mediterranean-like seacoast.

"Aw, nuts," Ranger said. "No orchestra for the matinee. Guess we'll have to make do with the Mighty Wurlitzer instead." We gazed down at an organ that looked as big as my bedroom, with enough bells, whistles, drums, and cymbals to make up an entire band. A gentleman in black tie and tails entered the orchestra pit and eased himself between the bench and the quadruple keyboard. Once he was seated, I could barely make out the shine of his balding head, low as a mushroom in the pit. "But it's almost as good," Ranger went on. "A Wurlitzer can do almost every sound in the world."

While the organist arranged sheet music, we killed time rocking back and forth in our seats until the lady behind us said, "Stop that, children. You're making me seasick." The lights dimmed, and the organ blasted into an overture that included national anthems of England, France, Belgium, and the United States, stitched together with march music. As the organ surged into "The Stars and Stripes Forever," a company of soldiers (or at least men dressed like soldiers) marched on stage and performed an elaborate drill to hearty applause. The footlights dimmed as they marched off, and the painted curtain parted over a still picture of a woman gazing forward under an enormous hat that looked like a whole flock of ostriches was nesting on her head, while another lady and gentleman peered around behind her. *Madam*, read the screen, *How would you like to sit behind the hat you are wearing?*

The lady behind us tapped Ranger on the shoulder. "A question I might ask you, young man."

Sighing, Ranger pulled off his dashing headgear as *Charlie Chaplin in "The Bond"* suddenly blazed up in white letters.

This was my introduction to the celebrated Charlie's work, and I was not overwhelmed by it. It wasn't a story, just a brief parable about different kinds of human bonds—friendship, love, and marriage—during which the main character wiggled his eyebrows and mustache. Then came the Liberty Bond, and a pantomime in which Kaiser Wilhelm threatens Lady

Liberty. Charlie (representing "the People") joined forces with a weapons manufacturer ("Industry") and Uncle Sam ("Bonds") to fight the Germans. At the end, Charlie hefted a huge Liberty Bonds mallet and brained the Kaiser with it, after which all joined hands in triumph.

"He's not so funny," I told Ranger in disappointment, just after the Kaiser got his.

"This is just public service claptrap to get people to buy more bonds," Ranger murmured back. "You should have seen *Shoulder Arms*. It starts out when Charlie's enlisted and he's training and can't get the drill—"

"Young man." The lady behind us leaned forward. "I came to see *this* picture, not hear all about another."

Ranger's voice, which had risen to its normal level, dropped back to sotto voce to tell me the rest of the plot. Which I didn't even care about. All the time he was twitching and tapping his feet and no doubt annoying the row behind us even more. But when the curtains pulled back farther and the huge screen glowed with the words *D. W. Griffith Presents*, he turned as still as a rock.

Hearts of the World began with two American families living side by side in a French village. One family is full of high-spirited youths; the other has only one girl, called the Girl in that idealistic Griffith way. ("Lillian Gish," Ranger said. "I told you about her.") She naturally falls in love with the Boy in the other family. ("That's Bobby Harron—he plays the Boy in *The Mother and the*—ouch!" The "ouch" was to a thump on his head, delivered by the lady behind us.)

The Little Disturber, a naughty street entertainer from Paris, makes trouble when she tries to steal the Boy away from the Girl but doesn't succeed, and the lovers are about to be married when war breaks out.

That's when my fingernails, fully recovered from the mauling they took during *The Mother and the Law*, came in for more abuse. Because of course the couple couldn't just get married and live happily ever after, with three more reels of film to run.

When the Germans invade, the Boy nobly enlists in the French army, even though he's an American. The Germans advance; there's a big battle on what was supposed to be the young couple's wedding day; and the Boy is wounded. After the shooting stops, his lover searches the battlefield for him, clutching her wedding dress and convinced that he's dead. She's half mad by the time she finds him in a touching reunion scene. Then she goes to get help—but he's missing when she comes back, which sends her all the way around the bend.

(By this point, I was clutching Ranger's hand as determinedly as he was mine.)

The Boy isn't dead; he was picked up by a Red Cross ambulance and taken to a field hospital. At the appearance of the "field hospital," I sat up and stared. "Just like Father!" I whispered excitedly to Ranger. "Do you think the real field hospital looks like—*ow!*"

I got the thump from behind this time, but Ranger's attention was riveted to the screen, where things had gone from bad to worse. The Germans had captured the little village and began half starving its people while forcing them to work like slaves in the fields.

Meanwhile the Boy, fully recovered, slips behind enemy lines to spy for the Allies and brushes against death's door yet again before making his way back to the village to be reunited with his intended. But of course the Germans are still there, and at least one of them has lewd designs on the Girl. The French army is advancing, but it appears they may not make it back in time to save the Boy's life and the Girl's honor. The scene cut from the frightened lovers huddled in an attic to the German officer breaking down the door, then to the oncoming army, and I was nearly wringing poor Ranger's fingers off.

Finally the Little Disturber throws a hand grenade at the lustful German. The French army arrives and beats back the foe. A ripple of applause began in the audience, but Ranger sat up sharply and grabbed my arm to keep me from joining in. "Listen!"

In the quick fading of applause, I picked up the rhythm of marching feet, distant yet steadily advancing: *tramp, tramp, tramp*. The music had ceased, and for a moment all we could hear was *tramp, tramp, TRAMP, TRAMP*, as real as if the rescuing army were about to burst open the doors of the theater. On screen the Boy and Girl clutched each other in their attic, scarcely believing they were to be saved. The organist began playing again, very softly, that jaunty tune everyone started singing last year:

Over there, over there;
Send the word, send the word over there
That the Yanks are coming,
The Yanks are coming...

The scene had shifted, and the lower part of the screen seemed to fade out. Vague moving shapes came slowly into focus and became marching men, row upon row.

I gasped out, "Americans!" and jumped to my feet. People were rising all around me, some singing "Over There," others silent like me, hands gripped over my heart as I scanned the faces. Our boys, our brave, hearty boys, were throwing themselves into the fray, laughing at hardship and scorning trouble, resolving to stay until the job was done.

And my father was "over there," patching up the wounded and cheering the fainthearted. The picture showed what his letters couldn't: what a noble enterprise and honorable mission looked like.

"And we *won't come back* until it's over over there!"

Ranger took my hand and pressed a clean handkerchief into it. "*Always* bring two to a Griffith picture."

Chapter 10
The Night the Stars Came Out

T hat's realism for you," Ranger gushed as we took the streetcar home. "I hear the crew shot some of those scenes in France, even while real battles were going on. That's *picture making*. That's what I want to do…"

Now that my heartbeat had slowed down and my hankie was mostly dry, I was feeling a tiny bit foolish about getting so caught up. While the picture was running I'd felt bigger and better, like I was part of the effort to chase the barbarians from France. But when the dark recesses of Clune's had spilled its audience onto the glaring streets of Los Angeles, the world seemed to be going on just the same as before, no matter how thoroughly my feelings had been worked over.

Ranger didn't notice, but raved about Mr. Griffith and his own humble film project all the way home. By the time we got off the streetcar in Hollywood, he was so warm to the topic that he was popping like corn.

"And another thing—you can't say we don't need a villain

after that. If you took that sinister Hun out of *Hearts of the World*, you'd have a hole the size of Rhode Island."

"Holes can be filled," I said cryptically.

"With what? Stories have to have a balance, you know—a yin and a yang."

"Mostly they need a beginning and an end, and you keep changing both."

"Now you sound like Sam."

"Ask Sylvie if I know how to tell a story." Even if I didn't know how to end them.

"All right, Miss...Miss Scheherazade. How do you tell a story?"

"For one thing," I said as we started up the drive, "if there has to be a villain in the picture, it should not be the father. My father is the kindest man in the world, and it would be very difficult for me to perform in a photoplay where he's a brute."

"For the luvva Pete, Isobel! It's *acting*. It's nothing personal. You seem to think—" He stopped abruptly and stared toward the hacienda as though it had grown two stone towers and a moat.

What I saw was a long, low touring car in an icy shade of blue, parked in front of the hacienda. Next, a man with very long legs, in a black suit with a string tie, who was slapping a white Stetson hat against his knee as he strode toward us.

"Ranger!" he called out. "How's my boy?"

With a start, I recognized the high cheekbones and wide mouth of Titus Bell.

I don't know what I expected. The way Ranger talked, his father never paid much attention to him or was especially interested in anything he did or said. So I was rather taken aback when Mr. Bell threw an arm around Ranger's shoulders and crushed him to his chest in a great bear hug.

"You're growing like a weed, boy!"

The boy, weedy or not, only came up to the clasp of his father's string tie. What I could see of Ranger's expression was curiously mixed. Briefly he clasped his arms around the man, then muttered, "Lemme go, Pa. I have to breathe once in a while."

Titus Bell let go with a laugh and a whack on the back that sent Ranger's breath the wrong way. Then he turned to me. "Is this the Isobel I've been hearing so much about?"

"Pleased to meet you, sir." I stepped forward, extending my hand.

"Likewise, young lady." Instead of merely squeezing or shaking my hand, he bestowed a gallant kiss on it in the same courtly manner adopted by his son on the day we met. What Ranger had said about resembling his father from the scalp up was only half true. They were startlingly alike in manner, down to the long, flourishing fingers. Even the flash in Mr. Bell's eyes was much the same, though the eyes were sky-blue instead of dark brown. "I've already met your charming sister. Got the bruise on my shin to prove it."

I jerked my hand out of his. "Oh, sir! I'm so sorry! She's—"

"Settle down, Isobel," he said, laughing. "Not all her fault. She heard the grown-ups talking about my arrival and thought it was her own papa under discussion. When I turned out not to be him, she kicked me. High-spirited little girl. I like that."

Good, I almost said, *for you will be getting more of that.*

"So what have you been up to, old man?" he asked Ranger, who shrugged in reply.

"Nothing much. Showing Isobel around."

"Lucky girl." Mr. Bell drew us into a happy triangle, one arm around Ranger and the other around me. "Nobody knows this town like my boy. Say, you kids arrived just in time. We've decided to throw a shindig tonight. Spur-of-the-moment thing. I got on the horn to Doug an hour ago, and by golly, he'll be here with bells on at eight. Bringing as much of the gang as he can rustle up."

Ranger caught his breath and looked at me. "Who...who's coming, sir?" I asked hesitantly.

Mr. Bell threw back his head in a powerful laugh. "Why, royalty, miss. King Doug and Queen Mary. Prince Charles too, if they talk him into it. Threw your aunt and mama into quite a tizzy. You young'uns better come pitch in."

With a warm clasp on our opposite shoulders, he left us, long legs disappearing under the porch roof. "Royalty?" I asked Ranger.

"Fairbanks. Pickford. And maybe—" His head snapped up, like a hound's catching a scent. "Pa! Pa, wait up!"

Then he was gone, and I was reeling with visions: Mary

Pickford herself and that handsome, overwhelming Mr. Fairbanks in this house. Tonight!

For all Mr. Bell had said about a casual "shindig," the atmosphere inside the hacienda was like Buckingham Palace being polished up for a visit from the czar. Mother was arranging fresh flowers on the sideboard while Aunt Buzzy was giving Masaji a shopping list, and by his quietly frazzled demeanor, it wasn't the first time today he'd been sent out on a desperate errand.

"…and stop by Wingates' for three bottles of champagne. And see if the farmers' market is still open and if they still have strawberries—but don't get them if they're green on the ends, or they're starting to get that purplish color. Oh, Mattie, there's something else. Can you remember?"

"Butter," said Mother, who had set the flowers on the fireplace mantel and was now dusting with a steely efficiency that didn't fool me for a minute. When she saw me, she paused, feather duster raised, and on her brow was that peculiar gleam I had noticed after the incident with Mack Sennett's greased intersection. "Isobel, you're needed in the kitchen to help polish the silver. You and Ranger can stay up for dinner tonight, but after that you're expected to excuse yourselves and go to bed. It's not a formal occasion, so your green organdy frock will do, the one with the violets around the neck…"

I glided past her, still in a daze. Pickford! Fairbanks! In this very house!

Sylvie had been packed off to the Theodore Cooper household to stay with Agnes of the ink-black hair. And, I suppose, to prevent any diving into laps or bruising shins. But after the sun set and the guests started to arrive, I had to wonder if she wouldn't have fit right in.

Not that it seemed anything out of the ordinary at first. Mr. and Mrs. Hiram Porter arrived unfashionably early, while the extra help were still setting the table. They were followed shortly by another banker and his wife, whose names I quickly forgot. But then Miss Constance Talmadge swept in with a gaggle of other young people, and the big front room of the hacienda blazed with light. Literally, for Titus Bell had just turned up the gas in the two bronze chandeliers, but also figuratively. Other guests flocked to Miss Talmadge like moths to a flame, while Aunt Buzzy helpfully whispered to me that she was a celebrated comic actress who'd made a name for herself in *Intolerance*.

That revered title made me wonder where Ranger was. After a glance around the room I discovered him in the musicians' corner, sitting by the piano. His expression startled me. He looked like the Great Stone Face or a shell-shocked veteran. I was about to go and ask him what was up—or down—when someone called, "It's Mary!"

"Five bucks says they're together," Miss Talmadge said, laughing and raising a champagne glass.

Shortly after, Mary Pickford herself crossed the threshold with a swift step, smiling briskly while sliding a snow-white summer coat off her glowing shoulders. "Delightful house,

Titus. And, Bea, how lovely to see you again. It's been too long." With her honey-colored curls pinned up and her feisty manner watered down, I didn't recognize her. She seemed too quick, her eyes too sharp as she glanced around. And she was tiny—she stood barely taller than me as she took my hand and said, "Delighted to meet you, dear."

There was a glitter about her that had nothing to do with the diamonds around her neck. I couldn't say a thing in return.

Behind her, a man leaped into the room—or seemed to. Abruptly I recalled Miss Talmadge's remark about *They're together*, and took it to mean Pickford and Fairbanks. Together, though I knew they weren't married. Not to each other, that is. Though Titus Bell towered over Douglas Fairbanks, they threw their arms around each other and laughed like hyenas. The next minute, they were trading punches.

"Doug!" Miss Pickford's voice rang out. "Do stop cavorting and come meet Titus's sister-in-law." Her tone made it sound like they were married. To each other.

Mr. Fairbanks bounded over and took my mother's hand with a bow. He started in surprise when he recognized me, but recovered with a quick wink and a swipe of one finger across his mouth, meaning his lips were sealed about when last we met. I saw Mother's eyebrow rise, but before she could ask about it, she was being introduced to another guest. This was a short man whose wavy hair was streaked with gray, making me think he was old until I saw his face—a youthful, unlined face dominated by wide, dark-lashed eyes.

"...and this is her daughter Isobel," Mr. Fairbanks was

saying, as he steered the short man over to me. "Isobel, believe it or not, this sorry piece of work regularly outsells me at the box office."

Without his busy mustache and bushy eyebrows, I didn't recognize Charlie Chaplin at all. He shook my hand like it was a pump handle and muttered something about being pleased. He didn't look pleased though. In the brief moment that our eyes met, I tried to see that character that made him so beloved: the Little Tramp, with his coal-black hair and ill-fitting clothes. But I couldn't. The real Mr. Chaplin looked like a cheeky English schoolboy—and talked like one too.

I recalled Ranger telling me he was a limey: "Everybody knows that."

A young lady was hanging on Mr. Chaplin's arm, someone whose name I forgot as soon as I heard it, though I recall her wild, red hair and tinkly laugh. The house suddenly bulged with young men and ladies whose wild hair and flashing eyes and reckless laughter broke the evening into sharp, bright little pieces, tumbling in kaleidoscope patterns. Titus Bell boomed, Aunt Buzzy buzzed, my mother glowed, and the young people twittered. But the night belonged to the stars.

After a few drinks, Mr. Chaplin snapped out of his dark mood. He did something with two dinner rolls that had the company almost rolling on the floor. He stuck a fork in each of them and tucked his fists under his chin and made the forks perform a little dance. The rolls looked like huge feet, and his face became the character's head, and it was so funny that I thought I might split a seam. (An old routine, according to

Ranger, but Charlie did it best.) Mother laughed with a hand over her mouth, a rare sign of near-abandon.

Meanwhile, at the other end of the table, Mr. Fairbanks was taking bets on his athletic abilities. He must have been, or why else would he have been doing handstands on his chair? Alcohol had nothing to do with it; so far as I could tell, he never touched a drop. Every now and then Miss Pickford would say, "Do sit down, Doug, and enjoy this splendid dinner." And he would obey, but not for long.

I don't recall eating any of the splendid dinner. As the dessert dishes were cleared away and the host was passing out brandy and cigars, Mother bent her eyebrow at me, meaning it was time for Ranger and me to excuse ourselves and go to bed.

We obeyed halfway: the excusing part but not the going to bed. For as soon as we departed through the west wing door, Ranger grabbed my hand in a viselike grip and pulled me around to the little side porch that opened directly off the front room. Here he dropped on a bench under the rose arbor and pulled me down beside him. The window was open, and a sparkly buzz of party conversation glowed like fireflies on the lawn.

"All right," I said. "What's the matter?"

He seemed to be having difficulty breathing. "The gig is up," he croaked.

"What?"

"My scoutmaster called today. Right after Pa got in. They had a nice long talk."

"Oh no!" Dire as this news was for him, I couldn't dismiss the consequences for myself.

"He wasn't going to tell me until tomorrow sometime. But I chased him down to ask if he'd invited Mr. Griffith to the party, or if he would, and that led to an altercation—"

"Why? Aren't they friends?"

"They were." Ranger's heel thumped hard against the bench board. "Pa used to be a pretty big investor in Fine Arts. He made a pile with *Birth of a Nation* but lost money with *Intolerance*, and now they're not speaking to each other. It's just sour grapes, is all. Pa's such a…philistine. All he likes are comedies and melodramas. D.W. has more craft in his little finger than Pa has in his whole…" Ranger paused and folded one crafty little finger into a fist. "I blew my last chance, Isobel."

"What do you mean?"

"I was on probation, see? If I pulled one more prank, Pa swore he'd send me to military school in Palo Alto. To smack some discipline into me. So… I did, and he will."

"Oh, Ranger!" Emblazoned on my memory was the time Aunt Buzzy had told me this. She'd asked me to be a friend and help him stay on the straight and narrow. Instead, I'd let him pick me up and carry me like a football down the twisty and crooked. "I'm so sorry. I—"

"Not your fault. By the way, I asked him not to tell your mother. It was all my idea, and you didn't want to go along. He said he wouldn't."

"Oh—well, thank you." This was a relief, though getting off scot-free didn't feel entirely comfortable. Especially when I hadn't been such a good guardian… But wait. Why should a twelve-year-old girl be given charge over a thirteen-year-old boy anyway? My thoughts were becoming thoroughly scrambled. "Did you get a licking for it?"

"Not this time—the school's my licking. The school's going to make me 'grow up.' He didn't even seem all that mad about the scout episode. That makes it even worse, that he can be so blasted *jolly* about the whole thing."

He gave the bench another savage backward kick. "If I could only finish the picture, it might… It might be my ticket to somewhere else. But without a camera, I don't have a bat's chance in hell of finishing anything."

"Snowball's chance," I murmured.

"What?"

"A snowball's chance in the flames of Hades is what you don't have." As bad as I felt for him, Sam's problems seemed greater. "School might not be as awful as you think. Only a year or two of your life."

He made a strangled cry and jumped to his feet, just as laughter burst from the front room. Through the gauzy curtains on the glass door we could see Mr. Fairbanks dancing a fox-trot with Aunt Buzzy—on the table.

"Is that what you call grown up?" Ranger demanded rhetorically. "It's a game to them. They just want to have fun. I'd like to know where their parents were when *they* needed discipline." His eyes narrowed as he stared through the window, and his next words sounded like they were directed at a single person. It wasn't hard to imagine who. "I'm not going."

"You have to."

"I'm not! I'll go down to San Pedro and stow away on a

China freighter before I'll get packed away to any puking military school." He nodded fiercely to himself before he turned and took a running leap off the porch. I could hear him whacking hydrangea bushes on the way to his room.

The air stirred agitatedly at his leaving, then drifted soft as petals while music and chatter fell in bright patches at my feet. At least with our motion picture on the trash heap and our director shipping off to China, the rest of the summer would be a good deal more peaceful. But quiet days on the window seat with a stack of library novels didn't have quite the appeal they would have had a few weeks ago, before Ranger had dragged me into the world of picture-making.

I stood up to go back to my room, pausing by the window for a last look. The party had broken up into smaller groups. One clustered around the piano where Aunt Buzzy was playing ragtime tunes, while another listened to Titus Bell explain how he acquired the jade Buddha on the mantel shelf. Three couples were dancing in the cleared space at the far end of the room.

Constance Talmadge was up for a round of charades. With the back of her hand to her forehead, she cried, "Ay me! All the perfumes of India…" until someone called out, "Sarah Bernhardt!" Then a man jumped up to imitate some equally celebrated ham.

I waited to see if Mr. Fairbanks would swing from the ceiling fans. Perhaps he would have—I wouldn't put it past him—but something else happened first.

The door to the porch opened, and my heart jumped up to my tonsils. There was no time to run and very little place to hide. With a pounding heart, I backed against the wall, shielded by darkness and twining vines, hoping that the intruder had only come out for a breath of fresh air.

"Ah, smell the roses," said a man's voice. "Pity I hate roses."

Then a woman's laugh, with a comment I couldn't make out. To which he replied, "We'll fix that. Smoke?"

Though he spoke softly, there was a vigorous quality in his voice that strode out from under the arbor. It strode with an accent, which I could not place until the sudden flare of a match picked out the piercing dark eyes of Charles Chaplin. The flame glided to a woman's soft lips with a small, vertical scar, pursed lightly around a cigarette.

I didn't even know Mother smoked!

My heart was beating so hard that I couldn't hear anything else at first, but gradually their voices came clearer to me, especially when Mr. Chaplin burst out: "Mack Sennett? He's low class. Barnyard comedy. I worked at Keystone until I couldn't take any more. What's a lady of your quality doing in a Sennett picture?"

"Oh my." My mother's voice had a peculiar lilt that I could only describe—with a squirmy feeling on my insides—as flirtatious. "What kind of 'quality' are we speaking of?"

"Mrs. Ransom...may I call you Matilda?"

"No, Mr. Chaplin."

"Or not yet?"

"That remains to be seen."

"Then allow me to say, as your disinterested admirer, that you're too good for Keystone."

"And allow *me* to say that you're making far too much of it. It was only in fun. And you won't see any more of me than my hat."

He muttered a response, and she laughed. The banter went on in light tones that seemed to mean more than I could figure out. It reminded me of some of those long conversations between Jane Eyre and Mr. Rochester (which I usually skip), where more seems to be going on than meets the eye or ear.

Then he said, "Here's what I'm thinking. Come down to the Triangle studio next week. See what I'm working on. I have an idea about a part for you."

(Gasp from Mother.) "What do you mean, 'a part'? I'm a doctor's wife on holiday, Charlie, not an actress."

I was relieved to hear "doctor's wife," but the "Charlie" didn't sit well, and his answering voice had a peculiar warmth that pricked like walnut shells: "I don't need an 'actress,' *Matilda*. I need someone with regal bearing and a quiet center. There's something about you: a vulnerable strength. That little scar—how did you get it, may I ask?"

"You may ask, but I will not tell." Her cigarette glowed fiercely, and the scar seemed to pulse in the limited light. I had never been brave enough to ask that question, but I'd put it to Father once while he was gently rocking a photographic portrait of her in his developing tank. He had cleared his throat and changed the subject.

"A woman of mystery, eh?" Mr. Chaplin teased. "Who could blame you? But about the part—it's just a small bit in couple of scenes. Come on, do say yes!"

No, no, no! I was saying for her. I felt a certain nervous quiver in the air and hoped it was Mother's discomfort with the situation. She tossed down the cigarette and ground it out among the geraniums.

And when she spoke I could hear my mother again, using the same tone that might be asking Sylvie how she had mistaken rouge for finger paint. "You're a silly man. And I'm a chilly woman, or fast becoming one. Shall we rejoin the company?"

His teeth flashed in the dim light. They were a bit large for his face. On the screen, I recalled, he showed them only in an occasional smile that was smarmy and cocky at the same time. "I don't give up so easily, you'll find."

He extinguished his own smoke and held the door open for her. Once they were inside, I let go of a long breath, feeling dizzy and only partly relieved. For she hadn't said no.

Chapter 11
Chips and Blocks

*A*fter a restless night, unsettled by dreams of being chased through the Keystone Studios by the Little Tramp, I was still in bed at eight fifteen the next morning. But not for long, for that is when a resolute set of knuckles rapped on my door. "Who—?" I called out irritably.

"Me," came the reply. "Can I come in?"

I sat up and reached for my wrapper. "You *may*. If you must."

Ranger flung open the door and flopped down on Sylvie's empty bed without ceremony. "Sam just phoned. He wants us to meet him in the projection room at Vitagraph, eleven sharp."

"What?"

"No, the question is *why*, not *what*. He didn't say, but he sounded just a little bit excited, and if you know Sam, that means a *lot* excited."

I pulled my hair out from under my collar, trying to wake up. "Do you think it's about the picture?"

"Sure, it's about the picture. What else?"

"Well…a lot has happened since last we met, as you recall. And last night—"

"I know. But something's up. I don't know what it is, but I've got a hunch it could change everything."

Never was a hunch more totally proved out. When we arrived at the stuffy little projection room off Prospect and Talmadge, Sam answered our knock with his eyes almost all the way open.

"What's up?" Ranger demanded without even saying hello.

"Not much," Sam lied. "Just some film I wanted you to see. Have a seat."

Inside that placid exterior was a barely contained, jackrabbity excitement. There was also, I noticed when he turned toward the projector, a rather livid bruise high up on one cheekbone. I took a seat in the front row, and Ranger dropped next to me while Sam flicked a lever on the projector.

Scratches of light appeared on the screen and then, so overwhelmingly that it knocked us back in our seats, the picture thronged with marching men. They seemed to keep coming on and on. The Lasky Home Guard wasn't that large, but the camera made it seem like legions.

"Sam!" Ranger exclaimed. "How'd you manage to loop the film?"

"Not now," Sam replied. "Watch this."

Looping the film (whatever that meant) was not all he'd managed to do. We watched with growing amazement as the camera caught hordes of feet swinging smartly around a corner, rows of helmeted heads swinging by the reviewers' stand, and even a view from above, booted feet striding proudly out from under the helmets in a way that reminded me of Mr. Chaplin's roll dance.

Then Ranger himself appeared on the screen, a rifle on his shoulder and a face like flint. It was as if the camera had crouched on the sidewalk, lain on the street, dodged near, backed away, and popped up like a hovering dragonfly, all in the space of a couple of minutes. Ranger had been popping up with exclamations the whole time, but I nearly fell out of my chair with the next scene—it was *me*! Weeping into a handkerchief in front of the broken-down picket fence on the way to Daisy Dell. I'd forgotten that scene, but here it was, smoothly "cut" into the rally.

Before I had fully taken myself in, the camera jumped back to the Home Guard, just as Ranger turned his head with a rueful glance. It looked for all the world as though he'd spotted me over by the fence. The Home Guard marched out of sight and the film came to an end.

Ranger jumped up, pulled the light cord, and attacked the cameraman, pounding him on the back. "You sly dog, you! That was *bully*! You cut those scenes together as slick as butter. But how'd you get past your old man?"

That was my question. Had Sam escaped from his house in the dark of night, developed all the film, and stuck the pieces together all by himself?

"Didn't have to get past the old man," he explained while rewinding the film. "He helped me do it. And one of those shots—the one looking down on the helmets? That was cut from a picture he worked on last winter. He gave it to me."

Ranger and I gulped in unison. The little room was stifling by then, so I turned on the ceiling fan. As we stood in the scissored light, Sam explained:

"Sure, he was mad—he yelled himself hoarse once we got home."

"Where did that bruise on your face come from?" I asked.

"This?" Same touched it and shrugged. "Got in the way of a fist, I guess."

"So how did you get him to come around?" Ranger asked.

"Well…once he was through yelling about the camera, he started yelling about me stealing the tripod. So I yelled back, 'I didn't steal it! I made it!'"

"You did?" It never occurred to me that the tripod hadn't come with the camera.

"Sure he did, right down to the panning crank," Ranger said proudly. "Sam can make anything."

"Shook the old man up a little," Sam remarked. "Had to take another look at the tripod. Then he finally got around to asking what the Sam Hill I thought I was doing with all this, so I what the Sam Hill told him."

Ranger jumped. "You *what?*"

"Don't get in a lather. Your secret's safe. He wanted to see the film, is all."

And once seeing, Sam went on to tell us, Mr. Service was rather taken with our efforts, especially the ingenious shot of marching feet that his son got by lying on the corner curb of Hollywood and Main.

"Did you tell him who you were working with?" Ranger asked, making it sound as though R. A. Bell were an up-and-coming Hollywood figure.

"Nope—just 'some friends.'"

Ranger punched the air. "Terrific! The mind reels!"

My mind was revolving in circles too. I'd spent the previous weekend viewing Sam as a tragic figure, a motherless, misunderstood boy with a heartless father who drank too much. He didn't stay in the miserable hole I'd dug for him. But neither did his father—a few hours with noxious chemicals and film, and all was forgiven.

I'll never understand boys—or men either, for that matter.

"Speaking of reels," Sam remarked, "I've got another one here."

Piecing together military scenes wasn't all that occupied his time over the last few days. It seemed that father and son had collaborated on a picture project featuring Jimmy Service himself, which Sam now mounted on the projector and set rolling.

It didn't amount to much, in my opinion: a man goes to an outdoor café where he's greeted by his chums, flirts with his bosom pal's best girl, and exchanges a few stagy, fake-looking punches with the pal. The flirtatious female brought hostilities to an end by pouring two mugs of beer on their heads—a twist that didn't seem to be part of the scenario. The image became very jumpy for a few seconds.

149

"Couldn't help it," Sam admitted. "Laughing too hard."

While I tried to imagine what Sam's laugh would sound like, he hurried on. "But here's the beauty part." He rolled the film back and stopped it at a point before the punch-trading and beer-dousing, with Mr. Service cheerfully lifting his mug while seated at a table. He had a long bony face, a little like Sam's, that didn't seem to go with a short torso and the restless legs of a boxer.

"I changed reels and rolled the film camera for a few minutes longer after he combed out his hair and called for another beer. He didn't notice I'd put a half-mask over the lens. Wasn't noticing much of anything by then. Before we develop it—"

Ranger caught his drift. Unable to contain himself any longer, he leaped up and pulled the overhead light cord. "A double exposure—you *genius*!" He attacked the genius again, with an embrace instead of a pounding. "Do you know what I'm thinking right now?"

They stared at each other with an identical gleam in their eyes, that precipitous look just before someone yells *Eureka*!

"Let me guess," Sam drawled, and together they shouted: "*We've got our villain!*"

It took me somewhat longer to understand what had lit such a fire under them. Sam had—very cleverly—taken advantage of the father-son project to solve one of our most persistent problems. With Jimmy Service on the left side of the frame, the undeveloped film could be shot again with his part masked and Sylvie and me on the right side. That would turn Good-time Jimmy into a heartless father mocking his poor daughters who are pleading with him to come home. There might even be enough film for Ranger to confront the old man, in a manner stern but just.

Ranger jumped up and threw some gleeful punches at that idea. "We're back in business!"

I suddenly remembered we were supposed to bring Sylvie home from her friend's house an hour ago. Before leaving, Ranger could not resist throwing his arms around Sam once more. "I'll say it again: you're a genius. But this is going to take lots of camera time. Is the old man good for—"

"He thinks the picture's finished, because that's sorta what I told him." Sam looked less than smug for the first time that day. "And he didn't exactly say I couldn't use it, but...better not take a chance on his mood next time. It's kind of...unpredictable."

On our way back to Hollywood, Ranger was over the moon. "I'm going to finish this picture, and D. W. is going to see it, and it'll be so brilliant that he'll take me under his wing. Bobby Harron wasn't much older than me when he started as a messenger boy for Fine Arts. After a few years, Mr. G put him in front of the camera. So he can put me behind one. Sooner or later."

His plan seemed as far-fetched as ever, but still I was rather glad to see the old Ranger back—and even gladder that we wouldn't have to give up the picture. Though for the life of me I couldn't say why.

When we reached the Coopers' house, Sylvie was hustled out with her hat and coat and satchel in hand, as though her hosts had been eagerly watching for our arrival and didn't intend to waste a minute. This made me suspect Little Sister had outstayed her welcome, but I didn't ask. And she did not tell—all she wanted to know was how late we'd stayed up the night before, and did Mr. Fairbanks sword fight with anybody.

"Not much happened," Ranger kept saying. "A dull party, really."

His thoughts were elsewhere. I'd almost forgotten the party myself, in light of this new frontier in picture-making that Sam had opened up, but I was abruptly reminded of it as a light tan roadster approached us on the drive. I didn't recognize the auto, but Ranger did, snapping his head around as the vehicle passed with a half wave from the driver. "That's Chaplin's Pierce-Arrow. Wonder what he's up to?"

I didn't wonder at the way my heart seemed to tighten, as though someone were pulling its corset strings.

The ladies were having tea under the grape arbor in the courtyard. "What was Chaplin doing here?" Ranger asked first thing.

"My, you're abrupt," Aunt Buzzy remarked, busily waving a palm-leaf fan. "He came to see your father—about money, of course. Oh, and he dropped off a scenario for your aunt Mattie to look at."

My mother was elaborately *not* looking at the large, white

envelope lying on a corner of the glass-topped table. "A scenario?" I repeated.

Mother waved a careless hand. "He has an idea about a part in his next picture. He thinks I have the perfect *maternal* quality."

"Which is a *silly* notion, of course," Aunt Buzzy said.

"Well, it *may* be, and it may not," Mother countered. "I haven't looked at it yet."

The stress they were putting on certain words made me think of rival boys drawing lines in the sand. Was there some sort of falling-out between them over Charlie's silly notion?

"You aren't going to do it, are you?" I blurted out.

"For heaven's sake." Mother sighed. "Will everyone stop behaving as though I'm about to run off to Cuba with the encyclopedia salesman? All is well, whether I decide to do it or not. How was your night, Sylvie? Did you have a good time?" Thus, by sticking an elbow in the conversation (Sylvie being the elbow), she turned it away from herself and a certain most-famous-man-in-the-world.

Chapter 12
The Rescue

*I*t was almost a week before circumstances converged to allow the kind of shooting Ranger wanted to do for Sam's innovation—"circumstances" meaning Jimmy Service's mood (or job), Mother's plans, Sam's work, the streetcar schedules, and the sun's disposition. In anticipation of which, Ranger explained to me how the double-exposure technique would work. We would shoot three scenes: one of Sylvie pleading with the villainous father to come home, one of me likewise pleading, and one of Ranger manfully confronting.

Villainous Father's part would be played unknowingly by Jimmy Service on the left side of the frame, which Sam would cover with a half-circle of black cardboard. Matching the action would not be difficult for the first two scenes, since the father was supposed to be ignoring us anyway. But Ranger's confrontation would be extremely tricky, because Mr. Service would have to show some response to the young man threatening to paste his ears back. Sam had taken note of his father's reactions as he shot them, and marked where they were on the film counter. Ranger would try to match them, and of course we would only be allowed one take of each scene.

But if all went well, when the film was developed it would appear that Jimmy Service had joined our company. "And what do you think his mood will be when he discovers that?" I asked.

"Who says he will?" Ranger replied, innocent-eyed.

Finally, on Wednesday afternoon the stars converged and we boarded the streetcar for Daisy Dell, where Sam was to meet us.

The boys had worked out when the light would best approximate the half of film that was already shot (four thirty) and planned to arrive early so we could find a spot as similar as possible to the beer garden. The stand of juniper that surrounded our shack would do.

While Sam peered through the viewfinder, Ranger marked the sandy ground with a carpenter's chalk line. "What's that for?" I asked him, as he snapped the string.

"That's the line we can't cross," he replied, "or we'll disappear into the left side of the frame." After winding up the string and putting the marker away, he coached Sylvie in how to plead with empty space, an idea she found difficult to grasp.

"Never mind," Ranger said at last. "I'll stand in for the old man." He hauled a rickety homemade stool from our props corner while Sam carefully fitted his cardboard mask over the left side of the lens, covering the half of film that was already exposed.

When he nodded, Ranger called, "Roll it!" Sam turned the

crank, and Sylvie played to the hilt, wringing her hands and squinching up her eyes. Her vocabulary was limited: "Please come home, Papa. Please, please, please come home…" After about a minute, Sam reached around to close the shutter and cranked a few more turns while watching the counter. "Looks good."

Ranger sat back with a heavy sigh, then jumped up and wrapped Sylvie in his arms.

"What about the ground?" I asked Sam, after he had stopped the film. "Will you have to tint out the floor too?"

He shook his head. "Won't show in a three-quarter shot. Camera's only got you from the knees up."

Ranger called my name, and I trotted obediently out to perform my turn with "Papa." He trusted I could do it without him standing proxy: "And you'd better keep a straight face while you're at it. Sylvie almost laughed a couple of times."

"I did not!" she protested.

My pleading was more sedate, with good use made of a handkerchief twisted in my fingers and dabbed at my eyes. That take also seemed to go well, so Ranger was feeling confident when setting up for his confrontation scene. He rehearsed it a couple of times as Sam stood in for his father, self-consciously copying the actions he remembered.

When the shooting began, Ranger quickly worked up an air of indignation. In fact, it seemed to me he was overdoing it. But soon it didn't matter, for Sylvie found a half-grown kitten lurking among the trees and gave chase, and the feral feline led her diagonally right across the camera lens.

"*Cut!*" Ranger yelled, followed by a few words I didn't even know.

Sylvie was devastated at her speedy fall from grace and tried to make it up to him by presenting the cat she'd managed to capture. But Kitty just scratched Ranger's face, and the situation was not improved until I had an idea.

"Why not shoot another scene in the house, where the youth comes to call, and Sylvie introduces him to the cat and it scratches him and… I tend to the cut on his face and we look at each other and…" My inspiration dried up at that point.

But Ranger calmed down enough to consider it. "What do you think, Sam?"

The cameraman, who had been taking some deep breaths to regain his composure after the shot was ruined, just tightened his lips and nodded shortly.

We shot two takes of the scene, and Ranger cheered up, even after getting a scratch on the other side of his face. No one seemed to notice that I had made my first original contribution to the picture—no one but me, that is—and I couldn't explain my inner glow on the way home.

A couple of days later Sam reported via telephone that the father-and-daughter scenes didn't look too bad, if something could be done to blend the backgrounds together. On Saturday afternoon Ranger disappeared until well after bedtime. Since he wasn't speaking to his father, he told Aunt Buzzy that he was helping a friend with a project. But I knew he was in the editing room at Vitagraph, hand-tinting frames with Sam until he was cross-eyed. I was the one who knocked on his bedroom door this time, after hearing him stumble down the hall.

"How does it look?" I asked.

"I have no idea." He yawned, not otherwise moving from a sprawled position on his bed. "Couldn't see anything but dots. That's how we filled the space in between people and trees: lots 'n lots o' dots. Dots everywhere. But say, since you give a darn now and my brain is fried, help me figure out a way to save Sylvie's life."

"Save her life? Is Sam still furious at her?"

"In the *picture*. Good night, Irene—hit that light on your way out, wouldja?"

Since our botched attempt at Santa Monica Beach, Ranger had given up the idea of rescuing Sylvie from drowning. Still, one of us had to be rescued from something. "What about a train?" he suggested the next morning. "Sylvie's playing on the tracks and doesn't see the locomotive thundering up, and I throw myself—"

"*No*," I said. "A locomotive wouldn't allow for retakes. And neither would getting hit by one."

Automobiles and other large moving objects had the same drawback, as did falling from great heights and plunging over waterfalls. Ranger came almost to his wit's end before hitting on a workable peril: "Sundance," he told me a day later.

"Your horse? What about him?"

"That's how I'll rescue Sylvie."

"Oh no," I began. "You're not going to subject my little sister to…" But not quite sure to what Sylvie would be subject, I could not complete the sentence.

"See? You don't even know what I have in mind. You just know you're against it."

"All right," I conceded. "What do you have in mind?"

His eyes snapped with their usual combustiveness. "We can use the film Sam already shot of me on the horse. Here's how it goes: you and Sylvie are taking a walk in the pasture behind our house, and Sylvie's attacked by Bone."

"Bone?" Sylvie was tighter with Ranger's dog than Ranger was himself. "He's her best friend!"

"I can fix that. Anyway, I'm riding my horse not far away and hear your bloodcurdling screams and ride to the rescue, leaping over obstacles—we've already got that on film, remember—and snatch her from the vicious creature's foaming jaws."

"Can we use the part where you fall off?"

"Ha-ha. Say what you will, it's surefire, with no public places and perfectly safe."

"But I thought you weren't allowed to ride yet."

He rolled his eyes. "When did *that* ever stop Michelangelo?"

Surprisingly, Sylvie was the one with objections. She would have cheerfully posed in front of a roaring locomotive or floated to the edge of Thunder Falls—"But Bone's my friend! I don't want to make him mad at me."

"You won't," Ranger assured her. "The way I'm going to

make him *act* mad is with catnip. The smell drives him crazy. We'll put some in your pocket—better make sure it's an old dress—and he'll be all over you. Mad with joy, really, but if you scream and act scared it'll look like he's mauling you."

Of course, once he explained, Sylvie thought it sounded like fun.

Meanwhile, I had been thinking. "So if we use the film we already have, then the shots we need are of Sylvie and me walking, and one of Bone spotting us, and one of you galloping toward us. And one of you hearing the screams, just before cutting back to us. And Bone attacking Sylvie while I call for help and wring my hands. And if this is the first time we meet, we'll need—"

Ranger laughed, holding up a hand. "Don't tell me. I'm just the director. Why don't you write it all down—and make a copy for Sam, okay?"

So I became a scenario writer. It was easy: I just wrote the shots in order with what was to happen in each one and made an extra copy for Ranger to deliver to Sam. More days went by before all the necessary elements lined up again, but we didn't have to travel far this time—just to the back lot behind the hacienda.

We would have to work fast to get all our shots in before eleven, when the light would be too glaring, so Sam was already set up by the time the rest of us arrived. Ranger was wearing the old Boy Scout uniform (that was already tight on him) and leading Sundance. Sylvie was in charge of Bone, and I came last, toting necessary props and supplies in a knapsack.

These included a pistol, a riding crop, a plug of catnip, and a bottle of hydrogen peroxide.

Sam greeted us with, "Better hurry. Dad's only working 'til noon today."

"Couldn't you say you needed the camera for cleanup shots?" I asked.

"If I don't say, he can't refuse."

"Let's get cracking," Ranger said. "What's your angle for the first shot, Sam?"

The setup was amazingly short—due, I say in all modesty, to the scenarios I had written out. We would do the scenes with Sylvie, me, and Bone first, then the two of us expressing our gratitude to Ranger, then Ranger solemnly pulling a revolver and shooting the mad dog.

That was not in the scenario I wrote, but Ranger put it in over Sylvie's objection, after assuring her over and over that the gun would be loaded with blanks and wouldn't be pointed at Bone anyway. I wasn't too comfy with a gun either, especially a real one. It belonged to Titus Bell, who had taught Ranger to use it. At least Ranger said so. At any rate, he insisted we needed it for realism.

The hydrogen peroxide was for making Bone's mouth foam like a real mad dog's. The first dose made him choke because he had the bad sense to swallow most of it. What remained fizzed over his jaws and dripped convincingly, even though he looked a little too happy while "attacking." Ranger was right about the catnip though. Bone charged with such abandon that Sylvie was truly alarmed, and her cries for help

sounded so real that I thought it a shame pictures couldn't be made with sound.

Next, with Bone safely tied to a stake in the ground some yards away, Ranger modestly accepted our thanks. He also insisted that I make eyes at him, since this was supposed to be our first meeting. I wasn't sure I knew how to "make eyes," so I narrowed them and looked sideways at him, as though inconspicuously checking his shirt for gravy stains, while Ranger grandly took no notice.

When it came time to shoot the dog, Sylvie cringed and covered her eyes while I turned half away with one hand lifted—very theatrical. Standing between us, Ranger raised and steadied the revolver with both hands. Aimed directly at the camera, the pistol roared.

"Cripes!" Sam jumped as though he'd been hit, though the crank never stopped turning. "Good thing you warned me."

"Cut," Ranger said and waited until Sam closed the lens cover before asking, "How'd it look?"

"Perfect. Flashed like a cannon."

Sylvie and I were trembling, the retort still ringing in our ears. "Sam, you didn't even stop!" she exclaimed in wonder.

"The camera *never* stops," he said solemnly.

He next turned his lens on Bone to establish what Ranger was shooting at. Newly dosed with hydrogen peroxide, the dog was supposed to look fierce but he mostly looked curious.

Then it was Sundance's turn. Since we already had film of the thrilling ride to our rescue, all the horse had to do was gallop to the spot and slow his pace while Ranger reached down with his riding crop. Sylvie was to grab the crop and use it for leverage while Ranger got a better grip on her with his other hand before sweeping her away to safety. Since we were short on time and everybody, including the horse, seemed clear on their part, Ranger proposed to do it without rehearsal. He swung into the saddle, folded his glasses into his pocket, and trotted away to a spot well behind the camera.

Rescues are easier said than done, it's safe to say. On the first take, Sylvie missed the riding crop altogether, and the second time she grabbed it but almost pulled Ranger out of the saddle when he didn't anticipate her weight. (She is small but dense.) The third attempt failed when her foot missed the stirrup and Sundance galloped away with a little girl hanging onto the pommel, legs dangling and bloomers showing. In a real rescue no one would mind about bloomers, but on film it would look silly.

"Are you sure you don't need some rehearsal?" I asked.

"I've only got fifteen minutes," Sam called.

"We'll get it this time." Ranger's face wore a determined look that the fates would do well to heed. "Isobel, pick up that stick and give the dog a whack. Pretend you're trying to fight him off. Ready, Sylvie?"

He was right: we got it that time. I could only see bits of it, occupied as I was, but the bending, grabbing, catching, and sweeping looked smooth. Or it did up to the point where Ranger was galloping away with Sylvie. Without his glasses, he failed to see a rabbit leap up from behind a half-buried boulder. Sundance saw it and shied so violently his riders fell off.

I raced over to Sylvie, who had landed in a patch of clover and seemed no worse for wear. As I turned away from her, an object in the grass caught my attention: a pair of glasses, glaring at the sun, the lenses in place but shattered.

My nightmare blazed up before my eyes—the blasted field, the strewn bodies, the artillery fire flashing behind broken lenses. I staggered and made a horrible noise in the back of my throat like my breakfast was coming up.

Then a light pressure on my elbow, a breath on my cheek. "Are you okay?" Sam asked. I could only look at him, unable to shape a single word. The mere sight of Ranger's broken glasses had released a flood of dammed-up feeling I didn't even suspect was there. It felt like absolute terror.

"Ranger's hurt!" Sylvie yelled.

He was flat on his back next to the boulder, staring up at the sky. "I'm fine," he insisted. "Just fine." But he didn't move until Sam came over and pulled him up by the hand.

Ranger winced and put a hand to his head. "Do we have time to shoot the dog?"

Sam eyed him narrowly. "We already did that."

"Oh yeah. I forgot."

"Are you sure you're all right?"

"Absolutely. Just a little dizzy for a minute." He shook Sam's hand, holding it longer than he needed to. "Good day's work, old man. Now you'd better get that camera home and… whatever you're supposed to do with it."

Sam packed up and hiked across the pasture, with a few backward glances. Ranger seemed all right as we rounded up the animals and started back to the stable. Then, at the corral gate, he stumbled against me. "Man-oh-man. It *hurts*."

"Did you hit your head on that rock?" I asked sharply.

"I may have. I mean, I did. Just a knock. I mean a knot. Maybe both. Go open the sylvie door, Stable."

"I'm Sylvie!" she protested.

"Right," he said, swaying.

"I think we should call a doctor," I said worriedly.

"Oh no. That won't be nessenary."

"Won't be *what*?"

He frowned at me before gently keeling over at my feet.

Chapter 13
Talmadge and Prospect

While I stayed with Ranger, fanning his face and calling his name—and slapping him when his eyes rolled back—Sylvie raced to the hacienda. A lifetime later (or so it seemed, though it was probably no more than ten minutes), Titus Bell came bounding over the pasture on his long legs, picked the boy up as though he were a bag of flour, and sped him to the hospital in the long, blue touring car, where it was determined that Ranger had suffered a mild concussion.

I was not allowed to see him until the next day, after he'd been released from the hospital and brought home in triumph.

For a boy with a knot on his head the size of a lemon, he seemed remarkably spry. I figured it was because he'd finally gotten his rescue scene. Anyone else might have said it was because he was propped up in comfort with Esperanza at his beck and call, a stack of Hardy Boys by his side, a cherry phosphate within easy reach, and a very relieved father who was promising to tan his backside as soon as he could stand up for it. I was pretty relieved myself, though I'd never admit it.

"'Oh what a tangled web we weave, when first we practice to deceive,'" I quoted to him.

"So, what did you tell 'em?" he asked with a grin.

I grimaced in reply. "Just that you were giving us a riding demonstration, which we begged for. I couldn't explain the scout uniform, but fortunately nobody asked. Your father is furious with you, and my mother is furious with all of us, especially me, for encouraging you."

"All worth it," he assured me. "It's a terrific scene; I can feel it in my bones. But wait—" He sat up too fast, then whistled with pain, clutching his head. "You're not grounded, are you?"

"Mother hasn't said anything. But I should be. It was bad enough going along with your lies, but when I start telling them myself—"

He waved away my scruples. "Don't worry, it's all for a great cause."

"Why don't you just tell them the *truth*?"

"I *will*. Soon as we're done, and we almost are. But I need you to do something. You know the old film of me on Sundance? It's stashed under the bed here. You need to get it to Sam tomorrow so he can cut it with the new."

"Can't it wait until you deliver it yourself?"

"Don't know when I can." He frowned, still gripping his forehead. "Pa could have me pinned down for a week. Saturday afternoon is the only time we can count on getting into the

Vitagraph studio, and that's tomorrow. Please, Isobel? You're our only hope."

As the reader may have guessed by now, I am a sucker for boys who look at me with dark pleading eyes and say I am their only hope. Especially if they've just suffered some injury to soul or body.

But how is a young lady to go traipsing around Los Angeles alone without raising any suspicions? By telling her mother she needs to shop for a birthday present for that selfsame mother, whose birthday was only two weeks off—no lie. Sylvie wanted to go, of course, but I told her she was needed to keep Ranger company. Fortunately she saw this as a high calling and didn't fuss too much. I saw it as exactly what he deserved.

Following Ranger's directions, I walked down the row of plain stucco buildings until I found the door marked *Editing*. Sam answered my shy knock. "Just in time."

The room was close and stifling, in spite of the ceiling fan blades turning slowly over our warmish heads. Sam took the film canister from me and opened it right away, snapped the reel on the projector, and threaded it without a pause. "How's Ranger?"

"Perfectly fine," I said. "Sharp as vinegar. You wouldn't think he had just escaped death by inches."

Sam spun the take-up reel, smiling with one side of his mouth. "He's a funny kid."

I agreed, but probably not for the same reasons. "How do you mean?"

"Pull that light cord, wouldja?" A beam of light shot from the projector as the room went dark. Several feet of film sputtered across the screen before Ranger appeared, loping along on the back of Sundance. "Look at him," Sam remarked. "He's got his own horse, servants, a dad who hobnobs with the likes of Griffith and Joe Schenck. But he doesn't act rich."

"How does he act?" I asked, curious.

Sam squinted at the screen, pursing his lips in concentration. "Hungry."

He stopped the film with Ranger leaning forward, half standing in the stirrups. "Right there. Looks like he heard something. We'll put your call for help right there." After slipping a piece of paper between layers of film, he continued turning the hand crank, more slowly.

"How long have you known him?"

"Met him at the St. Pat's parade on Broadway last spring. Seen him before though. He used to hang around here and at Fine Arts and Keystone too. Some of the cameramen and grips called him the Lot Lizard." Sam paused the crank. "What made me notice him at the parade was he was trying to shoot it with a homemade camera."

"A motion-picture camera?" I exclaimed. "He made it?"

"Yeah, from directions in *The Boy Mechanic*, I think. Just a tall wooden box with a reading glass for a lens and a reel that would hold about twenty feet of film. Less than a minute's worth. He hauled the camera back to an empty storefront and threw a black cloth over it to change the reels. You may have noticed he's not very mechanical. So I helped him a little, and we sort of struck up a conversation. As soon as he found out I had a real camera, one thing led to another."

"Do you…like him?"

"Like him?" He stopped cranking and stuck in another marker. "Used to think he was a snot-nosed brat. But money doesn't go to his head—I like that. 'Course, it doesn't seem to go much to his pocket either. Or else he wouldn't be trying to make pictures with a homemade camera."

"His father doesn't want to spoil him," I said.

"Yeah, I've heard all about that. His grandpa got rich in the Gold Rush selling pancakes. Then he moved down here and bought a ranch. That's how Titus grew up, riding the range and all. He wants his kid to be tough like him." Slowing the film just after Ranger cleared the ditch, Sam slipped in another paper and continued on. "Thing is, the kid's a lot tougher than he looks. And I've never known anybody so dead-set on getting his way." On screen, Ranger fell off his horse again. "Can't ride worth a darn though. Light."

That was a request. After pulling the cord, I noticed what I hadn't before: a long countertop down one side of the room and an overhead rod above it draped with strips of film in different lengths. The counter was not connected to the wall, so film could hang behind it all the way to the floor. The surface was littered with scissors, a knife, a glue pot, and bits of film. It was the first time I'd seen, with my own eyes, the fruits of our labor.

"How do you develop all this?"

"With difficulty." He lifted the reel off the projector and brought it to the counter, where he snapped it to an upright bracket that allowed it to spin freely. Then he pulled up a high stool. "There's a darkroom next door. I take it in there and wrap the film around a square frame. Then dunk it in the developing tank—"

"But where do you get all the solution?" I interrupted. "It must be gallons!"

"Yep, about a hundred. I know a fella who works at night. We've got a deal. He usually lets me put a rack of our film in with the batch he's developing for Vitagraph. Ranger and me never have more than two racks at a time, so there's usually room. After it's developed, the film goes in a fixing tank, and that's where my part of the deal comes in."

He paused to take a matchstick out of his pocket, which he stuck in his mouth. After a moment I prompted, "How so?"

"The film has to be washed off, and that's a messy job nobody likes. So the other fella goes home, and I wash all my film plus his. Then I have to wind it on a drying drum—looks kind of like a barrel—and keep rewinding it while it dries, so it won't pull up and break."

No wonder he often slept late or looked like impending death when he met us for a morning shoot. "Why do you do all this, Sam?"

He shrugged.

"No, I mean it. It's a lot more than just dunking film and winding film and hauling equipment all over creation. Every time you take the camera out, you risk breaking it or getting caught, and what if your father catches you again?"

The pale eyes flickered at me like the edge of a blade. "It's worth that risk."

"But *why*?"

Sam flipped a switch, and a square of thick, creamy glass on the countertop glowed with light. "Last time it paid off. Dad and me worked on something together, first time ever. He called me a chip off the old block. Might pay off again. Who knows?" He unrolled the film from the reel and scanned it across the light, studying the frames.

That was plainly all I'd get from him on the subject, but it was enough to chew on. Maybe the camera was the only common meeting ground Sam and his father could muster. I still didn't understand why they had to play their cat-and-mouse game with it, but maybe they didn't either.

"Are you cutting now? Could I watch you?"

Another shrug. "Suit yourself, girlie."

"My name's Isobel."

"So I hear."

Just when I was starting to like him. Nevertheless I pulled up another stool and climbed on it, watching as he pulled the film through his fingers, forward and back, back and forward. His overlong hair fell over his sleepy eyes, and his thin lips pursed in concentration.

"Right there," he muttered, picking up the scissors to cut between the frames. Then he laid the end of the cut film on a block, securing it on pins that exactly matched the sprocket holes.

He gently tugged a long section of film from the rack behind the counter. "This is you, yelling for help."

Leaning forward eagerly, I could see my tiny image repeated in the frames marching across the square of light. Sam scraped the last frame with a knife and brushed it with glue. Working quickly, he laid the glued frame over the piece that was pinned on the block so their sprocket holes matched. Pressing down, he announced, "Now you're in the picture."

I was intrigued in spite of myself. "Let me do one."

"Looks easy, huh? Watch this." He wound up most of the spliced film on a take-up reel by his elbow, then searched among the hanging strips for another section. "Here's a trick the old man showed me. This is the first take we did of you, same scene. You're standing in the same place so everything matches up. You can cut about one second of this film"—he paused to count twenty frames and pushed the scissors over to me—"and then you're going to paste it at the end of the shot. If we rolled the film real slow, we'd see a little jerk and then you doing exactly the same thing over again. But at projection speed, it goes by so fast nobody would notice."

"Why do it then?" I was holding the end of film I'd just cut, absolutely fascinated.

"It makes a smoother shift from one angle to another. Action doesn't look so jerky. Here, you need to take this knife and scrape that end of the film—careful, not too hard. Just enough to get the emulsion off." After scraping, I lightly applied the glue brush and lined up the ends on the splicing block.

The whole "rescue" episode went together like that, a bit here and a piece there, much of it in silence except for the scritch of the knife and the pulse of the overhead fan. We worked in the same murmury silence I remembered from Father's darkroom—otherwise known as the cellar—under the glow of his red lamp.

Father used glass plates taken with a folding camera, putting each through three trays of fluid. As he rocked the developing tank, shapes emerged: family portraits and reunions, street scenes, sunrises over Puget Sound. They were like frozen bits of time, snippets from the life we'd already lived.

But motion-picture film was something else entirely— something *un*frozen. Still pictures were the past, but film was, as Ranger always said, the future.

Sam straightened up and mopped his brow with a handkerchief. "We're making tracks here. All that's left is shooting the dog."

Glancing at the Seth Thomas clock on the wall behind me, I gasped. "It's been over an hour! How does Ranger sit still for this?"

"He doesn't much. I got more done with you in an hour than I could with him in a whole afternoon."

He said it as a mere observation, not a compliment, but I felt complimented anyway. In fact, I glowed like a little candle. "I like cutting film. It's...it's like rearranging time! Suppose your life was on film, and you could cut any part you wanted or move the pieces around to tell a different story."

"Um." He nodded, as though the thought was not new to him.

"Where I would cut would be when Father decided to enlist. Perhaps he could struggle in a manly way with his decision before he decided not to go—but no, it would be better if there wasn't any war at all."

"Cutting the war might be good." The smiling side of his mouth was up again, even while his head stayed down, scanning frames of Bone.

Remembering my moment of hysteria when I'd seen Ranger's broken glasses on the grass made a little extra warmth rise to my face, and I wondered if he remembered it too. "What about you? What would you cut?"

In spite of his talky mood, I didn't expect him to answer. So imagine my surprise when, after only a little pause, he did: "I'd cut a puddle of grease on the deck of the *Jersey Queen*."

I laughed, then realized it wasn't meant for a joke. "I'm... sorry?"

He cleared his throat delicately—the self-conscious noise of someone who's stumbled upon an embarrassing scene. "Um... Back in Jersey, 'bout four years ago, my mother and sister and I—"

"Your sister?"

"Little sister. About Sylvie's age she was then. Um, we were on a Hudson River excursion boat, headed out to Governors Island for a picnic, see, and she..." His voice seemed to dry up. I looked at him sharply, but his face seemed unchanged, except for blinking at a single frame. "She was playing tag with some other kids on the deck. Ducked under a guard rope at the stern end of the boat and slipped on a patch of grease. Before anybody could grab her, she fell into the paddle wheel."

"*Oh!*" I cried involuntarily. "How dreadful!" Clearly this was the family tragedy Ranger had hinted at.

"Yeah."

"Did you—I mean—did you see it?"

He shook his head, still staring at the film with a tight-lipped frown. "My mother did though." A pause followed, stretching longer than I thought a pause ever could. "She didn't handle it too good." So that was why she didn't come west with the family—the family had a sudden, gaping hole in it.

Abruptly Sam asked, "When are you supposed to be home?" Tactless, but I couldn't blame him.

"Oh dear!" I hopped off the stool. "I'm supposed to be shopping. Mother will look askance if I come home empty-handed."

"I'll walk you to the streetcar stop," he offered. "Could use some fresh air."

Fresh air was just the ticket after being cooped up with developing fumes and tragic memories. We walked down the row of blocky buildings and had turned onto Talmadge Avenue before I thought of anything to say. "Thank you for showing me how to cut. It was quite interesting."

"Don't mention it," he said shortly, sticking his hands in his pockets.

The time was already half-past three, which meant that the studios would be opening soon for their late-afternoon shooting schedules. Cowboys in chaps and bathing beauties in ruffles lingered over iced coffee in the studio café on the corner. Just ahead of us, an Indian in full headdress wandered out of a candy store with a little bag, pausing on the stoop to pop a jawbreaker into his mouth. I found myself wondering if I could afford a few jawbreakers for Ranger and Sylvie, and then it struck me: the whole scene no longer seemed strange.

How strange!

"There's Charlie," Sam remarked, nodding toward a couple coming our way on the sidewalk.

The Little Tramp was out of costume and blended in so well that I might not have recognized him except for his aggressive teeth. He ignored all greetings, deep in earnest chat with his companion—who seemed to be just as intent on him.

And that was a good thing, for she would have been as stunned to see me as I was to see her. As they passed us, Mr. Chaplin jabbering all the while, I turned my head to watch them disappear into the studio café.

"Wonder who's the dame?" Sam observed with a touch of disapproval.

What I wondered was why Charlie Chaplin was taking a late-afternoon stroll with my mother.

Chapter 14
A Love Story

My mood was pensive on the streetcar. Also on the street and all the way up the drive. It had been quite a pensive afternoon, especially at the end.

Surely there was a reasonable explanation for a doctor's wife and mother of two to be promenading with the Little Tramp, but I couldn't think of any. And when I walked into the great room of the hacienda, already somewhat overwrought, a Zulu warrior leaped from behind the Chinese lacquer screen and gave a wild ululating cry. I almost jumped out of my dotted-swiss summer frock.

But below the fierce wooden expression and animal-hair topknot I recognized Aunt Buzzy's sensible shoes. Laughing, she lowered her disguise. "Sorry, Belladonna. These masks just arrived—Titus's latest enthusiasm—and when I saw you coming up the drive, I couldn't resist. You should have seen your face—"

Seeing my face, her own expression changed. "Not a good time, obviously. Now I'm *really* sorry. What's the trouble, dear?"

What *wasn't* the trouble? Father in Europe picking bullets out of soldiers who wouldn't stop firing at each other—and perhaps dodging bullets himself! Mother gallivanting—well, strolling at least—with an untrustworthy show-business character. Sylvie besotted with picture-making and a boy we didn't even know six weeks ago, and me... I used to know what to think about most things, but that was before we were uprooted and set down in a strange land of relentless sun and make-believe. Now my thoughts lay in pieces like a pile of random film cuts.

Out of habit, I glanced at the palm-leaf table. "Nothing from Father today?"

Aunt Buzzy's blue eyes swam with sympathy as she set the mask on the nearest armchair. "I'm afraid not. You miss him, don't you, dear? No wonder you're feeling blue. Suppose I ask Esperanza to mix up a couple of glasses of lemonade for us?"

Soon after, I was sipping lemonade in the courtyard while she tried to cheer me up.

"I'm sure your poor father is too exhausted to write, even if he had the time. That was certainly clear from his last letter. But it'll be over soon—I read in the paper just this morning about a major offensive begun by the Allies, and they think the Germans have nearly had enough. Then your father can come home and rest up and get back to his old self. Which, by the way, hasn't changed much since he was a hopeful youth just out of medical school. I remember the night they met... You know that story, don't you?"

I knew it but didn't mind hearing it again. It was as cozy as a fairy tale, for in fairy tales you know the scullery maid will be recognized as a princess, and the children will find their way home, and the three bears will expel the intruder. (I never liked that Goldilocks.) And they live happily ever after. Aunt Buzzy even told it like a fairy tale:

"So. Many years ago, a young medical student named Robert Forrest Ransom Jr. took the West Coast Zephyr from Seattle to Newport Beach to visit his cousin Hugh between school terms. While he was there, Hugh received an invitation to a debutante ball in Los Angeles. The invitation was from Miss Gladys Russell, who was sweet on him. But the feeling wasn't mutual, so Hugh asked his cousin to go to the ball in his place.

"Bobby took the train to Los Angeles, then the trolley to Fremont Heights. From there he had to walk up a long hill, and when he arrived at the Pavilion, he discovered that he'd left his invitation behind on the trolley.

"Of course, he was mortified. They wouldn't have let him in without it, except that they were short of escorts that evening—and he looked so respectable, so *splendid*, really, in his black tie and tails. I was there, serving punch in my green taffeta dress with that scratchy organdy collar, and I can testify there was *quite* a rustle among the young ladies when he came in. When he and Mattie caught sight of each other, their eyes just *locked*." Aunt Buzzy sighed at the memory.

"They danced and talked the night away, and it wasn't until the party was breaking up that he confessed he was there by a fluke. 'I'm standing proxy for my cousin,' said he. 'There's a certain overzealous young lady he is anxious to avoid—Gladys Russell? Is she here?'"

"Your mother blinked in surprise. 'Gladys Russell? I don't know anyone by that name at the Academy.'"

"'The Academy?' said your father. 'Isn't this the Fremont Country Club Debutante Ball?'"

"Then it all came out—the country club was a little farther up the hill. He was at the Barlow Young Ladies' Academy Spring Cotillion—the wrong party!" Aunt Buzzy threw back her head and laughed, as grown-ups always did when they came to this part. "By then the die was cast though. And to think it all came about because he left his invitation on the trolley."

I found myself writing a motion-picture scenario in my head: an earnest young man in evening dress boards the car, tells the driver where he wants to go, and takes the invitation out of his pocket to be sure of his destination. But just then a lady asks him to hold her packages while she searches in her pocketbook for the fare.

Throughout the trip, every time he remembers to open the envelope, he's interrupted by things more and more fantastic: a little boy swinging on the bell cord, a bear on a unicycle, a funny little man in slap shoes selling flowers (but I nixed that idea because the epitome of funny little men in slap shoes was Mr. Chaplin). Finally, our hero would hear his stop, pull the cord, and step off the trolley. Close-up on the invitation, lying abandoned on the seat…

"…and they lived happily ever after," Aunt Buzzy concluded.

"What began as a mistake turned into a lifelong romance. Life is like that—the strangest or most unwelcome, even the saddest things that happen can come to make sense in the end." Then she leaned forward to put a hand on my knee. "It's a terrible strain with Bobby gone and the war and all, but this too shall pass, hmm? He'll be home soon and your family story will continue on its—its unpredictable, interesting path. Does that help, dear?"

I blinked, thinking of close-ups and film splices, trying to recall why I needed help. "Oh! Yes, it does. Thanks, Aunt Buzzy. I'm glad we had this talk." But the person I was now dying to talk to was Ranger.

Sylvie had brought in her dolls to perform a circus for him, and had rigged up a tightrope and trapeze over his bed. I thought it was clever of her, but Ranger considered himself too mature for dolls. Besides, there had been some trouble with the clown, whom Sylvie had made to juggle two lead soldiers and a juice glass not entirely empty. She wanted to tell me about it, but Ranger interrupted. "Why don't you see if the sugar cookies are done yet? I think I can smell vanilla."

That worked. Once she had scampered off to the kitchen, he said, "You sure took your time. What did you do, finish our picture and start on one of DeMille's?"

The cutting room seemed long ago already. "No. When I left, Sam was up to the part where you shoot the dog.

But that's not what I came to tell you. I have an idea about the scenario."

"You do?" Ranger straightened up, as I knew he would at the mention of "scenario." "What is it?"

"First, the father should not be the villain."

"Come on, Iz. We've settled this. Besides, we've already got him on film and it's terrific!"

"We can still use the film. All I'm saying is that the man at the beer garden is not the girls' father. He's their guardian or something. Maybe their uncle. Their father is a good, brave man who had to go serve his country. And…and the uncle promises to care for the girls, but instead he squanders their money on his own pleasures. Like the stepmother in *Cinderella*."

"What about the girls' mother?"

"She's passed on, like we have it already."

Ranger shook his head. "Won't work. The U. S. government wouldn't draft a man who has kids to care for."

"My father wasn't drafted. He volunteered."

"That's even worse. He wouldn't have volunteered if you didn't have a mother, would he? Think about it."

I was thinking he had picked an inconvenient time to start making sense. "But…but this makes the story *better*. The Dauntless Youth is even more outraged that the uncle's not caring for the girls as he should, and there can be a scene of Matchless showing him their father's picture and telling about him, and the youth is touched. And"—I paused, dramatically placing before his eyes the item I had stopped by my room to pick up—"we can use my father's real picture. See, he's in his uniform and everything. The Dauntless Youth can promise to search for him at the front, and…uh…"

Ranger was giving the picture more careful scrutiny than he ever had before. Father's level, serious gaze peered straight into Ranger's eager eyes as if it could do all the persuading. "So when he finds him," Ranger speculated, "the man is mortally wounded, and the Youth asks for Matchless's hand in marriage, and with his dying breath—"

"No!" I said, snatching the picture back so sharply that Ranger jerked in alarm. I hugged it to my chest. "The man's *not* dying. Field surgeons are too far away from the front to get wounded. Don't you know that?"

We glared at each other in silence until Ranger said, "Well, all right then. If you say so."

"Could we write the scenario?"

He snapped the bedcover, sending Raggedy Ann and Teddy and Bobo the clown tumbling into the abyss. "Grab that notebook over on the chest."

I will not go into the artistic process, except to say that a lot of paper wadding, eye rolling, and disgusted sighs were involved. What we finally settled on was this:

The girls' father has been called to France because he's developed a new surgical technique that will help save the lives of many brave, wounded lads. He's left the girls in care of their grandmother ("Where do we get a *grandmother*?" Ranger cried), who has most unfortunately suffered a stroke and is in the hospital. ("Maybe we can find an old lady on a porch," I slyly suggested.) That leaves the doctor's no-good brother in charge, and while he is not cruel he is certainly neglectful. The scene of Jimmy Service elaborately ignoring little Sylvie's pleas would show that side of him. Matchless struggles to make ends meet—

"Wait a minute," Ranger interrupted. "Wouldn't she try to get in touch with dear old dad to tell him what's going on?"

"Well, perhaps…" I thought aloud, "she doesn't want to worry him while he's doing important work. Or perhaps she writes to him but the letter goes astray. Close-up on an envelope slipping out of a mailbag and blowing into a puddle."

"I see," Ranger mused. "Write that down—establishing shot."

The Dauntless Youth, we decided, could make his dramatic appearance on horseback as planned and make friends with the girls before marching off to war—

"Where he is wounded," I improvised, "and taken to the field hospital, where the surgeon happens to be…" I spread my hands.

"Matchless's father!" Ranger crowed, almost leaping out of bed in his excitement. "That's *brilliant!*" His grin faded. "But how do we shoot it?"

"What if we find a tall man and dress him in a surgeon's coat and shoot him from the back?" I was stretching the fabric of possibility now but couldn't seem to help myself. "And when the Youth comes to after his surgery, he looks up at the man's face and it…it fades or somehow changes to an image of the picture?"

"Dissolves. You're thinking like a cameraman now," he said,

not without admiration. "But this calls for a big recognition scene with tears and all. And the only way we can end this thing is with Dad coming back and punching his brother in the nose and weeping over his mama in the hospital. You've let too many snakes out of the bag—we can't chase 'em all down."

"But suppose Father still has work to do overseas—"

"I can't figure you out! You want him out as a villain, but now you hafta stick him back in as a hero, and we don't have the time or the film for all this—and what is it with *Father* anyway?"

I couldn't tell him, because I wasn't sure myself. Only that the film-cutting with Sam had shown me something about stories, and I couldn't shake the sense that if we just told it right, it would prove true. "He can write a scathing letter to his brother or send some kind of legal document that takes the girls out of his control."

"I don't know," Ranger said. "A letter is weak—"

"Not if it's brought by Dauntless Youth, who comes home with a medal and his arm in a sling. Here's where your train scene comes in, Ranger. The girls meet him at the station and hear his story, and the Youth goes to confront Uncle at the beer garden… Maybe we don't even have to show you two together, but the Youth does his denouncing, and one of the uncle's pals is outraged and punches him—punches the Uncle, not the Youth—and we could cut that floozie in too—so full of righteous indignation she dumps a mug of beer on Uncle's head! The End, on a comic note."

Ranger chewed on the ending while I chewed my pencil.

"All right," he said finally. "It's not as good as a man-to-man knockdown, and there's a problem with shooting Father" (I couldn't help wincing at his choice of words), "but I like the field hospital. And if we can find an old lady in a sanitarium, that could work too. Tell you what: if you keep Sylvie out of my hair for the rest of the afternoon, I'll be so good Pa will have to let me out of bed, and tomorrow we can meet Sam at Echo Park."

Chapter 15
Miss Blanche

The price Ranger paid for getting out of bed the next day was a licking from his father for the Sundance incident. Oddly, this seemed to clear the air between them so they were on speaking terms again, even if the speech was not especially warm.

We couldn't meet Sam at Echo Park until the following morning. Ranger was so glad to be out that he turned a cartwheel on our way to the streetcar stop—though he had to limit himself to one because his head still hurt.

But Sam quashed some of those high spirits after hearing the revised scenario. "Way too complicated. Where do we get a field hospital, not to mention a field surgeon? Not to also mention an invalid grandmother—which we don't even need."

"We have to show that the girls have a good father," Ranger insisted. "A good father wouldn't leave them behind unless he knew they were in safe hands. And it wouldn't be his fault if the grandmother got sick after he left and ended up in the hospital so the no-good brother has to take over. Of course, we can explain all that in a title card, but pictures are for showing."

"A hospital is a public place," Sam pointed out. "What did I tell you about public places?"

"Only semipublic," I put in—obliged to support Ranger, since he'd accepted my scenario. "A place where most of the people are in bed couldn't exactly be public, could it? If we found a hospital or sanitarium where there's a porch or court-yard, and if we got there at the right time of day and explained to the nurses what we were doing…"

"Explain what we're doing," Sam repeated flatly. "What *are* we doing?"

"We'll tell 'em we're making a photographic record of the healing profession," Ranger said confidently. "It's true enough, and who wouldn't want to be in a photographic record?"

"I can think of a few," Sam muttered. "Besides, you've stuck in twice as many war scenes—before, we just had you marching in a parade and scouting on horseback. Now, we've got that, plus you getting wounded and toted to the field hospital—with Sylvie as the ambulance driver maybe?"

"All that might need a little more thought," Ranger admitted. "But Grandma in the hospital—that's easy, and it'll add pathos to the picture."

Sam made a very brief remark about pathos, and Ranger tried to change his mind with no evident success, and it ended up a most unsatisfactory meeting.

And I felt it more than Ranger did! On our way home, with Sylvie darting from one empty seat to another while the streetcar driver kept an edgy eye on her, I couldn't help fretting out loud.

"What if Sam backs out of the project?" I asked. "Is there any way we could get another camera?"

"Not that I know of," Ranger told me, disgustingly cheerful. "Sam gets foot-draggy every now and then. I'm used to it. He won't back out, believe me. But how come you care so much all of a sudden?"

"Who says I care that much?" The words came out snappish, and Ranger grinned at me. Because I did care, of course—a string of images on film had come to mean the world to me.

"I'll talk to him tomorrow," Ranger said. "He'll see the light."

Surpassing strange for Ranger to be the calm one, since he rarely was, but that state of affairs didn't last long. For when his father joined us for dinner that night, he brought news of particular interest.

After some random chitchat about Mack Sennett's latest run-in with the Santa Monica police (when Mr. Sennett ran a Keystone Cop car off the pier and caused a panic among church picnickers who thought it was for real), and some good-natured teasing about Mother's motion-picture career ("Don't make a federal case of this, Titus," she said warningly while I felt my ears getting hot)—after all that, and while the table was being cleared for dessert, Mr. Bell turned to his son and said, "By the way, I had lunch with D. W. this afternoon."

Ranger nearly choked on an éclair.

"Congratulated him on *Hearts of the World*. Glad to see he's back into solid, clean entertainment—though I didn't tell him that, of course."

"I should hope not," Aunt Buzzy said, laughing. "Let's not get started on the merits of *Intolerance*."

"Water under the bridge," Titus Bell agreed. "He has some interesting projects in mind. We agreed to talk further. Suppose we invite him over to dinner sometime in the next couple of weeks."

While he and Aunt Buzzy discussed dates, Ranger was struggling to force down his éclair, his eyes behind the glasses as round as nickels. "Say, Pa..."

"Yes, my son?"

"Would you... Could I..."

"Join us for dinner? I don't see why not."

Unable to sleep, Ranger slipped into our room after eleven. "I've changed my mind about fathers. Mine's not all bad."

"I thought he was a tight-fisted stuffed shirt," Sylvie murmured sleepily from her bed.

"Who said that?"

"You did."

"Perish the thought." Ranger waved away all previous opinions. "Know what I'm thinking? If we can have the picture finished by then, I'm going to ask him to see it. Mr. Griffith, I mean."

"Well, of course," I said. "That was the plan all along, wasn't it?"

"Yeah, but I wasn't sure how it would really happen. Now that I know when and where, well... We *have* to finish it, Iz. Soon as possible, so we have plenty of time for cutting. Better forget the war scenes: no time."

I grabbed my father's picture from the nightstand and held it up. "Can we still use this?"

"Sure. We'll make the Youth a member of the Home Guard who stands ready to defend his country, but in the meantime he vows to defend Matchless and Little Sister. I'll talk to Sam tomorrow and come to a meeting of minds. While I'm gone, see what you can do with the scenario."

Ranger left on his bicycle as soon as he could get away the next morning, after promising Aunt Buzzy he would pick up two pairs of high-top boots and a button hook at the shoe repair on Hollywood and Vine. Shortly after, I was trying to work up a scenario minus war scenes when Esperanza came to the drawing-room door to tell me I had a telephone call.

"For me?" This was unheard-of. "Who is it?"

"The young man who calls for Mr. Ranger sometime. I tell him he's not home, he say he'll speak to you."

Full of wonder, I followed her to the front hall where the telephone was. "Hello?"

I heard the operator's voice crackle, "Go ahead, Edendale."

"Isobel." Sam's voice sounded flatter than usual, or maybe that was just the wire. "Got a message for Ranger." I didn't tell him Ranger was on the way, but waited until he got some delicate throat-clearing taken care of. "For you too," he continued. "Forest Grove Sanitarium on Thursday. Meet me by nine."

"What?"

"Be sure to bring Sylvie."

"Of course we'll bring Sylvie. But, Sam, what made you—"

"See ya. 'Bye."

What made you change your mind? The question echoed long after he hung up so abruptly, and Ranger had no answers when he returned much later than Aunt Buzzy thought he should. At least he'd remembered the shoes.

"It's a mystery," he said, once we'd retreated to the rose arbor. "Sam just told me it's all set up, so we hashed out the shots. One of her and you and Sylvie, and a close-up of her and Sylvie, and one of you introducing me to her and she gives me her blessing."

"But what *her*? Who is she?"

"Search me. He knows somebody at the sanitarium, I'll bet. If she looks grandmotherly and takes direction, that's enough for me."

Forest Grove Sanitarium had a genteel but rundown air, like a French aristocrat reduced to washing dishes after the Revolution. An aristocrat, I might add, who did not bathe enough. It was a three-story brick building facing an ill-kept lawn with forlorn patches of grass spearing up unevenly. As we walked up the path, I noticed two wounded soldiers sitting under an alder tree, dressed in odd ensembles of uniform parts and pajamas. They made me feel a bit guilty, as though I should be visiting hospitals instead of making pictures.

Sam met us in the front hallway. "The camera's all set up. Light's only good for thirty more minutes, so we'd better hoof it. You can call the lady 'Miss Blanche.'"

He led us to the second-floor gallery, where "Miss Blanche" reposed in the very last chair. She looked elderly enough to be a grandmother, but the eager gray eyes she turned our way had none of that faded, rheumy look you see in the aged.

Sam introduced the three of us, and Ranger snapped to it, assuming his most winsome manner to explain to Miss Blanche what we were up to. Meanwhile, the lady's eyes fastened on Sylvie. They never left Sylvie for long during the shooting, even when I took her hand or Ranger knelt down before the chair as though asking for her blessing. At one point, she got in her head that I was the maid and kept asking me for a needle and thread so she could sew up a tear in Sylvie's dress. She nearly drove Ranger to distraction, but he persevered with various angles and sequences until Sam told him the film was almost gone. Sylvie had climbed up in the old lady's lap by then, and the two of them were getting along famously.

A fluttering sound in the camera like a frantic moth in a box signaled the end of the film. Sam straightened up, turned his cap around, removed the crank, and loosened the mounting bolts on the tripod in his usual efficient way. I noticed his eyes seemed brighter.

"Come on, Sylvie," I told her. "Say good-bye to Miss Blanche."

My sister kissed the lady on the cheek and began to ease off her lap, and that's when the trouble started. Miss Blanche tightened her grip, and our efforts to break it only made her frantic. "No, you can't have her. You can't take my pet away. Hold tight, Trudy. No!"

Sam let some pretty strong language slip just before he joined us. As he worked Sylvie loose, he told us to clear out. "Now! I'll wrap it up here—just go!"

With a last firm tug, he removed the lady's hands from my sister, who was crying by now (Sylvie I mean). Miss Blanche was crying too, and as we made our escape, her sorrowful wail followed us: "*Truuuudy!*"

"What was that all about?" Ranger exclaimed in the hallway. He paused to swing the sobbing Sylvie up in his arms.

Two nurses, alerted by the hubbub, marched past us with starchy disapproval.

"Fudge!" I stopped abruptly. "I left my pocketbook."

"Let it go. Sam'll bring it."

"But it has our streetcar passes! Of all the… I remember exactly where I put it, on the coatrack near the door. Go on. I'll meet you outside."

On the porch, Miss Blanche had caused quite a scene and the patients were buzzing with curiosity. I slipped behind them to get to the rack. I thought Sam had slipped away until one of the nurses around Miss Blanche turned aside with a hypodermic needle. There he was in a wicker chair, holding Miss Blanche's hand.

"I'd have thought you'd know better," another nurse was scolding him. "Any more pranks like this—"

I reached out and secured my pocketbook as the nurse with the needle bustled away. Miss Blanche, already much quieter, was moaning for Trudy as Sam hiked his chair closer and put an arm around her. Stroking her hair, he said, "It's all right now, Mama. It's all right."

I didn't think he had noticed me, but before I could slip away he raised his voice a little. "It don't work, Isobel. Some film can't be cut."

I stammered out something—I don't know what—but he never looked my way.

Ranger was pleased with the shots we got. Much to my relief, he entertained Sylvie in the streetcar so I could piece together what just happened. Rumor was that Mrs. Service had deserted the family after their tragedy. Maybe Jimmy Service himself had put out that story, once it was clear that a change in climate and scenery had done the missus no good. Not very noble, perhaps, but no worse than Mr. Rochester, who had shut his own wife in an attic and pretended she didn't exist.

The one I couldn't understand was Sam. Knowing the state of his mother's mind, what had possessed him to expose her to another little girl, only to tear her away again? The more I thought about it, the angrier I got. I was almost simmering when Sylvie bounced across the aisle and asked, "Who's Trudy?"

"She was Sam's… She was Miss Blanche's little girl, I think."

"Did she die?"

"Probably."

"Then," Sylvie declared, "I'm glad I could be her little girl for a while. She was glad too, don't you think?"

"Yes," I said. "For a while." The lady's face came to me unbidden, gazing at her little girl. If I were Sam, wouldn't I want to see her like that just one more time? On film forever?

But *some film can't be cut*. In life, some of it had to stay, no matter how desperately you wished it away.

By the time we reached our stop, the sun was at high noon and we were hot and starving. Halfway up the drive, Ranger caught sight of his father's long, blue touring car in front of the house. It was supposed to be on its way to San Francisco with Titus Bell inside.

"Maybe he's been delayed for an urgent meeting with D. W.!" Ranger cried and galloped toward the house. Sylvie was right behind him, but I took my time. If Ranger's life revolved around Mr. Griffith, I was pretty sure his father's life did not.

And I was right. What delayed him had more to do with us.

Chapter 16
News

The screen door banged behind me as I crossed the hall and entered the great room. There I found this tableau: Mother, pale-faced in the wing chair with a paper in her lap and Titus Bell by her side; Ranger near the door, biting his lip while Sylvie clung to his hand. Aunt Buzzy stood by the sideboard, a whiskey tumbler in one hand and a bottle of spirits in the other. Every eye, whether teary, shocked, or anxious, was on me.

It was my worst dream come true. I could almost feel the shuddery ground of that nightmare battlefield under my feet. "Has something happened to Father?"

"Dear Belladonna." Aunt Buzzy set down the bottle and glass and hurried over, putting her arm around me. "It's not so bad, and if we all pull together like troopers and put our chins up—"

"What is it?" I demanded, pulling away from her. Whereupon Sylvie let loose a wail and bolted across the room to dive into Mother's lap. I half noticed that Titus Bell rescued the paper just in time.

Aunt Buzzy reached out a hand, then dropped it. "We got a letter from your father today. He wrote it himself, so we know it can't be too bad—"

"*What* can't be bad?" I burst out again. "Someone tell me what happened!"

"He's been hurt." Mother spoke up suddenly. "On the front. It seems he's been going on ambulance runs instead of staying at the field hospital, but of *course* he would never tell us that, so we wouldn't be worried." She tossed her head in exasperation, as I recalled her doing when Father would come home late from a call without the pins or the half-dozen eggs she'd asked him to pick up for her.

"How bad is it?" My voice sounded echoey in my ears.

"Apparently his ambulance hit a mine." Mr. Titus Bell took charge, and I was never so glad for his resoluteness as I was then. "The problem is, this letter is dated a month ago, and he writes as if there was one earlier that explained everything. He hurt his right arm. That's all we can tell for sure. He says something about the bandages being taken off tomorrow, and... Well, here, Isobel. You're old enough to read it for yourself."

He crossed the room with his long stride and delivered the missive to me. Then he reached for his hat, informing Aunt Buzzy, "I'm going down to Western Union to send a telegram to the War Office. We'll raise a ruckus 'til we find out what's going on."

I was staring at the paper, which was in my father's

handwriting, but all the letters looked wobbly. Aunt Buzzy was talking, perhaps to me, and I could not concentrate with all the chatter.

"Excuse me," I said and took my leave with the letter clutched in one hand.

"Gosh, Isobel," Ranger said as I passed him, "I'm really sorry…"

"Let her go," I heard Mother say, as I climbed the steps to the east wing and passed wraithlike through the doorway.

The letter was short:

Dear Ones,

Well I finally did it—figured out a way to come home. Sorry to get beat up in the process but I'm feeling better now. The old right shoulder still complains but I expect it always will. The left side is almost as good as new, which explains the disgraceful hand. Behold the script of a lefty. They took the bandages off last week and I suppose it could be worse. If everybody will just stay to the left of me from now on I'll get along famously. I hear through the grapevine that discharges are coming down soon, tho' not too soon for me. When it happens I'll fight off all obstacles and limp down to Bristol and camp out on the docks until some U.S.A.-bound vessel lets me aboard. God willing, when I finally see my lambs again, I'll be the gratefullest, happiest sack of bones in the world…

By then I was blinking constantly and feared making a soppy mess of the letter. There wasn't much more to it anyway. For the rest of the afternoon, Mother pulled herself together—though she hadn't fallen that much apart, as far as I could tell. When Titus Bell returned from Western Union, the two of them got busy raising a ruckus. It was the most sedate ruckus I'd ever seen: mostly letter-writing, with calls to the local selective service board for names and addresses. Whenever the telephone was free, Aunt Buzzy used it to cancel engagements for the week, and Ranger kindly undertook to keep Sylvie entertained. That left me with nothing to do but think, and after a quiet evening meal, I tracked down Ranger with the intention of sharing my thoughts.

He was playing croquet with Sylvie, but with only half a mind since she was way ahead of him. An apprehensive look crossed his face at my approach.

"We have something to discuss," I said.

"Look, Isobel, I expect you want to drop the picture, and if you do, I understand, really. But all the same, if you'd just—"

"You *don't* understand, really," I said. "I don't want to drop the picture."

Clearly taken by surprise, he dropped his jaw instead.

"Ranger!" Sylvie called from the far end of the course. "It's your turn!" He knocked the ball absently and missed the wicket by a foot. "You're not even trying!" she complained.

"I want to finish it," I went on, "only with a few changes. We need to reshoot those scenes at the house, with Father's picture included."

"Uh-huh." He nodded. "We were going to do that already."

"And mention him more in the title cards."

"Sure."

"And when we shoot the war scenes in the field hospital—"

"We took the war scenes out, remember?"

"Oh." My brain may have been more disordered than I thought. "Well, of course I remember."

"Uh-huh." Ranger shook his head pityingly as he hit the ball again, bypassing the wicket altogether. ("*Ranger!*" Sylvie hollered in exasperation.) "If we even have a prayer of getting this thing done by the end of next week, one more day of shooting is all we can plan for."

"Well…" I began, wondering how to suggest he might have to forget his date with Mr. Griffith.

"So," Ranger went on, "we go back to the studio in Daisy Dell and we reshoot that scene where the Youth comes to call. You—Matchless—can show him your dad's picture. Sam can get a close-up on it, with flowers and a little flag. Sylvie can do something cute, and Matchless tells the Youth about her father and…uh…he's inspired then and there to take a vow on the old man's—I mean, on the noble dad's—picture to watch out for his girls until he comes home. That's all we have time to shoot, but I promise we'll do a bang-up job on it. Then we'll decide how to put it all together. What do you think?"

I didn't have to think long. "Get Sam on the phone."

Two days later we were on the streetcar again, all four of us, headed for Daisy Dell and what we fondly supposed would be our last day of shooting. Besides our usual equipment, we

brought a broom, a hammer, and a few extra nails in case
something had blown over or fallen down in the two weeks
since we'd visited our "studio." In Ranger's Boy Scout knapsack I had carefully packed Father's picture, plus some silk
flowers I'd borrowed from an old hat, and a small flag Sylvie
had bought last Fourth of July.

The bag also held an old gray uniform coat and a conductor's cap. Ranger had an extra shot in mind: me standing
beside the picket fence in front of the rundown house at the
head of the path. The postman approaches (Ranger, wearing
the conductor's cap and a handlebar mustache), tips his cap,
and hands me a letter. Upon opening the letter, I first register
surprise, then delirious joy. It imparts the news that Father is
on his way home.

"But where does that go in the story?" I asked.

"I don't know," Ranger admitted. "It just might be good to
have, as long as we're there and the film holds out."

Sam was quiet on the journey after telling me, "I hope your
father's okay." Being quiet was hardly out of the ordinary for
him, but from the way he refused to meet my eyes, he seemed
a bit rueful. I had to wonder if cutting his own mother into the
picture was one of the things he rued.

Someday, if the talking fit ever seized him again in my pres-
ence, I would ask him. For now, we had work to do. Getting
off at the Cahuenga Pass stop, we hauled our bulky baggage
to the end of the road, where the dilapidated little house stood
with its peeling picket fence. It looked as abandoned as ever,
and just as well, for Sylvie's clattering on the porch in her

hard-soled boots was enough to raise the most resolute invalid or corpse.

Sam set up quickly, and Ranger outlined the scene for us while attaching his handlebar mustache with a dab of spirit gum. I straightened it for him before taking my place.

With Sam rolling the film, Ranger approached along the path while I swept a walk that wasn't there. He smiled and touched his cap to me. Then he reached into his pouch and handed over an envelope. As he walked on, I ripped open the envelope and scanned the contents, showing surprise and then delight. I turned to Sylvie. "It's a letter—from Father!"

Taking her cue like a trooper, Sylvie ran over and joined me in a chorus of "He's coming home!" As we turned to run toward the house, Ranger yelled, "Cut!"

"That was fine," Sam said, closing the shutter.

"Wait a minute." Ranger hesitated. "Let's do it one more time. As a bad news scene."

His statement was met by silence. "Why?" I finally asked.

"I don't know," he said. "I just thought we might need one. What do you think, Sam?"

The cameraman merely shrugged. "It's your film."

"What do you mean by 'bad news'?" I pressed him.

"We just do the scene again, everything the same with the postman and all, only when you open the letter, you look sad instead of happy."

"What if I don't want to? What if I just refuse?"

"Come on, Iz. It's just one scene. Probably won't even use it. You think it's bad luck, or what?"

That's exactly what I did think—or feel. It wasn't rational or reasonable, and I knew he'd make that point if I admitted it, so I didn't. Leaving me no choice but to do the scene again, and upon opening the envelope, my face registered shock and sorrow.

"Good!" Ranger shouted from the side. "Excellent—we'll leave it at that."

We gathered up our stuff and pushed on.

Though it hadn't been that long since we'd visited Daisy Dell, the approach looked different. When we came closer, we saw why: tire tracks. The path had been widened by hacking brush and knocking down trees, and was now so ridgy that we struggled under the weight of our equipment.

"Sun's getting high," remarked Sam, who was in the lead. "Better hurry." We hurried, as sweat began to bead up on my forehead and trickle down my shoulder blades.

"I'm thirsty," Sylvie piped up.

"Uh-oh," said Sam.

He'd stopped on the edge of the clearing, and the rest of us pooled around him. What greeted our eyes was—nothing.

All the scrub cedar was cleared, the brush mowed. Most astonishing: the house was gone, erased, like it had been a figment of our fond imaginations. There was nothing left of it except scraps of curtain mashed into the ground. A *No Trespassing* sign fluttered from a post.

"Criminy!" Sylvie breathed at last. "Where did they put our house?"

Sam carefully set down the camera and tripod and crossed

over to the sign. "'Krotona Arts Alliance,'" he read. "'Future site of concert venue.' That's nice."

"Did they move it someplace?" Sylvie persisted. "Could we ask them?"

I stood at the edge of the clearing, clutching the knapsack to my chest, while my shaky faith in motion pictures' ability to change history gave up and burrowed right into the ground.

Ranger picked over the site in a desultory way, but there was nothing salvageable in it, and nothing to do eventually but traipse back downhill and wait for the streetcar, a most forlorn crew. Sylvie was reluctant to give up her notion that the house might still exist somewhere, but once I not-too-gently got it through her head that it was probably in pieces, she burst into despairing tears.

The only time available for a story conference was on the streetcar. Neither Sam nor I could work up much spirit. The project was back in Ranger's hands, and like a football player with the pigskin, he ran full-out.

"So," he began, "here's what we have:

"Opening setup with the girls' sad plight and scenes of the no-good uncle carousing with his chums.

"Scene of the girls at the hospital visiting their aged grandmother, including close-up with Sylvie." Sam shifted on his seat but said nothing.

"What about the father?" I asked. "Will he even be in it?"

"I was thinking about that," Ranger said. "What if Sam gets a close-up of your dad's picture, and maybe a shot of you and Sylvie looking at it with devotion? We can follow that with the Home Guard marching. Then we'll cut in one of ocean shots Sam got at Santa Monica Beach to show your father has gone overseas!" Ranger was getting his spirits back, and I acknowledged his latest idea with a wan smile.

Next, the rescue on horseback, followed by Dauntless Youth visiting the girls in their house (making Ranger sigh *Alas!* for its loss); maybe another shot of Father's picture, too bad we couldn't show it in the proper surroundings, but *Alas!* again.

Then the Youth marching with the Home Guard—

"But I thought we wouldn't use those, since you're not going to war," I objected.

"I can sign up, can't I? Every young man has to do his duty. Those scenes are too good to leave out."

"Even," Sam drawled, "if they don't add anything."

"Who says they don't? They establish my—I mean, the Youth's—character and show he's no coward because at the end..." He paused for a whole city block.

"What about the end?" I prompted at last.

"Well, I don't exactly know how to end it yet with what we've got."

I sighed, Sam rolled his eyes, and Sylvie leaped across the aisle to land on Ranger's chest, crying, "There has to be an end!"

Which had never bothered her before, but we were all a bit on edge. The problem with life, I decided then and there, is endings.

"Don't worry," Ranger insisted. "I'll think of something."

Next morning, as breakfast ended, the doorbell rang.

Shortly thereafter Solomon entered the sunroom. "It's the Western Union man for Señora Ransom."

Aunt Buzzy popped up from the table, cheeks ablaze, and Mother was on her feet directly after. A terrified glance passed between them—didn't Western Union usually mean something awful?

Mother was the first to make for the entrance hall, but the rest of us were as close as a cattle stampede behind her. As Aunt Buzzy tipped the messenger, Mother opened the telegram and scanned its brief lines, her face a cipher. Sylvie was bursting to ask what it said, but I kept a hand over her mouth.

Finally Mother looked up, her high color unabated. "He's in New York City. He has his rail ticket and itinerary. He'll be here on the westbound train, eleven o'clock on Wednesday morning."

That was just two and a half days away! After a moment of packed-solid silence, everything seemed to break loose. Sylvie screamed, Ranger exclaimed, and Mother and Aunt Buzzy started overlapping each other in listing things that must be done in preparation.

The telephone had not had such a workout since our party of the stars—ringing up florists and tailors, and trying to find extra help at short notice to do the cleaning and cooking. Plans were made for a welcome-home party, then scrapped when someone wondered if the guest of honor might not be in a party mood just yet.

Mother called a doctor instead to ask what to do about shell shock in case Father showed signs of it. Hobbies, the doctor said. Plan activities that interested him before the war. A search for photography equipment turned up only Aunt Buzzy's Kodak Brownie camera. I set to work making a list of the equipment we would need for a regular darkroom.

After several tries on the telephone, Aunt Buzzy located Titus Bell, who promised to come back from San Francisco as soon as possible so he could take dear Bobby fishing—even though dear Bobby hadn't fished since before I was born.

And Mother spent well over twenty minutes with my grandparents in Seattle, a conversation that sounded somewhat strained to my listening ear: "No, Father Ransom, we haven't talked about that. We haven't talked at all, because... I'm sure Robert feels the same, but he may not be in any condition to travel all the way to Seattle yet. Yes, sir, but his wife and children happen to be here, and he may just believe his first duty is to... Perhaps it's time to speak to Mother..." To my grandmother she was softer, even weepy toward the end, but the whole conversation wrung Mother out so much that she had to go lie down.

Ranger disappeared for most of the day. He didn't even show up at dinnertime, but that was all right since we didn't really have dinner, just sandwiches thrown together in the kitchen.

Sylvie and I were in bed, after Mother had tucked us in with the most perfunctory prayers, when Ranger tapped softly on the door and let himself in. "I've got an idea."

Chapter 17
The Perils of a
Life of Crime

*I*f ever I was not in the mood for one of Ranger's ideas, it was then. Not only did he have to tell me, but he had to drag it out to the utmost level of suspense.

He and Sam had spent most of the day at the downtown railroad station, watching trains. Why? To note where the passenger engines stopped, especially the 217 (which Father was scheduled to arrive on, two days hence). All the trains had arrived on time, and all had stopped at exactly the same spot, with the locomotive directly opposite the telegraph pole ten yards north of the station. And why was this important? The far edge of the platform lined up with the fifth car. All passengers unloaded from the third-to-fifth cars, which were closest to the station. *Meaning what?*

"There's a storage room on the second floor," Ranger explained, so excited he was twitching all the way to his fingernails. "We talked a clerk into letting us go up there. From the window there's a perfect view of the platform. Every passenger who gets off the train has to pass beneath its unblinking eye."

"Whose unblinking eye?" I prodded impatiently.

"The camera's, of course." Ranger said this with a quiet but pronounced flourish.

"I know!" Sylvie sprang up on the bed. "You're getting Daddy in the picture!"

Ranger just smiled modestly while the plan bloomed fat and full as a sunflower in my mind. "But—how—I mean, too many things have to line up exactly right. You have to know what car he's going to be on and where he'll get off, and there could be hordes of people in the way—"

"But that's what I'm telling you," Ranger said. "It's all worked out. The train unloads from the three middle cars, so that's all the space we have to worry about. And that window upstairs looks down on the whole platform—it almost doesn't matter how many hordes are in the way. So here's the plan..."

The most important problem was solved already. Jimmy Service was working on a Keystone picture and would be out of the way all week. The boys had made a deal with the baggage clerk (probably involving cigars) to get Sam into the upstairs storage room. Not once but twice: first on the day before Father's arrival, to shoot long views and establishing shots of passengers from the 217 milling about the platform.

The second time would be on the big day itself. Sam knew where he could borrow a lens that would allow him to shoot a close-up from the window. With it, he could capture the three of us pressing through the crowd, as well as get close on Father once he'd recognized the man. I would persuade Mother to let us girls greet him first. Then with any luck we would have time to introduce Ranger, who would manfully shake Father's hand, in mutual gratitude and admiration, before the ladies showed up.

"And how do we explain them?" I asked.

"A welcoming committee," Ranger answered.

"Even if Mother throws her arms around him and waters his collar with her tears?"

Ranger frowned. "You think she will?"

My mother wasn't given to flamboyant behavior, but she had surprised me rather often lately. "Probably not. But—"

"Sam can cut it, if she does."

"Can I throw my arms around him, and water his collar and all that?" asked Sylvie, bouncing up and down on the mattress as she'd been told many times not to.

"Absolutely!" Ranger grinned. "Tears and cheers, thrills and chills, the more the better. Dauntless Youth clasps Father's hand. The girls clutch him to their bosoms, and all's well at last. The End."

By then I was sold. Whatever it took, this was a scene that must be shot.

By the next day most preparations had been made, but Mother and Aunt Buzzy were as tense and fidgety as though a hundred things remained to do. Sylvie made such a nuisance of herself asking about shell shock (which to her impervious mind had something to do with seashells) that Mother finally threw up her hands and exclaimed, "Children! Please go out to play!" That, of course, is exactly what we were hoping for, and as a bonus she didn't even notice when all three of us left the house in our second-best clothes—that is, the clothes we intended to wear when welcoming Father's train on the morrow.

We met Sam at the station and got our establishing shots: the three of us waiting on the platform, the train's arrival in a veil of smoke and sparks, and Ranger and Sylvie and I plunging into the crowd, eager to greet the returning hero. Sam said he got it all and seemed anxious to be on his way.

When Ranger asked about the close-up lens, he said it was in the bag, just before hefting the tripod to his shoulder and setting off for home.

"What bag?" I asked as we walked back to our streetcar stop.

"That's just a figure of speech," Ranger said. "It means—"

"I know what it means. I'm also using a figure of speech to ask who this lens belongs to and how Sam intends to borrow it."

A little crease appeared between Ranger's eyebrows. "Sam was pretty dodgy about that. Must belong to somebody he knows. Or somebody who promised to borrow it for him."

One thing our endeavor did not need was the element of surprise. I was keyed up enough already, and the merest suggestion of something awry with our best-laid plan made me even jumpier. Still, my keyed-upness was nothing compared to Mother's. She came to tuck us in as usual that night but ended up reading the same Bobbsey Twins paragraph twice. I didn't notice; Sylvie did.

"Oh well." Mother sighed and closed the book. "That's enough for tonight anyway."

"Aren't you excited?" Sylvie asked in her demanding way.

"Of course, darling," Mother replied.

"But you're worried too, aren't you?" I asked. Mother was not uncomplicatedly happy, for sure.

"Worried?" I thought she was going to flat-out deny it, but to my surprise she said, "Well, perhaps a little."

"About what?" Sylvie asked, catching worry like a cold. "We prayed for his safety every night and he didn't get killed. So God listened."

"Yes, dear." Mother stood up, hands clutched together. "It's just that…your father's letter was not entirely reassuring. It appears some men come home more damaged than they let on—"

"*Damaged?*" Sylvie and I exclaimed together.

"Inside, I mean… Oh, never mind. I'm sure he's fine, or will be, but we may have to give him time. Now good night, sleep tight, and all that."

Give him time for what? I suspect Mother slept no better than I did.

Next morning the household was already in a tizzy when the telephone rang, and Solomon came to fetch Ranger. Ten minutes later, Ranger searched me out in our room as I was braiding Sylvie's hair. "Sam."

"Saying what?"

"He doesn't have the lens." I yanked a little too hard, and Sylvie yelped. "He had a deal with a guy at Vitagraph who was going to let him borrow it. Supposed to meet him this morning. But the guy didn't show. Sam thinks the lens might have been needed, or else the guy forgot."

"Can't he get one somewhere else?" I asked in a desperate tone. "What about at Keystone? He works there, after all—"

"That's just the problem. Everybody knows him there, and if he borrows anything like that, it's bound to get back to his dad." He shrugged sorrowfully. It was the most defeated I'd ever seen him.

But my mind was rolling like a Model T without brakes on a hill. "Is the supply room at Keystone locked?"

"Not usually. But there's a requisition man—nobody can just walk in and take stuff."

"What if the requisition man was distracted for a few minutes by one or two of us, and the other of us slipped in to secure the item. Is that possible?"

"It's possible, but... What's gotten into you, Iz? It wasn't but a month ago that you were crabbing at me about maybe kidnapping a camera. Now you're all game for whatever it takes."

"Nothing got into me," Sylvie offered. "I was always game."

"It doesn't matter what got into who—or whom," I said. "We *must* have that lens." We were down to the final shot, my last chance to make the story come out right.

"Must?" Ranger looked perplexed. "I thought this was *my* picture."

"It's *our* picture," I said. "And I have an idea."

My idea was not nearly as fleshed out as one of Ranger's, as he saw fit to mention. But soon the old gleam was back in his eye, and after thrashing out some details, he rang up Sam while we stood watch, ready to distract any passersby.

"I know... Yeah, but we'll take the blame. Cross my heart and hope to... Sure it's tricky, so what? Look, it's the *last shot*. Once it's in the can we'll clean up the mess... Of *course* it'll all be worth it."

He signed off with, "Meet you at the station."

Then we had to come up with a story for Mother and Aunt Buzzy as to why we wouldn't accompany them to that destination. "We'll meet you there at ten 'til," Ranger improvised. "We have to get flowers."

"Flowers? The house is full of them." Aunt Buzzy waved a hand to indicate the bounteous blooms.

"But these are special," I insisted. "Just from us."

"Let them go, Bea," Mother said in the abrupt way she was wont to lately.

And so we went—straight for the Keystone Studios in Edendale.

With so much ground to cover in less than three hours, I was never so grateful for the punctuality of the Los Angeles

217

public transportation system. On the way we discussed how to go about our heist, and I was only fleetingly surprised at how easy it was to slide into a life of crime with the proper motivation. Though we were only *borrowing* the lens, not *stealing*, the powers that be were not likely to grasp that fine distinction if they caught us. To make sure they didn't, the distraction we created had better be good.

"I could throw myself off something, like I did at the parade," Sylvie suggested.

"No," I said firmly. "We only want to distract one person, not the whole studio." That limited our possibilities, and we arrived at Keystone in an uncertain state.

The gates on Glendale Avenue were closed. On the other side of the street, a small crowd gathered about the fabulous panorama. Ranger grinned. "Looks like they won't be shooting anywhere close to the buildings today. All the attention will be over here. In fact—" His eyes lingered on the panorama. "I wish we could have used that in the picture somehow."

Several of the streetcar passengers joined the sightseers near the film crew, while we went in the opposite direction. A guard stood watch over the gate, but Ranger simply nodded to him and led us down the sidewalk to a loose plank in the fence where we could slip in. He still had the instincts of a lot lizard.

"Look like extras," he told us, after we had turned two corners and ended up on a narrow street lined with small adobe structures. We certainly looked "extra"—the street was almost deserted except for we three sore thumbs sticking out in the middle. Most of the buildings were labeled—*Prop 1, Prop 2, Prop 3, Wardrobe, Developing, Projection*, and finally *Technical*.

"This is it," Ranger announced.

"Now what?"

"I'll scope it out. You can pretend to tie your shoes"—he looked down at our tie-less Mary Janes—"or something."

He slipped away, and I pretended Sylvie had a rock in her shoe: kneeling to unbuckle it, shaking elaborately to discharge the imaginary rock, and carefully re-buckling. Ranger reappeared before I had to do it all with the other shoe.

"We're in luck," he said, panting. "The window's wide open and there's only one guy in there, Merle Ritter. He's a regular fellow. Move a little closer and try to get him to step outside. Tell him you're supposed to be extras in a picture directed by…um… Hampton Del Ruth, and you don't know where to report. String it out as long as you can—I don't know how long it'll take me to find the lens. Once I've got it, I'll give you a high sign behind his back and scoot out through the window. Meetcha at the streetcar stop—got it?"

I barely had time to nod before he squeezed my shoulder and ducked around the corner of the building. I took a deep breath and marched to the door with Sylvie in hand, ready for the scene of my career. "Mister? Oh, mister?"

He was tilted back in a desk chair, reading the *Police Gazette*. At my voice, the chair creaked mightily as he leaned forward. "Who's there?"

I launched into a long explanation of how we were reporting in as extras but couldn't find the lot, and I was afraid we were going to be late and we needed the work, and so on. Finally he got up and came to the little porch outside the door.

"Who's the director?"

"Mr....ah... I forgot—no, just a minute. Mr...." The requisition man was beginning to look a wee bit doubtful. Behind his back, Ranger slipped by like a shadow. "Mr. Ruth?"

"Hampton Del Ruth?"

"That's it! Can you tell us where he's shooting?"

"Nowhere today that I know of. No Del Ruth pictures on the docket this week."

"Oh no!" I turned a look of dismay on Sylvie, which she reflected admirably. "Did we get the date wrong?"

Sylvie whimpered, "But I saw you write it down!"

"Sorry, kids." Mr. Ritter did indeed look sympathetic. "Check with the shooting schedule on your way out. It's in the main office, right next to—"

"Our way *out?*" Sylvie cried. "But we can't go now! If we don't get work today, there won't be anything to eat tonight!"

She had learned her acting lessons well. Mr. Ritter was almost convinced, looking to me for collaboration. With the slightest of nods, I said, "Mother doesn't like us to talk about it, but times are pretty hard for us right now. Are you sure Mr. Del Ruth isn't shooting today?" He was shaking his head, while I desperately wished Ranger would pop in view with the much-anticipated high sign. "Is there any other director shooting today? Maybe we could still get a little work in. Just enough for a few potatoes?"

I should have left out the potatoes. The man stuck his

hand in his pocket, probably feeling about for spare change we could not in good conscience accept. "There's a Yukon picture shooting across the street," he said, "but girls aren't wanted. If it would help, maybe I can…"

"Oh pleeese!" Sylvie clasped her hands together. "Our step-father's gone on another bender, and he promised to beat us if we don't bring home money for booze. The last time I had bruises for days…" She was trying to fall to her knees, but I got hold of her arm and kept her upright, meanwhile shaking her elbow to make her shut up.

The jingle of Mr. Ritter's pockets ceased as he looked from me to her. "I'm beginning to think you have a future in the pictures, little girl."

"She exaggerates," I hastened to say, "but we do need work. Isn't there anything we could do? Maybe"—I was improvising desperately—"sweep out your office? Straighten the shelves?"

He'd had enough. "Good night, ladies. I don't know what you're selling, but I ain't buying. If you're serious about work, go ask 'em at the office. Otherwise—"

Oh joy! Ranger's hand popped around the doorway, fingers raised in a "victory" salute. Then it disappeared.

"We'll do that." I hurried to make amends. "I'm sorry for my sister, sir. She's seen too much Lillian Gish. Thank you for my time—I mean, your time…"

This was all covering action for Ranger's retreat. I needn't have bothered however, for firm footsteps were approaching directly behind us, and a nasally voice called out, "Mornin',

Merle! Would you have a thirty-five millimeter twenty-aught lens lying around?"

Mr. Ritter nodded a brief dismissal to us. "Step in and see what I've got, Jimmy."

There are a lot of Jimmys in the world, but when I turned, I was face-to-face with the last one it would be advantageous to meet. Not that we had ever met, except on film, but I recognized him. And I could tell that after a second look he recognized me.

"What the Sam Hill..." he began as Sylvie blurted out:

"Papa!"

Talk about getting caught up in a part! She had never even seen Jimmy Service on film but had guessed who he was, and that was the chief relationship she knew him by. But there was no time to marvel over that. I grabbed Sylvie's hand and took off running, as his voice bellowed after us, "Hey, you—*stop!*"

Chapter 18
Down at the Station

With a rabbitlike instinct, Sylvie somehow found her way back to the spot where Ranger had earlier led us in. We scurried through the gap in the fence, only to find that our pursuer had taken the more direct route, right through the gate. Once on the sidewalk, our eyes met. Again he bellowed, "*Stop!*"

Sylvie darted right into the street, and I had no choice but to follow. Behind us Mr. Service was yelling, "*I want to talk to you!*" Dodging tin lizzies and delivery vans, we safely reached the other side, where a throng of actors, prop men, and musicians provided temporary cover. Looking back, I saw Mr. Service by the curb, prudently waiting for a streetcar to pass. It was, I noticed distractedly, the nine forty-five northbound, meaning we had almost ten whole minutes before our car came by—ten minutes that we could not leisurely kill at the stop with Ranger. We had to keep out of sight at all costs.

Meanwhile, Mr. Service had crossed the street. "Doesn't he have work to get to?" I fretted.

"Maybe this is it," Sylvie suggested.

"We're going to have to lose him so we can slip away to the streetcar stop!"

"I know. Follow me!" While all attention seemed to be on the director, who was now shouting through his megaphone, Sylvie ducked right under the dividing rope and threaded through the musicians who were tuning up.

We edged around the platform of the panorama, hoping its sheer hugeness would give us cover to break across the wide lot behind it. From there we could disappear among the bungalows and cottages and work our way circuitously back to the streetcar stop where Ranger would be waiting. It seemed an excellent plan until I glanced back and met the malevolent glare of Jimmy Service, some yards away but closing fast!

"He's spotted us!" I gasped.

"Let's go under!" Sylvie leaped toward the platform of the panorama, but I grabbed a leg before she could get under it.

"That's the first place anyone would look! This is better—" I jumped up on the platform and darted over to a pile of papier-mâché boulders, placed in what was supposed to look like natural abandon. There was room in the narrow space to hide us, and a bushy cedar tree would give us additional cover. We flattened ourselves against the painted canvas. My pulse was pounding in my ears.

"What if they—" Sylvie began.

"Shhhhhh!" A man had just come around the curve, and

though his face couldn't be made out through the cedar, I knew who it was.

He paused. Then he crouched to peer under the bottom edge of the platform. I nudged Sylvie—*didn't I tell you?*

She whispered, "Isobel—we're about to be in the picture!"

A sudden stillness had fallen, and we heard voices calling for Jimmy Service. Sylvie's hunch was correct—he was the cameraman for this shooting. That seemed like a lucky break, but before we could make a run for it, a voice shouted, "*Go!*" and with a lurch the entire monstrous machine began to move.

"Keep still!" I told Sylvie, as the floor rumbled and the panorama crawled. "Stay down, and with luck nobody will notice us back here. As soon as we can, we'll jump off and make a break for the trees."

"Now!" she hissed.

"No!" I grabbed her arm and held her down. The little orchestra was coming into view, busily thumping out the storm music from *William Tell*, and if we jumped, we'd jump right into their laps.

"But we're almost in front of the camera!"

"I know—keep still!"

Easier said than done, for at that moment a very stiff breeze whipped my hair in my face and tore away Sylvie's bow, which had become droopy with all the running. We were headed right into a wind machine.

"What was that…?" I heard someone call, as the aforementioned bow sailed in front of the camera—and next, we were in the middle of a raging snowstorm!

225

White flakes caught by the wind machine swirled angrily by, and one of them caught in Sylvie's throat. My hair whipped around so wildly that it doubtless showed above the rocks—with that and Sylvie's coughing and her phantom hair bow, I was amazed the director didn't call for a cut.

Then I saw why, as a dogsled slowly passed in front of us—a sled with real dogs running on a treadmill, driven by a man in an Eskimo parka. The scene must have taken hours to set up.

"We'll make a break for it as soon as we're out of camera range!" I shouted over the wind.

But then, over the crank of the machine and wail of the motor and gagging of Sylvie and directing of the director, I heard another noise—the *clang-clang* of a streetcar bell.

We had no choice. "*Now!*" I screamed to Sylvie, and with a firm grip on her hand I pulled her to the edge of the platform and jumped off.

We had the clear advantage of surprise. The whole crew was stunned motionless as we dodged people and equipment. Once past the crew I raised a hand to wave frantically at the streetcar, shouting, "*Wait!*"

Ranger leaned out into the street, urging us on. The car was not up to full speed yet, and it looked as though we might make it—indeed I was sure we would—with just a smidgen more of effort—a last burst of speed—and suddenly something grabbed my arm and stopped me flat!

"*No!*" I screamed, as Jimmy Service began:

"All right, girlie, what's up—"

Sylvie's violent instincts are useful sometimes. She hauled off and kicked him in the shin.

Surprise and pain loosened his grip. We'd lost a couple of precious seconds getting free, so catching the streetcar was a near thing. Ranger had worked his way to the rear platform and leaned out as far as he could, reaching for us. Sylvie grabbed his arm and sailed aboard, right into the stomach of a curious passenger who sat down very abruptly with Sylvie in her lap. Then Ranger's hand swung out for me, and brushing his fingertips gave me the necessary jolt for one last surge.

We hung to the same bar, watching Jimmy Service shrink in perspective, still clutching his shin. "Is that who I think it is?" Ranger asked.

I nodded, too breathless to speak.

"Criminy. Don't tell Sam. I mean, not before. I'll tell him once we get the shot."

Sweaty and disheveled, I could only nod in reply. Not without a twinge of conscience: Sam's house was so close to Keystone that Jimmy Service could walk home between takes and see if the camera was where it was supposed to be. And since it wasn't there, Sam wouldn't have to guess about his father's mood this time. He'd be furious, with consequences fearful to contemplate.

But we *had* to get the shot at the station. It was unthinkable to come so far and not finish. "If Sam faces the music, we all do," I said. "We'll go over to his house—and explain to his father—"

"Calm down, Isobel," Ranger said, though I hadn't known

I was so obviously uncalm. "We'll work it out somehow...after the film's safe in the can." We rode a few blocks in silence before I could tell him what happened at the panorama, making his high spirits rise again. "That's bully—you getting right into the picture. Sounds like something I would do."

We got to the station with a few moments to spare. Aunt Buzzy's auto was parked on a side street with Masaji leaning against the door, but he didn't see us run around to the baggage agent's office for our rendezvous.

Sam was halfway through a cigarette—his fourth, to judge by the ends stubbed out on the baggage wagon nearby. On seeing us, he straightened up and stuffed something in his trouser pocket. It looked like rosary beads. "What took you so long? The train's due right now."

"Long story. Here's the lens." Ranger handed over his knapsack. "All set up?"

"Yeah, but it'll take a few minutes to get this on." Sam pulled the lens out for examination. "I hope the mounts match up."

"Golly, me too." Ranger gulped. "Better go. And, Sam—meet me right after. Pretty important, savvy?"

Sam shot him a wary look but nodded just before disappearing into the station.

"Now that is what I call cutting it close," Aunt Buzzy said, not bothering to hide her irritation as the three of us pelted up to the west platform.

"Where are the flowers?" Mother asked.

"Flowers?" I repeated, forgetting the pretext already.

"We stashed 'em—" Ranger began, at the same time Sylvie piped up with:

"We dropped 'em—"

"Look at you!" Mother exclaimed. "You look like you ran all the way to the San Fernando Valley to pick them yourselves. How did you get—" A loud whistle interrupted her.

"Mattie!" Aunt Buzzy shouted over it. "The train!"

Ranger took my arm and pulled me forward as the big, black locomotive clacked by, swishing steam. "Where's Daddy?" Sylvie shrieked behind us. "Boost me up, Ranger!"

He bent down enough to let her climb on his back, where she made so active a pilot that he had to keep saying "Cut it out" and "Stop kicking me." Finally she screamed.

"*There he is!* Down that way, talking to the train man. *Daddy!*"

I strained on tiptoe, peering in the direction she pointed. My heart leaped into my throat.

Three cars down, turning away to tip the porter— shockingly thin and pale, but undoubtedly him. I turned to Ranger and nodded wordlessly.

He let Sylvie down with a warning: "Don't get away from us. The lens has to get us all together."

"Ranger!" I blurted out. "Your glasses."

"Oh yeah." He hurriedly took them off and folded them away in his pocket. "Thanks."

We pushed our way forward. A quick glance upward at the station window showed a glint of sunlight off the camera's

229

single eye, trained on our object. I must have been breathing but didn't feel like it, especially when I caught a clear glimpse of Father through a gap in the crowd, smiling as the porter touched his cap and turned away.

Sylvie could no longer hold herself. "*Daddy!*" she cried again, breaking away from Ranger's grip.

"Nuts," muttered Ranger, who seemed as tightly wound as we were, for less reason. "Come on—we've got to keep up with her."

We were very close now. Sylvie shot through a gap in the crowd and jumped, wrapping herself around the man like a monkey.

Ranger sighed, squared his shoulder, and strode forward, right hand outstretched. Father turned at the impact of Sylvie hitting him, and I froze.

Or rather the world around me seemed to freeze, all except Ranger, still striding, perhaps so intent on his own part that he failed to notice at first that Father had no right hand to shake. In fact, Father had no right arm.

And his face on that side had been so rearranged that it no longer looked like Father at all.

Chapter 19
Another Way to Lie

My world stopped. And then it broke.

My memory of the next few moments is in pieces—or maybe I was the one in pieces. I remember Sylvie sliding off him and Ranger stammering and the smile that froze on Aunt Buzzy's face and the truly indescribable expression on my mother's. I saw them as though peering through those broken lenses on the battlefield.

I could not simply walk up and embrace him the way Mother finally did because my mind and my body seemed to be in two different places. One finally nudged the other forward, and my father mashed me briefly with his one arm against his uniform, scratchy and stiff. He felt different: thinner, less solid somehow. He even smelled different, of smoke and filth and bleach embedded deep in his clothes, or perhaps in his very skin. Only his nervous half laugh sounded the least bit like him.

I don't remember our ride back to the hacienda, crammed

into the Packard driven by Masaji, as reticent as ever. And once there, I had no idea what to do next.

Aunt Buzzy took over a role she understood, pointing out some of the curiosities of the front room. But when she wanted to show him the grounds, Father interrupted with, "If you don't mind, Buzzy—a little later? A two-day train ride…" He trailed off as she blushed and made apologetic noises countered by his reassuring noises, and after a painful second or two, she said, "Let your wife show you to your room—dinner's at seven."

Then Sylvie, who'd been admirably tactful thus far, burst out: "But, Daddy, where's your *arm*? And what happened to your *face*?"

Mother and Aunt Buzzy both cranked up the apologetic noises, but Father said, "I know you want to hear that, Kitten, but let's wait until dinner, eh? I promise to tell all."

Sylvie was clinging to his arm. Mother automatically reached for the other arm, faltered, and clutched his shoulder instead. They went off to the west wing, but Mother was back in the drawing room within fifteen minutes. Somehow, this did not bode well, nor did the intense conversation she and Aunt Buzzy engaged in after that, with warning looks every time a child came near.

The afternoon was desperately quiet. Sylvie sought refuge with Bone, and Ranger had not come home with us, generously announcing he would take the streetcar to allow more room in the auto for Mr. Ransom and his luggage. I knew he was on a mission to smooth the way between Sam and Jimmy

Service, but I'd broken my promise to go along. Nothing seemed to matter anymore, least of all the picture.

Some film can't be cut. What happened, happened, and there was nothing I could do about it. In the blaze of real life, I kept seeing Father's face. The missing arm we could probably stop missing; the shock of nothingness could wear off. But his face was the shock of *somethingness.*

From the left he looked the same: a mild blue eye, straight nose, strong chin, a mouth with a little upward tick at the corner. But on the right side, all those features mashed into each other, making him look like a battered bare-knuckle fighter: one eyelid glued shut over an empty socket, the lower lip bulged out, the cheekbone smashed. I kept remembering that soldier on the train during our journey to California—deprived of his mask, his face a thing to apologize for. *Sorry, miss. Sorry…*

At Esperanza's extravagant welcome-home dinner, which no one could eat much of, Father explained why the bad news had not reached us before he did. "I owe you all an apology," he said. Even his voice was damaged, the words a bit slurred by his twisted mouth. "I understood from the War Department that you'd been informed of what happened, but if they sent a letter, it must have gone astray somehow." (*Close-up on envelope in a mud puddle*, I thought.)

"That's no excuse though. I wrote you a long letter as soon as I was able but tore it up. It was weeks before I could write another, and by then I assumed you knew the worst and could read between the lines…"

"But what happened?" Sylvie burst out again, bouncing up in her chair. She was sitting next to Ranger, who put a hand on her head to push her down, though he obviously wanted to know as much as any of us.

"That's just what I was working up to," Father said. Another interval, and when he spoke again, the words came faster: "We got news of a cease-fire on the right flank at about seven p.m. That meant time to go out and collect the day's blood toll so everybody could settle in for the night." The good side of his mouth twitched, but it didn't look like a smile. "We were down by two orderlies—one sick and one dead. So I went out with the ambulance."

"Was this the first time you'd done that?" Mother asked in a tight, clipped tone.

My father hesitated, as though debating whether to lie. "No."

"But you told us you stayed in the rear at all times."

"I didn't want you to worry. What good would that do?" A sharp edge crept into his voice, which I had never known him to use with her. "We were often short on orderlies and drivers, and there were times I substituted for both. Men were dying on the field, but if the ambulance went out, some of them might be saved. A precious few compared to all who were lost, but it seemed a risk worth taking. You see? My Tilda?"

At the sound of his pet name for her, two spots of color appeared high on my mother's cheekbones and her scar flashed like a little dagger. "Do you think I might have understood if you had explained it that way? If you had told me the truth instead of treating me like one of the girls, who must be jollied along with silly jokes?"

Aunt Buzzy, who had been anxiously awaiting Esperanza to come and serve coffee, now jumped up to serve it herself. "There's no point in dwelling on what's past, is there, Mattie? Let him finish the story."

"There's not much to finish." When Father picked up the cup she had just poured for him, his hand trembled so that some of the coffee sloshed out. He set the cup down without taking a sip. "It was already dark, with a pall of smoke over no-man's-land, and we were going as fast as the bumpy ground would allow. I was standing on the running board of the passenger side, trying to direct the driver. He was listening to me more than watching the ground, so he didn't see the trip wire that went off, right under his front wheel. He was killed, and I joined the ranks of the wounded. Though I didn't really know that—or anything much—until I woke up in a hospital in Lyon two days later."

He took a deep breath, grabbed the rose-patterned china cup, and gulped half the coffee down. "And now," he hurried on, "I hate to pass on dessert, but I'm afraid I can't stay awake for it. If you'll excuse me—"

We couldn't linger long after that, and Esperanza looked reproachfully at how little we'd eaten when she cleared the table. Mother and Aunt Buzzy closeted themselves again, Sylvie raced off to find Bone, and Ranger looked meaningfully at me, a look I failed to answer.

So he cornered me in the rose arbor where I'd barricaded myself behind *Treasure Island*. "I have a *lot* to tell you."

"Nothing I want to hear."

"Oh, yes, you do," he insisted with every bit of his insufferable one-track-mindedness. "Unless you don't care about Sam."

After a moment, I sighed and lowered the book.

"When I told him about your run-in with Jimmy Service at Keystone, he turned white. I mean it—absolutely *white*. Then he started talking about hopping a freight train to Mexico. But cooler heads prevailed, meaning mine, for a change. What do you think about that?"

"Just get to the point."

"Right. I went home with him, and on the way, he unfroze enough to tell me he might have gotten something in the picture that would—"

"I don't want to hear about the picture. At all."

"But it's part of what I'm telling you!"

I picked up the book again and stared resolutely at its pages.

"All right!" Exasperated, Ranger reached over and slapped the book down. "So when we got to Sam's house, the old man was there, and plenty mad. I went in first, like a dauntless youth, and explained the whole thing was my idea but I couldn't have done it without that fine piece of equipment and he should know that his son is a genius and it must be because the acorn never falls far from the tree. I laid it on pretty thick. But it worked! Mostly. When Sam finally came in, the old man smacked him—not very hard, just to remind him who was boss and all that. But he was pretty interested in what we got, and when I told him about the station—"

"So Sam is not in danger?" I interrupted.

"Looks like it. Because when we were telling him about the station—"

"Good," I said, raising my book again.

"C'mon, Iz! Just hear me out." I pulled my feet up on the bench and curled around *Treasure Island* like a wad of obtuseness. "All right. You don't want to talk now. I understand. I'll wait." He hesitated, as though my mind might be changing already. But when it didn't, he sighed gustily and left me alone.

I uncurled enough to see the page before my face but not the letters, which were too blurry to make out. *You* don't *understand!* I thought fiercely, hugging my sobs tight. I saw my father off to war, but a stranger returned. Not the hero in the picture beside my bed, but someone ravaged and broken. Would I ever have my father back?

Mother failed to read to us that night, or even tuck us in. Aunt Buzzy did instead, with some twittering about how we all needed time and must be patient, and so on. Sylvie took it meekly, but soon after Aunt Buzzy had turned off the lights and said good night, she crept over to my bed.

"Could you tell me a story?"

This was the last thing I wanted to do, but as she crawled in next to me, I sighed and launched the old formula. "Once upon a time there was a little girl, six years old—"

"Not *that* one," she said. "Another story."

"I don't know any others."

She kicked me under the covers. "Yes, you do! You read all the time."

It was story or fight. But she'd been good all day—especially for her—so I began with something that started like *The Water-Babies* but grew into something else altogether:

"There were four children living peacefully in an enchanted garden—Flower Babies, I suppose—surrounded by fragrant orchards under sunny skies. Until the day that one of them discovered…an eye. Yes, a single eye, with lid attached, exactly like a human eyeball only bigger. At first it just blinked at them. Then it began showing them things: marble palaces like the Taj Mahal, and vast emerald oceans and exotic bazaars."

"How?" Sylvie asked. "How did it show them things?"

"Um… It would blink, and then a beam of light would shoot out from it, and they would see the pictures by gazing into the light. Then after a while one of the boys got the idea of putting up a screen, so the pictures would be clearer.

"They were so charmed with the eye that they kept it in a box lined with moss (where it seemed quite content), and every time they gathered around, it would show them more and more extravagant sights. They came to neglect their work of tending the garden and spent hours—days, even—gathered around the eye in its cozy box.

"And then, so gradually they didn't even notice at first, the eye began showing them things they didn't want to see. Spiders and snakes and hungry children in lonely attics and parents quarreling. Then men fighting and bombs exploding and other things too horrible to mention, until the children decided they must get rid of the eye.

"But after every attempt to leave it outside the garden, it always managed to roll back. Finally the children decided that the eye must be returned to where it came from. But where was that?"

I had to pause, because I didn't know. By this point in a story Sylvie was usually asleep. But not this time.

"Where did they have to take it?" she demanded with another kick.

"I'll tell you if you stop that!"

"I'm sorry, Isobel... Please could you finish the story?" She hardly ever apologized, so I had to come up with something.

"By watching and listening carefully, they gradually figured out that the eye belonged to a giant—a Cyclops—who was rampaging his way through the countryside looking for it. What they were seeing is what he saw. Or would have, if the eye were in his head instead of a mossy box. Since he couldn't see, he was blundering into things and causing random destruction: lots of shots—scenes, that is—of villagers fleeing in terror. Finally they recognized one of the villages nearby and understood that the giant had reached their own neighborhood. So they took their courage in hand, along with the box, and went in search."

"And did they find him?" Sylvie asked after too long a pause.

My well of invention was going dry. "Yes, they did, and he was just about to stomp them in a blind fury when his own eye winked at him. Overjoyed, he popped it right back in his head and was so delighted that he invited the children to his magnificent mountain to live with him, but they were smart enough to refuse. So they went back to their garden and lived happily ever after. The end."

Sylvie wasn't satisfied. "It shouldn't be that easy. To return the magic eye, I mean."

"Believe me," I said, "it won't be."

And indeed it was impossible to stop seeing things we did not wish to see. Next morning Father tried to talk to me—just light questions about what we'd been doing all summer, but it was so hard to look at him that I made an excuse about overdue books at the library. As the hours dragged, I couldn't help noticing how he and Mother continued to avoid each other or how hard Aunt Buzzy was working to keep everyone's spirits up. Even Titus Bell's arrival on Tuesday failed to lighten the swampish atmosphere.

An awful silence prevailed inside me, though Father tried one more time to break it, two days after his arrival. He chose the hour carefully. I was hiding behind a book in the grape arbor when he slipped up and took a seat.

"So, Isobel…" he began, and then awkwardly paused.

I was supposed to say something, but my mouth had gone dry. I swallowed instead.

"Yes, well," he went on finally. "Seems to me we have some catching up to do. Your mother tells me you know your way around here as well as any native now. Think you could take me on a little tour?"

I tried to smile, even as the bottom dropped out of my composure. How could I go out with him in *public*? I had always been proud of him before—he was so handsome and distinguished-looking—but now everyone would stare at us and pretend they weren't. I was immediately ashamed of myself for thinking these thoughts, but the thoughts came anyway.

"Um… I suppose. Only not today. Sir."

"All right." His left hand raised in a very familiar way, pushing forward slightly with his head to one side as though disowning whatever he'd just said. He used this gesture a lot, only with two hands. He caught my involuntary glance at his right side and made a rueful grimace.

"Funny quirk of anatomy—I can still feel this arm. All the nerve patterns set in my brain haven't got the message yet. You and Sylvie had better not do anything naughty since I've lost my spanking hand."

Just one of his little jokes; he'd never so much as swatted us in our lives. Again I attempted a smile.

"Yes, well." He looked down, fumbling in his coat pocket for a small, blocky parcel wrapped in white tissue paper. "I… didn't have much time for shopping while I was in France, but before heading to the front, I came across something I thought you might like."

"Thank you." I took the parcel from his extended hand and held it uncertainly for a few seconds.

"I'd be pleased if you would open it," he said with the slightest edge to his gentle voice.

It was a glass globe about three inches across—a paperweight on a lead base. The globe was filled with water and tiny white flecks that whirled about like snow when I turned

241

it upright. Inside the globe was a tall evergreen tree with lacy, sweeping branches.

As I stared, Father leaned toward me with a trace of boyish eagerness. "Do you see what I saw in it? It's like the hemlock tree down at the corner, the magnificent one where you always wanted to stop and pick up cones when you were little—remember?"

I nodded.

"Look at the base," he prompted me.

An inscription scrolled around the base of the globe: *Et dont les feuilles servent à la guérison des nations.*

"Can you read it? *Parlez-vous français, mademoiselle?*"

I nodded. The quotation was a familiar one from the Bible, and I had just enough French to recognize it: "*And the leaves of the tree are for—were for—the healing of the nations.*"

"Right!" He sat back, smiling. That twist to his mouth made the smile horrible; I had to glance away. "Funny thing—when I bought it, I didn't recognize the quote. I just thought you'd like the tree. Turned out to be rather appropriate, don't you think?"

I closed my hands over the globe and saw that stately hemlock tree of my youth splintered by cannonballs. The work of a moment. If something is destroyed, can it ever be healed? I choked down a surge of bile and said nothing.

After a painful moment he straightened up and cleared his throat. "Yes. Well... I expect it's naptime for me. Still taking a little something for the pain. Keeps the worst of it down, but around this time of day I can barely keep my eyes open." He stood. "I'm off to the Land o' Nod."

"Thank you," I said again.

"You're welcome, Isobel." He leaned in to touch my shoulder, and I never moved.

After that I spent more time at the public library with Little Eva and Tom Sawyer, avoiding a house that was either dead silent or ringing with pointless chatter—and Ranger was a wellspring of pointless chatter, as far as I was concerned.

On Monday, he cornered me urgently. "Isobel. There's something about the picture—"

"What picture?"

He blinked at me. "Why, our picture that we've been working on for the last six weeks."

"You mean that excursion into fantasy we've been amusing ourselves with?"

That brought him up short. "What the heck does *that* mean?"

I couldn't explain how trivial our project looked to me now, so I maintained a stony silence.

"It's all coming together!" Ranger insisted. "If we could just do another shot or two…" He trailed off, staring at my face. "Golly, you look like your mother right now."

For some reason this made me furious, if I wasn't already. "What do you mean?"

"Nothing. It's just an observation, for Pete's sake. Listen, we don't have much time. If—"

I slammed my book shut. "*Wake up*, Ranger. Even if the great Mr. Griffith agrees to see your picture, even if he raves about it to your parents, it won't save you from military school or whatever else it takes to make you grow up. Because you have to, you know. Everybody does."

He sputtered, "That's not—"

"And I'll tell you something else. I think the pictures are just another way to lie. *Hearts of the World* and 'Over There' and the Lasky Home Guard—cheering and crying and jerking your feelings all over the place—*it's a lie*, and I don't want any more to do with it, ever."

A boy of his complexion could not be said to turn pale. Rather, he turned dusty—all traces of pink draining from his face to leave a grayish tint.

"Have you talked to your father?" he demanded. "I mean, besides when you have to? I have. And you know what? He's swell, just like you always said. Did I show you the Iron Cross he gave me?" He had, but pulled it out of his pocket again. "The highest German military honor, and a kraut colonel gave it to him in gratitude—gratitude!—for saving his life. That's the kind of man your father is: magnanimous to his enemies. His face—the way it looks now—doesn't change what he is. If you'd come out of your sulk, you'd know that."

Now *I* was surely pale. Even my voice sounded blood-drained. "I don't need you to tell me about my own father. I knew him before, and you didn't. I am not sulking—I'm mourning."

"But he's not dead! That's what I... Listen, if you just hear me out about the picture—"

"Ranger Bell, if you say one more word to me on that subject, I'll... I'll set a match to the film, I swear."

That scared him off. What's more, he made a point of avoiding me for the next two days. Sylvie didn't try to avoid me, partly because Father had brought her a mechanical bank, a painted tin clown who hopped on one foot and juggled three colored balls whenever a coin was dropped into the base. Every waking moment she was begging for pennies. But that night, after the lights went out, she began, "You should talk to Ranger about—"

"The picture is done," I said. "As far as we're concerned."

"No, it's not," she said eagerly. "You see, we've got this idea—" I cut her off again, with a well-aimed pillow this time, and heard no more from her that night.

On Thursday afternoon, I returned from the library to a house oppressively silent, except for the ticking of the alpine cuckoo clock in the entrance hall. A huge vase of yellow roses on the side table grabbed my attention. Unfurled in Byzantine splendor, they splashed gaudy dabs of color all over that dark corner of the room. As I came closer, I noticed the card stuck under the vase. I wriggled it out and read the simple message: *To Matilda: Thinking of you. Hope all ends well, Charlie.*

Very thoughtful, harmless, and sweet, which can't explain the absolute savagery with which I picked up the entire vase and dashed it to the floor.

That was horrible enough, but then something truly horrible happened.

A monster rose up from the floor in front of the big wing chair at the west end of the room. Trembling, it seemed to swell to half again its normal size. It was my father. "*Isobel!*" he roared. "What in God's name—" He must have hurled himself to the floor at the sound of breaking glass, taking cover as though he'd heard a shell screaming overhead.

The shell was me. Days of suppressed fury had finally exploded, sparked by bright yellow roses.

Father recovered first, after a fashion. "I'm—I'm so sorry. Forgive me, Isobel. I shouldn't have…"

"*Don't!*"

I saw him take a deep breath and clench his fingers as he tried to speak calmly. "Dear Isobel… What do you mean? Don't what?"

"Don't come near me. Don't call me 'dear.'"

He took a step toward me, warily. "Please, Isobel. Get hold of yourself. I've changed, I know. I will take some getting used to. But we'll do this together, won't we? I know I can count on you, my smart, responsible—"

He took another step, and I lost all control.

"Don't touch me!" I backed away. "You didn't have to do it. You didn't have to go away and leave us, but you did it anyway, and now you're back all broken and things will never be the same—and none of it had to happen!"

All these accusations seemed to register on his face, as though I were punching him again and again. He took a deep breath. "All that may be true. But what will make it better?"

"Nothing. It can't be fixed, and I can't stand it! I hate all this"—waving wildly at the spilled flowers and china shards. "I *hate* it!" were my last words before bolting for my room. I could not bring myself to say *I hate you*, a small mercy. Because in that moment, I did—almost as much as I hated myself.

Unfortunately, the vase was rather valuable, a relic of the Chin Dynasty and a favorite of Aunt Buzzy's. She was inclined to go easy on me, given the strain we were all under, but Mother made me go out and cut a willow switch, then stand with my hands out while she rained blows upon them.

It was almost a relief, after weeks of half-truths and dodges, and about time for me to stand up and take punishment for something. It hurt like coals of fire, but I almost wished it could hurt more, in between Mother's short, tight statements: "Regarding Mr. Chaplin (*whap!*), I think you are behaving in a very (*whap!*) childish manner. He made a thoughtful gesture (*whap!*), which I accept in grateful spirit (*whap!*) and expect you to do the same (*whap, whap!*). Is that understood?"

It was, and it wasn't. Mr. Chaplin flickered like his image on the screen, barely real. The real problem was buried deep in my own family—what if Father's face now was his true face and all of our placid life in Seattle was just us pretending to be a happy family?

He kept out of sight for the rest of the day, pleading a peckish stomach at suppertime and declining the round of bridge Aunt Buzzy tried to set up afterward. My conscience was telling me to apologize, but I just couldn't.

The next morning at breakfast, the tension sputtered like a fuse.

Forks clinked on china plates and spoons rattled in coffee cups and conversation faltered like fledgling sparrows. Ranger got permission to take Sylvie to Griffith Park for the afternoon—*a likely story*, thought I. The glances they kept sending each other told me something was up, but I would never ask. Father mentioned an appointment with a doctor, and Titus Bell made a joke about doctors seeing doctors. Father attempted to play along, and I put both palms on the table to push my chair back.

"No, you may not be excused," Mother said abruptly. She'd been staring darts at me all through breakfast. "Not before you apologize."

"I'm very sorry about the vase," I muttered, staring down at my hands where the welts she had laid on yesterday still showed. "I already—"

"That's not what I mean, and you know it."

Father mumbled something, and she snapped back, "Why *isn't* this the time? It's a perfect time, as far as I'm concerned."

Aunt Buzzy started to speak up and then thought better

of it. Mr. Bell folded his napkin, took her hand, and escorted her from the room—leaving the battlefield clear, so to speak.

I stared across the table, our no-man's-land, fixing my gaze on the right sleeve of Father's jacket, pinned to the breast pocket with a tie clasp. The clasp was a little crooked because he hadn't yet mastered the trick of one-handed pinning. How would he manage a camera now? Drive his Model T? Do surgery?

"Isobel, I think it's high time you dropped this tragic heroine mien," my mother said.

Father sighed. "Go easy on her, Matilda. We all need more time—"

"It's past time. She's indulging herself." Mother picked up a piece of toast and began slapping on butter like a bricklayer. She plopped the toast on his plate, and he stared down at it as though it had magically leaped out of thin air.

Her words hurt. "I'm not indulging. I'm just...feeling. I can't help how I feel."

"Of course you can't," Father said. "They've been a lot of wild feelings ricocheting off the walls lately, but that's only to be—"

"Bobby, please stop acting the peacemaker. All that does is paper over problems that must be dealt with."

"And you're a fine one to talk about indulgence!" I burst out. "What have you been doing the last few weeks, all chummy with Mack Sennett and silly Keystone comedies, and flirting with Mr. Chaplin. I saw you with him one day, strolling on Talmadge Avenue, so wrapped up in each other you didn't even notice me."

That sucked the air out of the room. I felt a little breathless myself, and Mother blanched as pale as porcelain. Father turned to stare at her, and since the good side of his face was toward me, I raised my eyes. From that angle he looked like my father again, reluctantly confronting his wife on the rare occasions when she was in the wrong. "Flirting?"

"It wasn't flirting—that's ridiculous. He tried to charm me into appearing in one of his pictures, some heartwarming drama where a desperate mother abandons her baby on the Little Tramp's doorstep and he goes on to raise the boy—a *mother*, not a romantic..." She trailed off, looking agitated.

"Strolling?" Father asked in the same inquisitive tone.

"Yes. We met one time, and that's when I turned him down flat." Mother took a deep breath. "I won't pretend it wasn't flattering."

"And the yellow roses... I expect those were very flattering too."

"That was just a thoughtful gesture. Though perhaps a little flashy."

"From what I hear of him," Father said drily, "'thoughtful' is not the word that first comes to mind. 'Pushy' may be more like it."

She did not reply. After a pause, Father awkwardly folded his napkin with one hand and placed it carefully beside the untouched slab of toast. "Is it time we returned to Seattle?"

"Almost. At the end of the month—"

"The end of the *month*?" His tone sharpened. "That's over two weeks. Why wait?"

"It's as long as the girls and I originally planned to stay. We'll be back in time for school, and I'll have a few weeks of sunshine up there before the rain and gloom set in."

"It's your home, Matilda. Rain and gloom and all. Or perhaps it isn't really. Perhaps *I* should go back in a few days, and let you decide when you're ready. If ever."

This was certainly over my depth. "May I be excused?"

Mother practically glared. "You may be excused to your room. And stay there for the afternoon. You might want to ponder the trouble you've caused."

Sulkily I pushed back my chair and left the table. Was I the cause? Or just the pointer-outer? I stomped down the hall and slammed my bedroom door, and the moment I was alone, my mind began sprouting the seeds of a plan.

Chapter 20
Love's Wait Rewarded

O ne thing I was grateful to Ranger for: a knowledge of the greater Los Angeles streetcar schedules. That was how I knew they began at five-thirty in the morning so I could be at the corner of Fifth and Vine at that time on Saturday. Behind me, in our room at the hacienda, were a soundly sleeping Sylvie and a roll of blankets meant to represent my soundly sleeping self. Under my arm was a carpetbag with the few necessities for a twenty-hour train ride—and, as a last-minute thought, Father's picture from the nightstand.

Scraping together money for the ticket was not easy. I confess to "borrowing" some of it from Aunt Buzzy's pocketbook, with a promissory note to pay it back as soon as I could. Perhaps I could do extra chores for my grandparents, once they'd heard my story and agreed to let me live with them. I would make it up some way, but one thing was certain—I could not stay another day in that sprawling house so stuffed with pretense and passion. I had to get home *now*.

Stepping off the streetcar at the railway station, I squared my shoulders and marched to the ticket booth feeling like Joan of Arc—and when I heard that the Daybreak Limited had been delayed for half an hour because of a rock slide on the track, I felt like a popped balloon.

Also, the agent seemed disinclined to sell a ticket to a lone underage girl, in spite of my best efforts at grown-upness. "I'm going to join my father, the wounded veteran," was the lie that finally worked, especially when I described my father. The agent remembered him from the week before. From now on, I realized, anyone would.

Resigned to waiting, I found a seat in an alcove off the concourse, opposite a thin gentleman in a gray suit and Stetson hat who was reading a newspaper. The hat and the newspaper were all I saw of him for several minutes—that and a curl of cigarette smoke hanging sulfurously above. My carpetbag held two books, the ubiquitous *Jane Eyre* and a copy of *Red Rover* I was sure Aunt Buzzy would not mind me borrowing. But I was saving those for the train, and regretting my lack of reading matter, when the gentleman abruptly lowered his paper.

"Are you traveling alone, young lady?"

Startled, I could only nod.

"Why so distraught, if I may ask?"

That startled me even more, because I couldn't see how he'd noticed anything from behind that newspaper.

"Oh! I'm not—that is, well…"

He had a long, horsy face with very keen eyes. It might have been the eyes that soon pried the story out of me—or maybe after days of me holding in, it was ready to spill. All of it: my father at the station, the shock of his appearance, the dreadful silence that had swaddled our household until yesterday, and the rift between my parents that threatened to grow wider. Even the scene I'd made hurling the roses, and the hateful words I had hurled after them.

The stranger nodded as I spoke and murmured, "Yes, I see." What did he see? More than I could, probably, being a grown-up and part of their club.

"I don't know if it's right or wrong," I concluded. "But if my family's splitting apart, I can't stay and watch it happen."

"Yes," he said again. "It's a story to wring the heart. There are many such out of this war. I should probably advise you to go back to your parents and give them time to work it out. But you look so brave and determined, sitting there all alone. Yet so vulnerable. I wish I had a picture."

This was not a typical grown-up response, and I was emboldened to go on. "Could I ask you a question, sir?"

"Certainly."

"Do you think... If you were my father, how would you be feeling about me right now?"

The man put on a rueful expression. "Sad...and guilty."

"Guilty?" My mouth gaped in an unlovely manner. "But *I* was the one who was nasty to him." There it was—my own guilt.

"Nevertheless. If I were your father, I would feel I had forced you to take on too great a burden at a tender age. I would curse the fates that brought us to it."

That sounded rather grand, as much as sad, and I saw it in

a three-quarter shot, followed by a close-up of Father's melancholy countenance, followed by his hands on my face, and a title card reading—

Stop that! I told myself.

My companion folded his newspaper and laid it beside him on the bench. "Framing is everything, you see. How you look at a situation, the angle you take." He held up his hands, flat and parallel to each other, then shifted their position: forward and back, upright and sideways—like a camera lens, I abruptly realized. He reminded me of Ranger on the day we met. "You, there in the station, waiting for a train: are you running toward your future or running away?"

I frowned. "Should I go back then?"

"Back where? Back to Hollywood or Seattle?" While I hesitated, thinking this over, he added, "Go home, child. Wherever that may be."

"Sir." A young man was standing by my companion, holding a ticket. "Everyone else is aboard the eastbound. You said to wait 'til the last minute to call you, and this seems to be it."

"Thank you, Grayson." The gentleman stood, draped a summer overcoat over his arm, and picked up a leather bag. "I'll be right along." Then, to me: "By the way, young lady, I work in the pictures. I can't help noticing you have a rare quality of strength and pathos, combined with right expressive eyes." I blinked at the word "pathos," which I'd heard only one other person use in actual conversation.

The man had reached inside his jacket. "In a few years, if you are at loose ends, consider looking me up. I may be moving operations soon, but I daresay you'll be able to find me." So saying, he handed me a card.

"Thank you, sir." I accepted the card. "Especially for listening."

"An honor and a privilege." He nodded and touched his broad-brimmed hat in salute, then strode down the aisle between seats with a country man's gait—an easy lope that reminded me, for the third time in our brief acquaintance, of Ranger. Belatedly I turned the card over and saw it contained no address or telephone exchange, just a name. And the name was:

David Wark Griffith

I might have decided on my own not to board the train after all. The vision conjured by the master, of guilt and sorrow and cursing the fates, seemed too rich for my digestion just then, and that was surely what awaited me in Hollywood. But where it "home"?

I only wanted things to be as they were, and perhaps that was the real reason for my ticket to Seattle. Even though "things as they were" was a vain hope. And striking out alone in brave-but-vulnerable mode might not be the best way to nudge our family back together. Anyway, the decision was taken out of my hands only a few minutes later when Mother suddenly appeared in front of me.

First she slipped the ticket from my unprotesting fingers. Then she sat down, in the space Mr. Griffith had vacated, and gazed at me from under a black straw hat with a veil that obscured her eyes. "Your father suggested you might be here."

"You're the one who should have been here first."

She sighed. "When we go back to Seattle, we must all go back together."

"To stay?"

"Of course to stay. What else?"

"Some of us might want to follow a film career." I half expected her to look about for a willow switch. Instead she bit her lip, and the mark on it blazed palely.

"You were thinking about it!" I accused her. "Really thinking! Mr. Chaplin was egging you on, and you liked it! I've seen how people notice you here, especially the men, and you *like* it. Even that scar—it gives you an air of mystery, and it makes them wonder—"

I stopped because she had pushed back the veil. Her dark eyes were red-rimmed and smudgy and far from mysterious. "Would you like to know how I got this scar?"

I'd always thought I would. But now, oddly, I didn't.

"Your father gave it to me."

My hand went to my mouth. "Mother? Please don't…"

"An accident, of course. It happened during our honeymoon, as we took the ferry to Victoria Island. We were standing on the quarterdeck on a beautiful, sparkling day in September, and—in an excess of high spirits—he seized a davit hook and pretended he was going to swing out over the water on it, only it slipped out of his hands and slammed into my face. The point of the hook went right through my lip.

"It could have been much worse, but at first we couldn't tell how bad it was going to be because my face was swollen like a tomato for the rest of our trip. He felt terrible about it. But then, so did I. It was not one of the more blissful honeymoons in the annals of history, I'm afraid. But the swelling went down, and the bruises and cuts faded—" She touched her upper lip. "All but one."

"I'm sorry, Mother. I didn't mean—" But I didn't know what I meant.

"He's a good man, a loving husband, a fine father... But Isobel, he left us first, and he didn't have to. It's all very well to hear the call of duty and serve one's country, but that wasn't the reason. His own father goaded him into it: Major Robert F. Ransom *Senior* of the First U.S. Medical Corps, battling camp fever in the Philippines. Dr. Ransom Senior set a standard your father felt he could never measure up to. So he went. In my opinion he far surpassed that standard. But at a cost."

All this was much more than I wanted to know, and it struck me dumb. After a moment, she stood up and crossed the aisle between us, took my hands and pulled me to my feet. She pushed my hair back, and then her arms encircled me tightly. "We all have our scars, Isobel. Usually they don't show. But knowing that they're there, we can be kinder to each other, can't we?"

I didn't answer because I was crying so hard. I clutched her in return. While we were standing thus, my train was called, but of course I made no move to get on it. After a while my mother wiped her eyes. "And now, dear, we should take no more of Masaji's time—he's waiting at the curb. I'll exchange this ticket of yours for next Tuesday and buy three more."

"Tuesday?"

"Yes. Your father and I had a very long and frank discussion last night. After that scene at breakfast yesterday, it was that or nothing. We've worked out a way forward, and it does not include a film career."

I sniffed into her shoulder. "I'm sorry about the yelling... and stomping and door-slamming."

"I forgive you." Briskly, she tucked a wayward lock of hair behind my ear. "Your father has an apology due, I believe." I bit my lip and nodded. "You must learn to see him differently, Isobel. As we all must."

She picked up my bag and led the way out to the concourse. That's what Mr. Griffith had said, I suddenly realized. *It's all in the framing*. But that was Ranger's specialty, not mine.

"I forgot to tell you," Mother remarked over her shoulder. "Ranger has reserved our time tonight. He insists on it, and you know how determined the boy is. He and your sister have been thick as thieves, and now your aunt is in on the scheme too. Do you have any idea what it's about?"

Oh yes, I had an idea. But then I remembered: Mr. Griffith, for whose benefit this whole scheme had been devised, was at this moment headed in the opposite direction.

"I know," Ranger said when I told him. "I've known since yesterday. Pa says he's decided to move his studio back east."

For a youth whose dream had just been shattered, he seemed awfully composed. "Then who is the picture for?"

"You," he replied without hesitation. "And me, and Sam and Sylvie. And for itself. Just wait."

That was all the time he could spare. Even my conversation with his hero seemed to rouse no interest: "No time now. Tell me tomorrow."

For most of the afternoon he was down at Vitagraph with Sam and—to my astonishment—Aunt Buzzy, who left for the studio immediately after lunch and returned two hours later with a preoccupied expression and a large book of piano scores entitled *Motion Picture Moods*.

"I'm sworn to secrecy," she told her sister and husband. "I can't tell you what it is, but I will say that it's rather remarkable. Titus, I suggest you get Ranger what he asks for tonight."

Ranger's chief need was a projector and a screen, which his father could summon with a single telephone call to one of his business associates. It arrived around five o'clock, and Ranger shortly afterward. With Sylvie's help and Aunt Buzzy's permission, he unrolled the screen and tacked it to the east end of the great room—the side where the piano was. Then they set up the projector on a serving cart and arranged eight chairs in three rows.

And where was Father all this time? I had made up my mind to apologize, even though I still dreaded having to look at him and felt all the more guilty for that. But he made himself scarce all day. Whenever I asked, I was told he was taking a walk or taking a nap, and when I finally caught sight of him late in the afternoon, he was chatting it up with Ranger like a regular old pal. I knew what would happen if I approached them—Father's easy manner would drop like a loose shingle, and we'd be back to stiff words and awkward pauses. It made me feel jealous of Ranger and angry all over again.

After a subdued supper in the courtyard, while shadows lengthened into twilight, Sam arrived. Under his arm was a single reel of film in a round metal case.

He had dressed up for the occasion, in a jacket and a starched collar and tie, but his hair could have used a dab of brilliantine to keep it out of his face. I would have expected him to be somewhat ill at ease, having been flushed out in public, so to speak. But he was dignifiedly grave as he shook Titus Bell's hand and my mother's, and suffered Aunt Buzzy to put an arm around his shoulders and smooth back his hair. To my surprise, he seemed to know my father already. They nodded to each other with an attitude of mutual respect.

Ranger was the ill-at-ease one. Like a theater usher, he seated us in the three rows of chairs: Esperanza, Solomon, and Masaji at the back, then my parents and his father, and me and Sylvie in front. Aunt Buzzy sat at the piano, which had been turned so that she could see the screen, and opened her score book. I'd taken a peek at it before supper. Each page had a column running down the outside margin, with page numbers for themes suitable for "Monotony," "Battle," "Horror," and so on. Aunt Buzzy had stuffed it with bookmarks.

When we were all settled, Ranger stood before the screen holding a handful of square cards. He cleared his throat.

"I know you're wondering what this is all about," he began and, in a voice thinned with anxiety, went on to reveal what we'd been up to with our streetcar jaunts and late-for-dinners. He left out the more lurid parts, such as my turn as a Boy Scout and Sylvie's near-drowning and our raid on the Keystone supply hut. During the recital he was plagued by a fly that took a liking to him, and at the fourth or fifth swipe, all the cards tumbled to the floor. When Sylvie bolted out of her chair to help pick them up, she jerked the projector plug out of its socket. All of which prolonged the introduction and created something other than the mood of high-minded anticipation Ranger wanted for his work of art.

"*Anyway*," he said after regaining his feet, "it's not very long, and what we ended up with is not what I... That is, it may be even better than... Never mind. I guess that's up to you to decide. Oh—we didn't have time to shoot the title cards, so I'll just read 'em. And Buzzy will... Sorry, Mrs. Beatrice Bell has graciously consented to provide the musical moods. Thank you for your kind attention to our humble efforts. Amen. I mean, roll it, Sam."

Aunt Buzzy struck the opening bars of "Song without Words." That's when I felt the butterflies in my stomach—very rowdy, obstreperous butterflies, for I had no idea what Ranger had done with my flickering image. I glanced back at Sam, as though to stop the projector by force of will. My mother and Titus Bell wore expressions of amused curiosity, while Father slumped forward and peered up at the screen from under his eyebrows. In the last row Solomon stifled a yawn and Masaji frowned and Esperanza gazed in openmouthed expectation. Sam was a mere shadow behind the projector's powerful beam.

When I turned back, that beam was reflecting owlishly off Ranger's glasses. Beside him unfurled the words *LOVE'S WAIT REWARDED*.

"What?" I queried the screen.

Sylvie could hardly contain herself. "Ranger thought it up," she whispered, squirming. "Isn't it grand?"

Our names then blazed up: *Matchless – Isobel Ransom. Little Sister – Sylvia Ransom. Directed by R. A. Bell. Photographed by Samuel Patrick Service.*

Scene One was a view of the ocean from Santa Monica Beach, and in an unnaturally high voice, Ranger read, "Waiting is life's great trial. Families wait for loved ones to return. Soldiers wait for the enemy's advance... How oft would we fain to speed the hands of time."

My mother suppressed a small groan. A neatly dressed colored woman and her little son showed on the screen. Who were they? I belatedly recognized the train platform they stood upon as *the* platform. Was this shot taken on the day of Father's arrival?

"They're waiting," Sylvie whispered helpfully. Ranger himself was the next one waiting, watchfully posed on horseback.

"Ah-ha," Titus Bell murmured as the scene changed again, this time to Sylvie and me walking on the beach. My expression could pass for anxious expectation, I suppose. Ranger continued: "But nothing can be more difficult than awaiting a loved one who's serving his country in far-flung battlefields."

Matchless, her father's pride (close-up on me, to my intense discomfort). Little Sister, her father's joy (close-up on Sylvie, who barely stopped herself from squealing, "That's me!").

Murmurs of amusement abruptly stilled when Father's picture appeared—his photograph, that is, the one I so longed to include in our at-home scenes. As "My Country, 'Tis of Thee" transitioned to "Over There!" he faded into views of marching soldiers, including the overhead shot contributed by Jimmy Service.

All murmurs, chuckles, and rustlings had stopped, I noticed.

The unfathomable ocean filled the screen again: "Sorrow came to this house long ago, with the tragic loss of a mother. Now the father has departed as well, and their loving grand-mother, in whose care they were left, has been cruelly stricken." Miss Blanche, in her bath chair, fussed over Sylvie while I hovered nearby. Then the shot of Sylvie in her lap, which in the context seemed unbearably touching.

"Little Sister is a spritely spirit, unbounded by care—" Sylvie ran toward the Santa Monica Pier, coming closer in view, passing, and receding as the camera turned to follow. I had not anticipated how her personality would leap off the screen.

"But Matchless bears burdens unseemly for one so young." I dragged the picture into gloom with a series of sorrowful shots: fretfully tending Miss Blanche, searching the house for a morsel of food, anxiously standing by the picket fence, pleading with the oblivious Jimmy Service ("The Landlord," Ranger intoned) as he caroused with his chums.

"Food is scarce, the money dwindles, sickness threatens, the wolf is at the door…" Sylvie and I were walking down the path in the woods, starting at every sound, clutching each other fearfully. Closer and closer, as my eyes widened and Sylvie's grip tightened: "Where will it all end?"

More marching men thronged toward us, like inexorable fate. Then rows of boots, swinging smartly around a corner. A turning point in the story?

As if in answer, the ominous music shifted to hopeful rippling chords. "One day, the long-awaited news arrives from overseas: *Father is coming home!*" I received the word from a mustachioed postman, and Sylvie and I rejoiced together. The relief I felt while watching was exactly as though the future were unknown. But not for long.

"On the long-expected day, Matchless and Little Sister eagerly await their father's arrival. Others also wait." There was the shot that began the picture, of the mother and child on the platform. A cut to the locomotive's approach on the tracks, and back to the woman's head turning as it passed her. I expected to see the three of us next, in our eager pose, and then it struck me: where was the Dauntless Youth?

He appeared in the shot of us waiting on the platform, but with no preparation or "establishment," he might not have belonged to us at all. The passenger cars were sliding to a stop alongside the platform, and I felt my heart tightening, exactly as it had the week before while we waited for Father to step off.

The camera caught him early. Not in a true close-up at that distance, but a standard three-quarter that painfully showed his state of mind. His left hand hovered awkwardly about the right side of his face as though to shield it from the other passengers, who avoided glancing his way. My heart went out to him as he stood anxious and alone, looking for us.

I was dreading the moment when Sylvie would throw herself at him, but something else happened first. The porter walked up on Father's right side, carrying a little boy. With a start, I recognized the same child we had twice seen waiting with his mother at the edge of the platform.

Beaming, the porter introduced his son to Father, and vice versa. The two men must have become acquainted on the journey. Father put his hand in his pocket, but the porter waved away the tip. Perhaps the little boy was being told what an honor it was to meet a hero who'd risked his life to save others. The child seemed more interested in the hero's face. As the porter talked, his son's little hand went out and cautiously rested on the man's puckered cheek. All three were very still for a moment.

Then Sylvie shot into the picture, wrapping herself around Father. He turned in surprise, revealing his face and the lack of an arm. A gasp ran through the audience, as though we were seeing him for the first time. Sylvie slipped from his unsteady grasp.

The picture jerked; people would appear and suddenly disappear, or magically skip from one spot to another. That was the cost of eliminating Ranger's handshake and mother's welcoming kiss, but it reflected my jangled feelings at the time. In the shuffle I was the only one who didn't move. My face did not show, but my back—rigid and shocked—told all. The moment when Father finally had to walk up and embrace me wrung a strangled cry from my throat—a cry I couldn't even muster when it actually happened.

The camera never stopped, recording the little procession we formed with Ranger and Aunt Buzzy in the lead. Sylvie grabbed Father's left hand; Mother reached automatically for his right arm and drew back in confusion when it wasn't there. My face showed briefly as I watched them pass—a stony mask. The camera turned to follow us down the platform, nearly empty now. I brought up the rear, falling farther behind all the way to the corner of the station.

Ranger's voice startled us all. "So the long wait is over," he read as Aunt Buzzy began the first movement of "Moonlight Sonata." "But what now? Will our little family sink in the rising tide of despair?"

Cut to two heads bobbing in the ocean—at this distance it was impossible to tell that one of them belonged to a dog. Next was me on the beach, screaming. I remembered calling to Sylvie to hold on because Ranger was on the way, but it looked like I was furious, hurling outrage at the uncaring sea.

"Or will they reknit their bonds and learn to take the bitter with the sweet?" Ranger's voice had been gaining strength and now rang out like a revival preacher's. I was wondering if the sermon was for me when a new scene appeared: two wounded soldiers sitting under an alder tree. Sam must have shot it at his mother's hospital. Then Sylvie was skipping beside a pond I recognized from Echo Park, while holding Father's hand.

I straightened up in my chair, staring. When had they shot this? Next, they were sitting in the grass, and after a pause, she raised her hand and laid it on the damaged side of his face—exactly like the porter's boy, but lovingly.

A youth in an outlandishly checkered cap wandered by, tossing a ball. It took me a moment to recognize Ranger, as he caught sight of the pair and did an elaborate double-take. His lips moved.

"'Pardon me for staring, sir,'" Ranger read from his card. "'But I must ask, have you seen action?'"

Father looked down at the grass with a little smile. It was the way grown-ups often responded to Ranger, and it seemed beautifully natural and commonplace. With a jolt, I saw for the first time that he was *still there* behind that face. I knew that smile from the many times Sylvie was being outrageous and I was striving too hard to act grown-up.

Then Father looked up again and patted the ground. The youth eagerly flopped and began a lively (on his side, at least) conversation with the wounded veteran, during which the Iron Cross medal made an appearance. Meanwhile Sylvie crept into Father's lap and rested her head (close-up) on his chest.

The music shifted to "Morning," and the camera began to back away, as though tactfully suggesting we had intruded on these nice people long enough. The smoothness amazed me, as if the tripod was on wheels. Which it probably was—another of Sam's innovations? Back and back it went, taking in more and more: ladies and gentlemen strolling, a boy rolling a hoop,

269

little girls jumping rope. If all was not right with this world, there was still plenty of good in it.

"'While the earth remaineth, seedtime and harvest, cold and heat, winter and summer, day and night, shall not cease.' So time heals all wounds."

Ranger was reaching into his pocket as he read the last card, and the next I knew, he was holding something out to me: a handkerchief. "I keep *telling* you to come prepared," he whispered.

I blew my nose with a discreet little "honk" and glanced behind me. Father's chair was empty. The camera was still rolling and piano chords still rippling as I sprang up in a panic. Where was he? I had to see him, had to tell him the angle had shifted and I didn't want to run away anymore. Light from the projector silhouetted me against THE END, and I spotted a slump-shouldered figure in the doorway to the east wing.

I don't remember covering the ground between us. Slamming into his chest was the very next thing I knew, his one arm holding me up, his one word my name, and my one thought: *I'm home.*

Epilogue

When the lights came up, I gradually realized that the sounds of sniffling at my back came from Mother. Esperanza too. The men appeared unmoved at first, but moving back into the room, I saw Masaji's jaw work as he swallowed, and noticed Titus Bell blinking rapidly.

He was the first to speak after many seconds of shifting, shuffling, and quiet sobs. "Well, old man"—to Ranger—"I'll say this. You young'uns have certainly made creative use of your parents."

"Yes, sir," Ranger answered warily, as though he wasn't sure if he was in trouble or not. Then, with one of his quick, bright smiles: "But after all, that's the best material we've got."

After an impromptu reception with punch and cookies, I ran to fetch something from my room. Now I clutched it with both hands in my lap as we sat together under the low roof of the hacienda's front porch. "We" being Ranger, Sylvie, and me—Sam too, though he wouldn't sit down and kept saying he had to go. He'd removed his collar and tie and looked more like the Sam we knew. But I think he was, for once, fully satisfied with an accomplishment and was taking time to enjoy it.

He told us how he'd aimed at the porter's wife and child only to focus the close-up lens, having no idea who they were or that the boy would later appear in the scene. "That was luck. Having Sylvie echo the action later was Ranger's idea."

"*And a little child shall lead them.*" Ranger was spilling over with biblical quotations tonight.

So was I: *And the leaves of the tree shall be for the healing of the nations.* Between my hands was the smooth, cool glass of the snow globe. There would be healing; I was sure of it now. We had left the grown-ups in the front room, where they were now sipping wine and discussing grown-up things in a normal, easy manner they'd not been able to before. I kept glancing at them over my shoulder, and once, through the glass of the double doors, I saw Father reach out and take Mother's hand.

"Whose idea was it to back up the camera at the end?" I asked.

"Ah!" Ranger said eagerly. "That was Captain Ransom. He said the thing that helped him most after he got hurt was getting out of himself and trying to see a bigger picture. Sam thought we could show that if we put the tripod on wheels, but he'd have to have an absolutely smooth surface to roll on."

"Sam made a railroad track!" Sylvie said.

"I found a couple of planed four-foot boards on the lot and nailed guide rails on 'em for the tripod wheels," Sam explained. "At the park, we got a couple of kids to help us. When the camera rolled off one board onto the other, they picked up the first board and ran it around behind the second so we'd have a continuous track. Took a few tries to get it right, and the jump between the boards isn't perfect, but…" He shrugged, reluctant to heap praise on himself.

"It *looked* perfect," Ranger said.

It did, I silently agreed. "Weren't you worried about attracting so much attention?" I asked Sam.

He shrugged again. "Not anymore. If you're thinking about my dad, I'm back to being a chip off the old block. He got the projection room for us on Wednesday night—even printed some of our rough cuts so we'd have a little extra film to play with. But that's this week. Next week, if he finds the camera missing again…" Sam trailed a forefinger across his neck.

"So's your old man," Ranger scoffed. "His bark's a lot worse than his bite. You won't scare me with him anymore."

Sam made a little snort, then remarked, "I'd better shove along." But he stayed in the same posture, one foot on the ground and the other on the bottom step.

Sylvie threw her arms around me. "Weren't you surprised when Daddy showed up in the park with us?"

I nodded. Titus Bell had taken Ranger aside and told him he had a lot of brass, getting a war veteran to expose his wounds to public view. But there was an admiring lilt in his voice when he said it. My feelings were more mixed—and Mother's too. I could tell by the enigmatical way she complimented the boys: "It would certainly seem you have a future in pictures. Though not perhaps in subtle diplomacy."

273

Au contraire, I thought, *if diplomacy was the art of getting what you wanted without bloodshed.* I hugged the globe to my chest. Sylvie had begged me to let her make it snow, but I wouldn't give it up. "That's the burning question," I said. "How did you talk him into appearing in your picture?"

"Just got to know him, like I told you. Since he's interested in photography, it wasn't too hard to get him down to the projection room. Seeing himself on film—that was tough. But from then on, it was easier."

Ranger was brassy indeed, and where it would take him was probably limited only by his imagination.

"How about that Sylvie?" he said, reaching over to tickle her. "Ain't she sweet on screen?" For an answer, she threw herself at him and nearly knocked him over.

"She's photogenic all right," Sam agreed. Almost everyone had remarked on this—with some surprise, for I was always considered the beauty. But my personality did not charge off the screen as hers did, and it wasn't just a matter of liveliness—it was a Mary Pickford–like quality the camera adored. "Maybe she oughta be in pictures."

I recalled how Ranger had launched this project on my appearance, but the one who ended up contributing the least was me. Perhaps I had received the most though.

The night was soft but clear, with stars (the real kind, not the Hollywood kind) blinking sleepily down on us. A light breeze carried the faint, sweet scent of orange blossoms, and I missed California already, though we wouldn't be leaving for another three days.

"I'd really better go." Sam finally removed his foot from the step. "The old man's waiting up. At least he said he'd be. Wants to know how it went."

"Will I see you around?" Ranger's brashness seemed to slip for the first time since *The End* had shown on the screen. "I mean, before?"

"Before you get shipped off to Palo Alto? Sure, why not?"

"You're a genius, Sam. I mean it."

"Well…" Briefly abashed, the genius looked at his shoes. Then, turning away with a sly smile that took up both sides of his mouth: "You're no slouch yourself, Aloysius."

Ranger sputtered with outrage as Sylvie shook him by the arm. "*Aloysius?* What's that?"

"What the *A* stands for. My grandfather, Aloysius Bell, the Gold Rush flapjack king. *You weren't supposed to tell anybody that!*" he yelled at Sam's retreating back.

Sam turned around, and somehow I could tell he was still smiling, though the darkness had claimed him already. "Say, Isobel?"

"What?"

"You have the eye of a first-rate film cutter."

"…I do?"

"Yeah." I could hear his voice receding as he backed away. "If you come back, I'll show you how to do a split screen. So long."

Sylvie nudged me. "He likes you!"

"Hush!" I whispered, blushing lest her piping tones reach Sam's ears.

"You know," Ranger mused, "I think maybe he does. He doesn't give knowledge away to just anybody."

I thought of a way to change the subject. "Speaking of film cutters, why did you cut yourself out of the picture?"

"Well, if you hadn't been so stubborn there at the end, we might have settled things between Matchless and the Dauntless Youth—"

"That's not it. All those scenes you agonized over…the rally, the rescue…all gone. A boy with your fertile imagination could have worked them in *somehow*."

"For one thing, there wasn't enough time. But more than that…the story just went somewhere else. I couldn't argue with it. It was one of those times when you feel like you're part of something bigger, and you just have to go along. You know what I mean?"

I did know. That's what his little picture had helped me see, by cutting up our story and rearranging the parts. There were still a lot of pieces to pick up, but now I had a bigger frame to fit them in.

"Besides," he said in a lighter tone, "I never wanted to be *in* pictures all that much. I just want to make 'em."

"It was good," I said most sincerely. "And…it didn't lie."

"Thanks," he replied. Then, after a hasty clearing of his throat: "I couldn't have done it without you. Both of you."

"But I gather it doesn't save you from military school."

"Nope. That was wishful thinking all along, I guess." His face took on a mournful cast in the twilight.

To make him feel better, I said, "Try to imagine it in the

worst possible terms. Like the prison in *The Count of Monte Cristo*, or something. Then it won't seem so bad when you get there."

"Oh, yes, it will. It'll be just as bad as I think. But I'll have something I didn't before."

He meant the picture; I knew that without asking. It was something we all had now that we didn't before.

"I still think you're the wonderfulest boy I've ever met." Sylvie crawled into his lap, knocking his chin with her head.

Lest we drown in sentiment, I said, "Hollywood will still be here when you get back."

"I know," he replied. "This too shall pass. Onward and upward."

I nodded. "It's always darkest before the dawn."

Sylvie caught on. "A penny saved is a penny earned."

He made a noise of disgust. "You girls have no sense of artistic expression." Then he grinned his broad-beamed grin, and I got the idea that our story hadn't ended yet.

Acknowledgments

What inspired me to start thinking about movie-making in early Hollywood was a statue outside the entrance gate of Universal Studios. It represents a sound stage around the mid-1930s, with two actors, a cameraman, a director, and a sound tech holding a microphone on a crane. From such humble beginnings, *King Kong* and *Star Wars*, *Casablanca* and *The Avengers*. Might there be a story here?

But sooner or later, when constructing a plot, you come up against the cold hard facts—or rather, lack of cold hard facts. A bunch of kids making a movie would need some technical know-how and equipment—chiefly, a camera. And more specifically, a camera that two teenage boys of not-especially-prepossessing size could haul all over Los Angeles County without attracting much notice. Books couldn't give me that information; I needed to talk to somebody. So I contacted Shannon Perich, a curator in the Division of Culture and the Arts at the Smithsonian's National Museum of American History.

The Smithsonian is called "the nation's attic," and if the nation is looking for a particular object in connection with a particular project, it is welcome to come in and rummage around. Ms. Perich connected me with John Hiller, then retired, whose long career had included studio work in the film industry as well as cataloging for the Smithsonian. On a lovely day in July, I met Shannon Perich and Mr. Hiller at the entrance to the American History Museum in DC and we drove together out to one of the many Smithsonian storage facilities in Maryland. There I found the Prestwich Model 14 in its cherry-wood case, light and compact enough to carry to the battlefield. Just talking to John was worth a trip: he was a wellspring of little-known facts and telling details like double-splicing film to make for smoother transitions. Thank you both for such extraordinary helpfulness.

Thanks to Vicki Grove, whose husband's grandfather kept a diary during his service as a World War I field surgeon, copies of which she shared with me. Thanks to Aubrey Poole for relentlessly carving out unnecessary material in my manuscript (which seemed so necessary at the time!), for holding firm on the title, and for responding to my own suggestions about the cover. Thanks to the outstanding production team at Sourcebooks for making this book as handsome as Douglas Fairbanks. Thanks to Charlie Chaplin and Buster Keaton for making me laugh, Bobby Harron and Mae Marsh (of *The Mother and the Law*) for making me cry. Thanks to D. W. Griffith, Mack Sennett, King Vidor, Cecil B. DeMille and many, many others for stretching the limits of storytelling by film. And thanks to the Lord, who plants deep within us a love of stories.

About the Author

J. B. Cheaney was born in Dallas, Texas, sometime in the last century. In school, her favorite subject was making up parts for herself in imaginary movies and plays. Too bad they don't give grades for that. Fortunately, her second-favorite subject was history. All that daydreaming and history-loving finally paid off with five published novels, the latest of which is *Somebody on This Bus Is Going to Be Famous*. She lives and daydreams in Missouri with her husband.